LETHBRIDGE-STEWART
THE DREAMER'S LAMENT

Based on the BBC television serials by
Mervyn Haisman & Henry Lincoln

Benjamin Burford-Jones

Foreword by Shaun Russell

CANDY JAR BOOKS   CARDIFF
A Russell & Frankham-Allen Series
2017

The Dreamer's Lament © Benjamin Burford-Jones 2107

Range Editor: Andy Frankham-Allen
Editor: Shaun Russell
Cover: Martin Baines
Editorial: Lauren Thomas
Licensed by Hannah Haisman

Printed and bound in the UK by
CPI Anthony Rowe, Chippenham, Wiltshire

ISBN: 978-0-9957436-5-6

Published by
Candy Jar Books
Mackintosh House
136 Newport Road, Cardiff, CF24 1DJ
www.candyjarbooks.co.uk

My Journey to Ben

I used to love *Doctor Who*. As a child I would draw Tom Baker fighting the Darleks – well, that's what I called them. I am from Bristol after all! And when Weetabix started to give away *Doctor Who* cards I was staying at my nan's house. We went shopping and she asked what breakfast cereal I liked. In reality I wasn't the biggest fan of Weetabix, but I convinced her that I absolutely loved it, just to get the *Doctor Who* cards inside.

In 1982, after relentlessly doing my paper round every week, I caved in and bought *Doctor Who* Magazine issue 68, which had been gathering dust on the newsagent's shelf for months. I don't know why it was still there, but in hindsight, I'm glad it was.

In 1985 (age 14) I wrote to *Celestial Toyroom*, the magazine of the *Doctor Who* Appreciation Society, and my name and contact details were included on the pen pal page. Soon I was writing to a number of fans from across the globe, including Tino in New York, Alice in Glasgow and Nancy in Texas. This was great, but I still didn't really know any fans nearby. That was until I created my own fanzine about the series. It was called *Metebelis 3*, and I managed to flog some to Forever People.

Forever People was a sci-fi shop, halfway up Park Street, that had a fantastic range of comics, toys and *Doctor Who* memorabilia. I used to visit it almost every week. I didn't buy anything. I just popped in to read the latest edition of *Doctor Who Bulletin*.

One cold Saturday afternoon I got talking to James McGregor. He was a couple of years younger than me, but his breadth of knowledge of *Doctor Who* totally surpassed mine. He even had stories on VHS, so I arranged to meet him the following week, hoping that he'd bring along the copy of *The Daemons* that he'd promised.

He was late, but I later discovered that he was always late. He wasn't on his own though. He had brought a friend. And it was another *Doctor Who* fan. Fantastic!

James introduced him as Ben Jones, and we began to talk. Ben had the same encyclopedic knowledge of *Doctor Who* and I felt quite intimidated, although I didn't show it.

And then they cancelled *Doctor Who!*

Michael Grade pulled the plug just as I was making friends.

Thankfully this did not matter. We had twenty-two years of the series to discuss. Ben and James lived in Keynsham and I would visit regularly, watching stories, and we all became close friends. And we always thought that Keynsham would be a good place to set a *Doctor Who* story.

*

As the years passed sadly James drifted way, but Ben continued to be a friend.

Fifteen or so years ago Ben wrote two books – a children's novel called *Hoppers*, and *Doctor Who* book called *Corpse*, featuring the Second Doctor, Victoria and Jamie. I was so impressed with both these titles that in 2013 Candy Jar published *Hoppers* as *Beware of the Mirror Man*, and now *Corpse* is this book you are reading.

It was a long process turning *Corpse* into *The Dreamer's Lament*, a process I was ordered to stay clear of (rightly so!) by Andy Frankham-Allen, the range editor. A certain level of detachment is needed when hiring someone you've known for a long time. I've suggested several people to Andy over the last few years, and it's a wonderful feeling knowing that the only one who passed Andy's exacting standards is Ben! By the time I read the book, it had been rewritten from scratch, gone through several drafts, and only loosely resembled the book I remembered. Which, I think, is a good thing.

The book you're holding is a much superior book than the original version from the late '90s, and it's one that I am proud to present to you. Not only as the owner of Candy Jar Books, but also as Ben's friend.

So, here we are, a story set in Keynsham finally. And I still love *Doctor Who*!

Shaun Russell, July, 2017

Desecrating graves was not much of a job. Yet it put a few pounds into the filthy pocket of Tom Sawkins, with no questions asked. Grunting with effort, Tom thrust the grimy spade into the soft earth, and this time he was confronted with the hollow thud of wood. Nervously, he glanced upward, out of the six-foot deep hole. His bloodshot eyes searched for even the slightest clue that he was being watched. At this late stage in the game it would be impossible to plead innocent of any crime.

The graveyard was still and quiet, just as it ought to be at four twenty-two in the small hours of the morning. The dim light of a half moon, partially obscured by night-time clouds, cast ghostly shadows over the marble crosses and headstones. But there were no watching eyes. No lynch mob ready to put a noose around his neck.

Gritting his teeth, Tom clutched the spade tightly and thrust down onto the hinges of the coffin below his feet. The noise of splintering wood filled his ears. Once more the spade was brought downwards, this time with even more force. To Tom's current nervous disposition, the sound felt like an earthquake. Surely somebody must have heard the noise. If he was caught, he'd swing for sure.

A sudden blur of movement caused him to freeze in

panic. His heart sped up, racing to pump his seemingly congealed blood around his body at an alarming rate. The delicate squeak of a mouse and a flurry of wings, followed by an eerie hoot, explained the activity neatly to the body snatcher.

Blasted owl nearly gave him a heart attack!

Pausing in his grisly employment, Tom let his heart slow and pulse return to its customary leisurely rhythm. Patting his dirty clothes, his fingers searched for the only item he knew that could return him to some state of normality, and aid him to complete the job he had started. To his satisfaction, the comforting metal was easily found.

With a flourish, Tom brought the battered and tarnished hip-flask to his lips. The cheap gin burned his throat, causing him to cough and splutter, but it was a welcome sensation of ordinariness. It was a sensation that reminded him of his wife, just before he'd slap her for not having dinner ready the second he returned home. He could almost hear the muffled sobs of the hag, as she hurriedly served up the slop that she'd call food onto his plate and await another blow.

It also reminded him of his many walks from the pub, where he often drank with fair-weather friends. He had a lot of these now he had the coins from this job to flash around. Good money too, although he kept his wages far away from the missus.

She had no idea of his nocturnal activities. If she ever became nosy, a hard punch would put paid to her questions. As for his fair-weather friends, they knew better than to enquire about his ill-gotten gains. All it took was a few well-placed pennies to oil over any doubts. He knew that the regulars at *The Ship Inn* didn't really like him, but he knew they loved the beer that he bought for them. He had ulterior motives, of course.

It was the perfect excuse to get close to little Rosie Porter, one of his so-called friend's wives – a buxom lass, and so much prettier than his own ageing wife. He was going to have his wicked way with her soon, whether her free-loading husband liked it or not. If he had to commit murder to cover his tracks, so be it. After all, he knew where to get rid of the bodies and get paid for them – seven pounds ten shillings per cadaver with no questions asked. It would be just like the vagabond he bludgeoned last year, when there were no fresh graves to be had. The more he thought about it, the greater the appeal. Perhaps he could get rid of that nagging wife into the bargain. He'd be looking at a fortune.

It would certainly be no more horrific than his current position, standing on the coffin of Mr Edgar Wells who had passed away from smallpox a number of weeks earlier.

Tom glanced at the headstone. *'Swept into the arms of our Lord,'* it read. *'A dear husband and father. To be forever missed. 1761-1815.'* He felt it would have been more accurate for the inscription to read, *'Swept into the arms of Tom Sawkins. To be sold for profit, with our Lord none-the-wiser.'*

The blasphemous notion destroyed Tom's air of confidence. He was not a religious man, yet there was no point in condemning himself if there was indeed an all-powerful deity listening to his every thought. Yet again he turned to the comfort of gin. Another swig, and another. He felt the wave of giddiness sweep over him, like a warm blanket. Confidence crept back. Now he was ready for the final stages of his employment. It was time to open the coffin.

Tom discarded the spade and lifted his stocky frame out of the grave. With practised ease, he flipped the coffin's lid open, displaying Edgar to the world he had departed from so tragically. Although he had done this job dozens of times before, Tom recoiled from the body. The rancid smell of decomposing flesh, combined with the sight of wriggling white maggots, was a sight that he had never been able to get fully used to, and tonight it was worse than normal.

He'd been forced to take an older body than he would have preferred. Choking back the vomit that insisted on jumping from his gut, Tom held a handkerchief to his nose and leaned into the coffin. His fingers swiftly pocketed the encrusted pennies that had been placed over the deceased eyes. There was no point wasting currency on the dead. Then, seizing one of Edgar's arms, he gave a series of almighty pulls and the corpse rose from the grave, flopping onto the damp earth.

With no respect for his wares, the body snatcher roughly pushed the carcass away from the hole. Tom smiled. All that was needed was to fill in the grave and nobody would know he had ever been there. The deceased's relatives would be blissfully unaware that the wooden box buried beneath their mourning feet held nothing but soil and dust. Squinting in the dim light, he probed for his spade, eager to finish his business.

As he searched on his hands and knees, he heard a soft cracking sound behind him. It was almost inaudible – no more than the snapping of a twig. Tom glanced around for the source of the unexpected noise, but saw no movement. Taking another swig of nerve-building gin, he peered into the gloom of the graveyard. Was somebody there?

Dread crept through Tom's alcoholic haze, as the outline of a body stumbled out of the protection of the trees at the edge of the graveyard.

He'd been caught!

His hand thrust into the inner pocket of his jacket and thumbed the handle of the knife hidden within. He would not go down without a fight, but he would need to wait for the right moment to strike.

The person came closer, and the soft moonlight lit him up for Tom to see. It was a man in his early twenties with long hair, a shaggy beard, barefoot, with strange clothing. His shirt was a multi-coloured mess – as if he had recently had a fight with his local painter. Across his forehead was a nasty gash, and blood tricked down towards his cheek.

'Hey, man, I've been in a train crash. Heavy, right? Where's the nearest phone?'

Tom stayed silent. What was this madman babbling about?

'Come on, man, there must be a telephone box somewhere?'

'A telephone box,' Tom repeated. The term was unfamiliar.

'Yeah, come on, man. There must be one.'

Tom's hand gripped the handle of his knife. It didn't matter who the stranger was, he had to be dealt with, and now was the time.

'What about your mate? Maybe he knows where a telephone box is?'

Tom's hand paused. His mate?

The body snatcher only became fully aware of the figure behind him when a shadow blocked out the moon's feeble

5

light. The babbling stranger's eyes went wide, and much to Tom's amazement he fell backwards in a dead faint.

Tom turned around. Much to his brief regret, a lynch mob had not discovered him. But with a sickening crack, a lopsided figure shuffled slowly forward.

Paralysed with horror, Tom closed his eyes and took his final breath.

Merciful blackness swiftly overcame Tom Sawkins, as he felt the caress of a mouth clasp around his neck and teeth sink in.

CHAPTER ONE

On the Right Track

'Would you like another garibaldi?'

Alistair Lethbridge-Stewart looked at the plate, full of golden brown glazed biscuits, offered by his mother, Mary. He was tempted, but shook his head instead.

'Best not,' he answered, before patting his stomach. 'Must keep fit you know.'

'It's been good to see you,' his mother said. 'I don't get to see you as often as I would like.'

It was true that he wasn't able to make it to his mother's very often, but that was the nature of his job. The regular army was a tough partner, but working for the Fifth Operational Corps protecting the world from extra-terrestrial threats was even worse. He was an army man, even when off duty and dressed in civvies. Family life often took a back seat. Still, he was here now and hoped that the time off could help heal the wounds of his failed relationship. He had ended his engagement with Sally Wright. The relationship had run its course, but that didn't make it any easier. After his brief and unexpected visit to Bledoe recently to deal with the Comfort Bot, he decided a peaceful weekend away from his worries was all that he needed.

Alistair took the last sip of his tea, and set the bone china cup carefully down onto the coffee table. It was a mistake. To his horror, his mother was looking directly at his ring finger. He hadn't told her about the break-up. The memory was so fresh he didn't want to talk about it. In time, he would. But not yet. Quickly, he withdrew his hand, but it was too late.

'Alistair, your engagement ring! Have you lost it?'

So much for his peaceful weekend away. 'Everything's fine,' he lied, attempting to end the conversation. It didn't work.

'I can always tell when you're fibbing. So you've split up?'

Alistair just sat there, but his silence confirmed the worst to his mother.

'Things were going so well at Christmas,' his mother said as she tried to point out the folly of his actions. Her words caused a stab of regret to pierce Alistair's heart. Things were indeed going well back then.

'How is it between you and Mr Cooper?'

'Don't change the subject, Alistair. It's going well, as it happens, but it's you and Sally that are important right now. You're just going through a bumpy patch, that's all.'

A bumpy patch? It was considerably more than that. It had ended badly, and Sally had said she never really loved him. He didn't know if she had said it to hurt him or if it was true, but whatever the reason her words had cut him to the core. But he had been ordered to reassign her to the base at Imber, another strike against him as far as Sally was concerned. He missed her. He couldn't help it, but it was over. There was no way of repairing the damage that had been done.

To shield himself from his mother's probing questions, Alistair glanced at his watch. The hands were stuck at ten to one. He had been so preoccupied with his thoughts that he had forgotten to wind it. He glanced at the carriage clock sat on the mantelpiece. It was six o'clock.

'I need to watch the news now. It's about to start.' It would be a distraction from his mother's prying.

Alistair bent over to turn on the TV, feeling his mother's eyes boring into him as he did so. With a click and a high-pitched whining, the television sprang to life. The picture was grey and fuzzy at first as it warmed up, but soon the glorious black and white spinning globe filled the small screen.

'And next on BBC 1 it's the National News and Weather.'

The main story concerned a train that had apparently gone missing. He tried to listen, but his mother refused to be put off. Throughout the programme she continued her cross-examination. He busied himself setting the time on his watch, and blocked out her questions as best he could.

'You know what? I think I *will* have another garibaldi.'

'Are you sure you're ready for this?' Bill Bishop asked, looking at Anne Travers and still only seeing a shadow of the woman he'd come to... love? Well, he decided, if that's the first word that came to mind, then perhaps it was true. Despite all that business with the Silhouettes, their first date had gone very well, and they'd only grown closer in the couple of weeks since.

She glanced over at him, and shook her head.

'Listen,' Bishop said, turning as best he could in his seat.

9

'You don't have to. If you like, you stay in here, and I'll go and speak to your brother, explain things to him.'

Now Anne smiled. It wasn't much, not as broad and vibrant as usual, but it contained at least a glimmer of the old Anne. 'Thank you, Bill, but I should do this. I... I have to.' She reached out and squeezed his hand for support. 'But, thank you,' she said, and climbed out of his car.

Bishop watched as she pulled her coat tight, and opened the umbrella to protect her new hair-do against the rain. It may have seemed odd, treating herself to such a luxury so soon after the tragedy, but Bishop and Sally had encouraged her to take some time out. Reluctantly, she had given in and accompanied Sally to a swish hairdresser's in the middle of Edinburgh. The pampering had done her good. But still there was a cloud of sadness hanging over her, and Bishop just didn't quite know what else he could do to help.

He had spoken to Samson, who himself had lost both parents, and he'd told Bishop that all he could do was what he was already doing. Be there for her. 'It'll take her a while, mate,' Samson had told him. 'It's only been six weeks. Eventually the loss will just be a normal part of her everyday life. It'll always be there, but she'll only notice when she stops to think about it.'

For the first few weeks Anne hadn't been herself at all, but their little adventure with the Daughters of Earth had helped to bring some of that old fire back. Of course, at the time, Bishop hadn't known that Anne had caught up with an old friend of hers; that had helped a lot too. And once the Corps had finally taken care of that business in Motherwell, Bishop had finally been able to approach the subject he'd been wanting to talk to her about.

Her father's funeral.

Bishop could see the thought of that was too much; the finality of it all. So he had persuaded her to go to Oxford to inform her brother of the death. She had plenty of family out there, all whom could take some of that weight off her shoulders. It had taken a few days, but eventually Anne had relented. The Travers weren't a tight nit family, and Anne was closer to her mother's side, but that didn't matter so much at a time like this. They were all kin, and whether or not they knew it yet, they had all lost someone in January.

The evening's conversation had been awkward, with his mother continually reminding Alistair why Sally was the perfect woman for him. More often than not, the television simply provided a background noise while his mother attempted to prise more information than he was willing to share. He had a small reprieve when his mother had insisted on silence during *The Kenneth Williams Show*. It was a favourite of hers, and as the end credits rolled, Alistair was dreading her renewed interrogation.

'And now on BBC 1 Robert Powell in *Doomwatch – Tomorrow the Rat*,' intoned the TV announcer.

As the dramatic theme tune of the next programme began and his mother prepared her next assault, the harsh *bring-bring* of the telephone cut across the living room. His mother stood, brushed down her skirt, and picked up the telephone receiver from its cradle.

'Hello... Oh... Yes, he's here,' she said, noticeably irritated. She held out the receiver to her son. 'Alistair, it's for you. Didn't you tell them you had the weekend off?'

Time off, Alistair thought. *If only!*

Holding the telephone to his ear, he answered the call in his usual clipped manner. 'Lethbridge-Stewart.'

'Hello, Brigadier, I hope this isn't an awkward time to call.'

Alistair recognised the nasal tones of Harold Chorley immediately. He was a nuisance. The last he had heard of Chorley was when Samson and Professor Travers had waylaid him up in John o Groats, some months ago now. They all knew it was only a matter of time before the journalist crept out of the woodwork again, and it was typical of him to pick Alistair's time off to do so. It was not a voice he normally would have wanted to hear, especially on his mother's telephone, but to Alistair's great surprise it came as a blessed relief. If he played his cards right, Chorley's unexpected phone call might save him from an entire Sunday of his mother's questioning.

'Chorley! How did you get this number?'

'Well, I am a journalist, old boy.'

'What do you want?'

'Is that any way to treat an old friend? After all we've been through?'

'Just get to the point.' If he was to avoid his mother's cross-examination, Alistair had to make it look as if he had no choice in the matter, or he would never hear the end of it. 'I am on leave, you know.'

'Only until Monday.'

Alistair shook his head, irritated. 'How the devil do you...? Oh, it doesn't matter. What are you after?'

'Straight down to business, is it? I suppose it's best to dispense with the niceties. Get to the heart of the matter. Save time by being direct.'

'What on earth are you talking about, man?' Alistair snapped, finally losing his composure.

There was a slight pause on the other end of the line, before Chorley answered. 'Well, there's something very strange going on in Bristol. I'd like you to meet me there ASAP. Well outside Bristol really. Practically next door to Keynsham.'

'You'll have to give me more than that.'

'I've found something you really need to see,' Chorley said, before adding, 'By the way, don't go by train.'

Alun Travers had to sit down. It was a moment he'd expected for some time, but never really wanted to admit it. And now it was here.

'How?' he asked, not even sure he really wanted to know, but what else could he say?

Anne just looked at him. 'Alun, I don't know if—'

'Don't!' he snapped, cutting her off. He took a deep breath. 'Sorry, Annie, but please don't obfuscate. I daresay it's all hush-hush, and you know normally I wouldn't even ask...'

Anne turned away, and picked up the picture of Alun and his family. His wife, Julia, and their daughter, Anna-Margaret. The last picture taken of them as a family, before the pile up on the M4 had claimed the lives of his wife and child. Alun had survived, mostly with minor wounds – except for the hearing deficit in one ear, which led to him wearing a hearing aid. A constant reminder of a much greater loss.

'Please,' Alun said, 'just tell me.'

'It's the anniversary soon,' Anne said, still looking at the picture.

'I'm aware.' He stood up and walked over to her. The last thing he wanted to do was talk about that. He gently took the picture off his sister, and placed it back on the mantelpiece. 'This is obviously a work thing, but I still want to know. I deserve to know.'

'It's… complicated.'

Alun didn't doubt it. Their father's life had always been complicated, a seemingly endless stream of adventures. Growing up, both Alun and Anne had heard so many stories, which, as children, they believed, but as they both became adults they looked back on the tales as just that… *Stories.* But things had changed last year, when Anne had found herself slap bang in the middle of one of Edward Travers' adventures.

Things hadn't been the same for them since.

Or at least, not for Anne. Alun chose to keep away from it all. He didn't even want to know. The closest he had come was when he'd spent Christmas with Anne and their father. During the festivities he had met some of the people Anne worked with up in Scotland. That was close enough, as far as he was concerned. It had been nice to meet her colleagues, and some of their own families. Nice to be around the laughter of children again, and even nicer to meet William Bishop, who was clearly very soft on Anne. Not that she seemed to notice.

'I'm a smart man, Annie,' Alun said, and offered her a smile. 'History is a very complicated thing. And if I can teach that without going nuts… Tell me.'

Anne nodded and they both sat down. Alun listened as she explained about Tibet, about the Great Intelligence, and about saying goodbye to their father on the astral plane. It was a strange tale, and if Alun hadn't been brought up with such tales, then he may have thought Anne was laughing at him. Although he found some of it hard to believe, he knew enough of their father's obsession with Tibet and the monastery at Det-Sen to at least accept it as fact.

'So…' Alun shook his head at the odd words he was about to speak. 'Dad's consciousness survives on the astral plane? But his body… has been emptied, and filled up by this Great Intelligence?'

'That's more or less right.'

'More or less.' Alun tried to take it in. Maybe it would never make sense to him, and maybe that didn't matter. The end result was the same. He stood up. 'Maybe we should have some tea, and …'

'Not for me. Bill is waiting outside, and I…'

'…we should discuss the funeral, and…' Alun stopped at the same time as Anne, as her words filtered passed his own. 'Bill is…?' He had to smile at the indecision on Anne's face. It was so unlike her. So, for a change, Alun decided to take charge. 'Then you put the kettle on, and I will invite him in. He's like family now, isn't he?' He almost laughed at the look of surprise on her face. 'Anne, it was just a matter of time. I may seem like I'm in a world of my own, but I am still your brother.'

Leaving her to puzzle over that, Alun headed to the front door of his house, a million thoughts running through his head.

Lethbridge-Stewart pulled his silver Mercedes left into Durley Lane. He was almost at the rendezvous point just outside Keynsham, having driven for much of the morning. He just hoped that this wouldn't turn out to be a waste of time. It was certain that Chorley had his own motive for sharing any information he had. As with all members of the press, it was always wise to treat Chorley with care and suspicion. If he was true to form, he would try to fish for any information he could use for a story.

Part way down the lane, the road intersected with the railway line that spanned between Bristol and Bath. With military precision, Lethbridge-Stewart pulled into a lay-by. He pulled on his sheepskin jacket and perched a flat cap on top of his head, before exiting the car. It was his weekend off, and he'd be damned if an unsolicited phone call from Chorley was going to force him into his restrictive army uniform. After all, this whole caper could turn out to be a wild goose chase.

Chorley was already waiting, his tall waspish frame leaning against an ash tree, while looking decidedly bored. No doubt he thought he looked dapper in a dark blue suit, lilac shirt and a bright red dickie bow, but the suit was crumpled and the tie crooked. The journalist looked up at Lethbridge-Stewart's approach, pushed his glasses to the top of his nose, attempted and failed to straighten his bow tie and then extended his hand in welcome.

'Glad you could make it, Brigadier. Spot on time too.' The journalist's eyes scanned over the civvies before adding with a small smirk, 'Anybody would think you're in the army.'

The corner of Lethbridge-Stewart's mouth twitched as he shook Chorley's hand, but he did his best to ignore the feeble attempt at humour. 'Is this to do with the missing train by any chance?'

'Oh, you heard,' Chorley said, deflating a little, as if the punchline from a fantastic joke had been taken away from him.

'Barely. There was something on the news about it last night, and it probably would have passed me by if not for your comment about not getting the train here. What do you know?'

In true media style, Chorley recovered quickly. 'A few days ago the 23.45 from Paddington to Bristol Temple Meads vanished, along with all the passengers.' He paused briefly, before leaning in conspiratorially. 'It's not one of your hush-hush undercover things, is it?'

'Not to my knowledge. It's my weekend off. If the Corps is looking into it, I'll find out when I report in tomorrow morning.' Lethbridge-Stewart considered Chorley for a moment, then asked, 'Were there many on board?'

'It was the last train of the day, so not many by all accounts. As I recall, there was a young man on his way home from a Hawkwind concert, plus a few businessmen. And the train crew themselves, of course. The entire railway line has been searched and there's no sign of any wreckage whatsoever. Isn't that strange?'

'Yes, I suppose it is rather odd,' Lethbridge-Stewart agreed. 'I would have thought they would have found it by now. Unless it's been stolen, of course.'

'But stolen en route to Bristol Temple Meads, full of passengers?'

'They may have been in cahoots with whoever nicked the thing, and it's down a siding somewhere. Still, I must admit that seems very unlikely. I assume that you have some

17

other explanation? There has to be a reason you called me in.'

'Have you ever heard of the Keynsham Triangle?'

'Keynsham Triangle? I don't believe that I have.'

'You must have heard of the Devil's Triangle, though.'

'Devil's Triangle?' The name rang a bell. 'Isn't that another name for the Bermuda Triangle? That place in the Atlantic where loads of ships have disappeared.'

'Planes too,' Chorley added.

'Well, no ships or planes have disappeared here. It's the middle of the English countryside, man!'

'Would it surprise you to know that in 1815, when Keynsham was still just a village, a sizable portion of the population vanished overnight? Just disappeared. And since then something like fifty-five people have disappeared in this very part of the English countryside. Some locals, some visitors. Despite various missing persons reports, the police have never been able to find any of them. And then there's the stories...'

'The stories?'

'The usual stuff – ghosts and ghouls. Seeing people in old fashioned garb out of the corner of your eye, but when you turn to look they're gone.

Chorley reached into the inside breast pocket of his suit and took out a battered ordnance survey map. Spreading it out as well as he could against the trunk of the tree, he beckoned Lethbridge-Stewart closer.

'Look at this.' Chorley moved aside so he could get a better view. Three place names had been highlighted and lines faintly drawn between them. The journalist jabbed a finger at each one in turn. 'The Somerdale Frys Chocolate

Factory, Portavon Marina, and the edge of Willsbridge. If you plot lines between these coordinates...'

'I see,' Lethbridge-Stewart said, nodding his head. 'It looks like a triangle, and right next door is the town of Keynsham.'

'Hence the name,' Chorley confirmed, before motioning with his finger to a particular spot on the map. 'Have you seen anything odd about what's inside the Triangle?'

Lethbridge-Stewart's eyes swept to the tip of Chorley's finger. It was just a blank spot. 'What am I supposed to see?'

'You should be asking what should be there,' Chorley said with a small chuckle. 'Within the Triangle there is nothing. No pylons, no houses, nothing at all. You see the river there. It should continue right through this grid reference. But it doesn't.'

'A mistake surely.'

'Would you believe that the whole area has never been surveyed?'

'What, in this day and age?' Lethbridge-Stewart mused, raising his eyebrows in surprise. 'Surely not!'

'Nobody ever goes there, and that includes the survey team for this very map. I tried it myself, and every time I needed to call my editor, chase up a different lead, even go for lunch, there was always somewhere important I needed to be instead. If you go to the edge of the Triangle, all you can see are open fields – with grass that never appears to grow and crops that are never harvested. But try as you might, you always turn away without entering.'

Lethbridge-Stewart sighed. It was intriguing, but there wasn't much substance. Chorley seemed to be clutching at straws. 'Would you kindly get to the point? What has all this got to do with a missing train?'

'The theory goes that something happened here in 1815 that warped reality, creating the Triangle. Sometimes people stumble in and are trapped, and that's what happened to the missing people over the last century or so. I think that is what happened to the train.'

'There are many reasons why people might disappear, and people going missing in such a large timeframe is hardly unusual. However...'

'...We now have a missing train,' Chorley said, finishing his sentence. 'The Keynsham Triangle takes another victim.'

Lethbridge-Stewart did his best to ignore the melodramatic remark. It sounded too much like a headline for his comfort. Instead he pointed out the very obvious flaw in Chorley's reasoning. 'I hate to point this out to you, but the railway track isn't in the Triangle.'

Much to his irritation, Chorley turned away and started off down the railway track. 'There's something I want you to see!' he shouted over his shoulder.

For a few seconds Lethbridge-Stewart just stood there, watching the journalist walk away. He was tempted to walk in the other direction. Then, in resignation, he followed Chorley. This had better be worth it.

They hiked down the railway line for some time, and now that Lethbridge-Stewart had escaped from his mother's well-meaning interrogation the loss of his day off was beginning to grate. Then, just as he was reconsidering his course of action, he saw people on the tracks a little way ahead. Chorley was not at all impressed.

'Damn! They weren't there yesterday!'

The track was cordoned off, with two bored looking policemen guarding the way forwards. So far, the police hadn't spotted them. To Lethbridge-Stewart's surprise, Chorley darted to the thick undergrowth that lined the railway line and began to force his way through the brambles.

'Quick, before they see us.'

Lethbridge-Stewart sighed, and followed. To his great relief, while the brambles at the edge of the railway track were thick, the thorny branches thinned out in the middle. If they kept low it might be possible to crawl past the cordon. Together they skulked through the undergrowth as silently as possible, thorns threatening to rip into their flesh if they did not pay the plants the proper respect. They had almost made it when a nettle brushed across Chorley's hand. He yelped with the unexpected pain, and rubbed the reddening patch on the back of his hand. The pair froze at the sound of a policemen's voice.

'What was that?'

'Dunno.'

Lethbridge-Stewart and Chorley lay still, as the policemen peered into the brambles. Five uncomfortable minutes passed before they finally gave up.

'Probably a weasel. Do you have any more tea? I'm parched.'

As the policemen helped themselves to a cuppa from a thermos flask, Lethbridge-Stewart and Chorley made the most of the distraction.

Before long, they were past the cordon and away from prying eyes.

As they strode down the railway line once more, much to Lethbridge-Stewart's surprise Chorley did not utter a single word. He thought it was likely that the journalist was attempting to build tension, ready for a big reveal. Then, at long last, he saw what Chorley was so eager to show him.

'Good God! The track is missing!'

'I think the Triangle has been expanding slowly over the years, and now it has reached the railway line,' Chorley said, waving his arm to the distance. 'Why don't you go and take a closer look?'

Lethbridge-Stewart's eyes surveyed the countryside. There should have been rail tracks snaking into the horizon, crossing the bridge a short distance away, but they halted abruptly less than twelve feet away from where he stood. If the missing train had come past this point it would have been derailed for sure, but there was no indication that the train had ever been there. All he could see before him was the rolling countryside of Bristol; but something wasn't quite right. There were no farmers going about their daily business, no livestock grazing the fields, not even a solitary car winding down a country road in the distance. Indeed, there was no sign of any industry at all – just masses of new looking grass and crops swaying in a non-existent breeze. Perhaps Chorley was right, and the Triangle had expanded to the railway track. It certainly warranted closer inspection.

He had almost reached the end of the track when he suddenly stopped dead. This was obviously a matter for the Corps, and the sooner a platoon from Imber was brought in, the better. He turned on his heels and strode past Chorley, back in the direction of his car. It would be a simple matter to pop into Keynsham and put a call through to Major Leopold in Imber, and it was important that it was done right now.

'We need to call backup immediately. If another train—'

'Don't you watch the news?' Chorley asked, his smirk becoming a grin. 'The line's closed. Has been since the beginning of the weekend.'

'But...'

'A few minutes delay in calling in your people won't make a jot of difference.'

There was no point in denying Chorley was right. Otherwise there wouldn't have been a police cordon, and he had to concede that it made sense to check the area out before calling in backup.

'Oh, very well,' he grumbled, before striding towards the end of the line. Less than a foot away he ground to a halt once again. This was a waste of time. It was just an empty field, and he had better things to do with his day off.

'I told you that would happen!' Chorley exclaimed, clearly enjoying himself. 'You can't go near it. I know. I've tried.'

'I've never heard such nonsense,' Lethbridge-Stewart said, swinging his arm in a round arc to point directly at the missing train tracks. 'If I thought this was important I would—'

'Brigadier, *your hand*...'

'What is it now?'

'Your hand! Look at your right hand!'

Lethbridge-Stewart's eyes darted to the end of his right arm, still pointing towards the missing train tracks. His mouth dropped open in surprise. It ended in a stump. His right hand was missing.

The first thought that went through Lethbridge-Stewart's mind was, *well that's my career over. What good is an army man*

23

missing his right hand?

The thought was swiftly replaced with the realisation that if he had really lost a hand, then there would be pain. There would be blood. Lethbridge-Stewart felt no pain, and there was no blood. There was no severed hand on the grass, nothing nearby that could have caused such a terrible injury. It all pointed to one thing. It must be an illusion of some sort. It had to be.

He tried to raise the stump of his arm, but it didn't want to move. He reached his left hand across with the aim of pulling his right arm back towards him. To his horror, his left arm disappeared below the elbow.

There was a lurch as he was pulled forward.

He felt himself toppling. Lethbridge-Stewart was dimly aware of Chorley, as the journalist grabbed his belt, attempting to prevent him going over. Then he was tumbling, with Chorley's scream of terror ringing in his ears.

CHAPTER TWO

The End of the Line

Anne sat in the back garden of Samantha Brook's Mitcham home. It was the early afternoon and the kids were in school, while Samantha and her husband, Jarryd, were at work, leaving Anne and Bill the run of the house.

Bill joined her, with a freshly brewed pot of tea.

'So, this is where you grew up?' Anne said, sliding her cup towards him so he could fill it up.

'Well, hereabouts, yeah. Not this actual house. Jarryd and Sam bought this just after they got married.'

Anne sipped her tea. It was nice of Bill's sister and brother-in-law to put them up for a couple of days while they sorted things out with Alun. The Travers' family home was in London, of course, but Anne couldn't quite bring herself to visit there just yet. Seeing Alun on Saturday had been difficult enough, although it seemed Alun had dealt with it better than she had.

'I think I'm going to have to keep you and Alun apart,' she told Bill. 'You two are incorrigible together.'

Bill chuckled. 'Sorry, but a bit of light relief is good. Especially at times like these.'

'Speaking of...' Anne hesitated. It was a thought she had been considering for the last two days, and one she didn't really want to voice. But, if they were going to have a funeral, and Alun insisted on it, then they were missing one key component. 'What do we do about a body? We can't bury an empty coffin.'

Bill studied her face a moment.

She smiled slightly. 'I'm okay. At the moment it's all so abstract, and the idea of holding a funeral for an empty coffin just helps to make it even more so.'

Bill nodded. 'Fair enough. But you know it won't always be so abstract, and I... Well, I want you to be ready for that.'

'I'll be fine, Bill. Or I won't.' Anne sighed. 'Soon find out.'

A moment of silence passed between them, and then Bill spoke.

'A body should be easy enough to sort out. There are plenty of homeless deaths, people buried in unmarked graves.'

'Oh, Bill, that's horrible. To die and nobody there to care.'

'It is.'

'Well, at least one of them will get a decent send off,' Anne said, deciding to make the best of it. Her family, and friends of her father, would be saying goodbye to him, while another poor soul would be laid to rest with the respect they'd never really had in life. A tragedy on more than one level.

'That's one thing off the list, at least.' Bill sipped his tea. 'What else is there to do?'

'Alun's going through the family he has contact details for, and a few personal friends of Father's. I'm going to have to contact those who he knew in professional circles.' She tapped the side of her cup with a nail. 'Oh,' she said.

'What is it?'

'There is one person who's going to be hard to track down. Not someone Father had much time for, but… Well, he should at least be told.'

'Who's that?'

It was someone nobody in her immediate family really spoke of. Someone neither Alun nor Anne knew very well at all. 'It's Father's brother.'

'Ted had a brother? I never knew that.'

'No. Nobody really did. As you know, Father was never particularly close to his side of the family. Much more interested in Mother's side. And I'm afraid Uncle Vincent took particular exception to that.'

Bill nodded. 'One of the worst things about a death in the family. Old skeletons come out.'

It was something Anne had been trying to avoid. One of many reasons she hadn't wanted to tell anybody about her father's death. Her family was very difficult at the best of times. And this was far from the best of times.

Lethbridge-Stewart came to with the bitter taste of soil in his mouth. With the world still spinning, he opened his eyes and slowly lifted his head off the ground. Spitting the loose earth from his lips, he took in his surroundings. He was still in the same spot, sprawled on the grass near the railway tracks. He heard a whimper from behind and turned to see Chorley on his hands and knees, frantically searching for something.

'My glasses… Where are my glasses?'

Bit by bit, Lethbridge-Stewart's head returned to normal. It took him a moment to realise that his hands were present and correct. It was a blessed relief. Regaining his composure, he pulled himself to his feet just as Chorley managed to locate his misplaced glasses – slap bang in the middle of a cowpat. The journalist pulled a disgusted face, as he delicately retrieved them with a handkerchief and wiped the thick black plastic frames clean.

'What the dickens just happened?' Lethbridge-Stewart asked.

'No idea, old man. At least we are both all right though.'

'This place looks different.'

Chorley put his newly cleaned glasses back on the end of his nose. 'What are you getting at? Oh… I see.'

They were standing in the same spot as before, but the missing railway tracks had miraculously reappeared. Behind them, the railway line that they had been following had vanished to be replaced by a couple of grazing cows.

'I do believe we've found our missing rail tracks,' Lethbridge-Stewart said. 'However, we've now gone and lost the other ones.'

'I don't recall there being any cows here.'

'That's hardly significant,' Lethbridge-Stewart said, dismissively. There were far more important things than cows. 'We still have a train to find.'

Again the two men set off down the railway line, but they didn't need to walk far. Once more, the tracks abruptly ended. The final few feet of track protruded over the edge of a steep slope. Lethbridge-Stewart and Chorley peered over the edge at the small wooded area below. Beneath them was devastation.

At the bottom, the once majestic sycamore trees were twisted and crushed as if they had been hit by a great force.

Some had been uprooted. Ripped from the ground, they lay interwoven together with their branches matted into the thick undergrowth. Something must have caused all of this destruction. Lethbridge-Stewart scanned the carnage for any sign of the train. Then he spotted it. Hidden deep under the branches of a tree, the blue paint of a British Rail train glinted in the sunlight. They had found the 23.45 from Paddington to Bristol Temple Meads.

They carefully scrambled down the steep slope, gripping the broken branches to prevent the loose soil from causing them to tumble downwards. When they finally reached stable ground, the pair wasted no time in exploring the train wreck. The door on one carriage hung open, inviting them inside.

On first impression, the carriage appeared to be empty, but when they reached the end they found a man in a pinstriped suit slumped across the last two seats. If it wasn't for the smell of decomposition, he would have appeared to be asleep, with his bowler hat tilted forward, covering his face.

Lethbridge-Stewart hesitated, before slowly pushing the bowler hat away from the man's face. Whoever he was, he was in his fifties, with greying hair. His lifeless eyes stared up at them, and a small dribble of congealed blood ran down the side of his mouth.

'Probably died during the crash, poor man,' Lethbridge-Stewart said darkly. 'I wouldn't be surprised if we find more bodies.'

He returned the bowler hat to its previous position, to give the unknown business man some form of dignity, and together they left that carriage and entered the next.

It took some time to check them all, but each one was the same as the first. There was no living soul among the twisted remains.

'Let's get back to my car,' Lethbridge-Stewart said, once they had finished the grim task. 'I should call this in.'

The loose soil made their progress back up the slope difficult, but the branches aided them once again in the climb. When they eventually found themselves at the top, Lethbridge-Stewart immediately strode ahead, leaving Chorley to hurry to catch him up. Before long, they were back at the spot where they had woken sprawled on the ground. There were still a couple of cows, happily munching away at the grass.

Lethbridge-Stewart marched towards them and stopped dead. Maybe they should check the rest of the land first. Chorley walked straight past him and then suddenly stopped as well.

'Oh no, not again,' Chorley said. 'What now?'

'I was thinking that now we have the chance, we should reconnoitre the place. You?'

'Well, *I* was thinking that I should go into Keynsham, find a pub and wash my glasses properly,' Chorley admitted.

'So the same problem as before then.' Lethbridge-Stewart sighed. 'Although this time I really do think that we need to check the place out. Maybe somebody escaped from the train crash.'

'Oh, that's a point.'

'Then that's our first course of action,' Lethbridge-Stewart said firmly. 'We'll check the surrounding area, and see if we can locate any survivors. Hopefully we can circle around back to my car afterwards. Which way should we go?'

'Frys Chocolate Factory is that way, and Keynsham High Street is just beyond it,' Chorley said, motioning his arm towards a field to their right.

Lethbridge-Stewart set off in the opposite direction. They needed to see what else was inside the Triangle, so there was little point heading towards Keynsham.

The pace was easy going, and when they reached a small wooden stile at the boundary between two fields, Chorley went first. He was half way over when he hesitated.

'There's something bothering me,' he said, swiftly regaining his composure and swinging his right leg over the stile. 'People don't normally return from the Keynsham Triangle. Do you really think we can circle around back to your car?'

'Your guess is good as mine,' Lethbridge-Stewart replied. Did they really have a choice?

Still looking unconvinced, Chorley jumped from the stile into the field beyond. Suddenly, the journalist yelped, with an expression of distaste splattered on his face. Lethbridge-Stewart nimbly hopped over the stile and joined Chorley's side, immediately seeing the reason for his revulsion. At their feet lay the mutilated carcass of an animal. The black leather of Chorley's shoe was dotted with beads of thick red blood, intermingled with white strands of wool and flesh. He had, in the truest sense of the phrase, put his foot in it.

Determined to salvage his dignity, Chorley swallowed hard and did his best to ignore his spoiled footwear, while Lethbridge-Stewart kneeled down to study the remains.

'It's a sheep,' he said matter-of-factly.

The animal was a bloody mess. Its entire head nothing more than a mash of crimson tissue.

'Do these look like bite marks to you?' Chorley shuddered, pointing to the small wounds covering the dead sheep's body.

Lethbridge-Stewart studied the injuries. They certainly looked like bite marks. 'Rat bites I would say.' Something he was, unfortunately, all too familiar with.

'Seem too small for rat bites,' Chorley said. 'Mice maybe? And there must have been a lot of them; those bites are everywhere.'

'Are you saying that this sheep was attacked by a gang of field mice?'

Catching the hint of mockery in Lethbridge-Stewart's voice, Chorley shook his head. 'Of course not.'

No doubt the bite marks were from scavenging rodents after the sheep had died, Lethbridge-Stewart mused, and straightened up. It was unpleasant, certainly, but not something that needed to concern them. The only person likely to be concerned with the animal's death would be the farmer that owned it.

'We're wasting time. Come on,' he said, setting off across the fields towards the town.

'Thank God.' Chorley sighed. 'This gives me the creeps.'

Early Monday morning a military Land Rover pulled into the lay-by a short distance up Durley Lane, just where the lane intersected with the railway track. Two men climbed out, and looked at the silver Mercedes a few feet away.

'Just as we were told, sir,' said the older of the two men.

The other man, darker of skin and the superior of the

two, nodded his head with a frown, and regarded the Mercedes through his sunglasses. This was Sergeant Major Samson Ware. Usually he was stationed in Stirling, training the troops of the Fifth Operational Corps' 1 Battalion, but he had been at Imber, Wiltshire, inspecting the new recruits of 2 Battalion when word had reached them of Lethbridge-Stewart's disappearance.

Which was just as well. They were all good men at the Loony Bin, in particular Major Leopold, and Samson's equivalent, RSM Greenland, but none of them knew Lethbridge-Stewart like him. They went back years, and if anybody was going to look into Lethbridge-Stewart's disappearance, it felt right that it should be Samson.

When the brigadier had failed to report in a few hours previously, Colonel Douglas up in Edinburgh had put a call through to Imber to see if Lethbridge-Stewart had turned up there instead. It was very unusual for him to not report in after a weekend off, but nobody had heard a word since Friday night. Calls had been made, and they discovered that Lethbridge-Stewart had left his mother's the previous morning to meet up with Harold Chorley at Keynsham. The mention of Chorley set off alarm bells. If he was involved, then trouble wasn't far behind.

Further calls to the authorities in Keynsham revealed a few interesting pieces of information; not only had a train gone missing, some of the track had been stolen as well. And nearby on Durley Lane there was an abandoned car. Up to that point, the missing train hadn't registered on the Corps' radar; no threat to the UK was suggested, domestic or alien. But the description of the car had secured their interest.

And now here Samson was, along with Sergeant Barry Dovey.

'What do you think, sir?' Dovey asked.

'Not sure at the moment. But that's definitely the brigadier's car.' Samson rubbed his chin and walked over the Mercedes. He tried the door. Locked. So, Lethbridge-Stewart had intended to leave it for some time. The odds of his disappearance not being connected to the lost train were very low. 'Let's take a look at these missing tracks. Perhaps we'll find something the local plods missed.'

'Why would the brigadier go along with Mr Chorley anyway?' Dovey asked as the two soldiers set off along the rail track.

'I haven't met Chorley, but I've heard plenty about him from Gwyn; none of it good.'

'I'll admit it is a bit odd.' Samson smiled. 'Chorley's not all bad. Pain in the rear at times, but I spent some time with him back in October. He's not the man his reputation would suggest. Well, not entirely. Still, the Brig has done a good job of avoiding him for the last few months.'

Dovey was quiet for a moment. 'Something to do with the missing train?'

'Seems likely. Kind of story Chorley would follow. Not sure why the Brig would be interested, though.'

The men continued in silence for a while. Up ahead loomed a police cordon set up in an attempt to keep nosey locals at bay, but it seemed a little pointless. There was nobody around, and no roads or other rights of way anywhere nearby. Nobody in their right mind would normally be walking down the middle of a railway track. Perhaps it was intended to keep kids away.

'Let's take a closer look,' Samson said, and moved the cordon aside.

They walked a small distance past the cordon until they neared the end of the line – literally. The land before them showed no sign that there had ever been any rail tracks laid, never mind that they'd been stolen.

'It's like the rail track just stops.'

Samson nodded at Dovey's observation. 'And not even at the end of a beam. Look, if we...' He trailed off and stopped walking, glancing back the way they had come. 'Perhaps we should take a recce of Keynsham itself?'

'Yeah, the brigadier and Chorley are probably there.'

Agreed, the two men retreated away from the end of the track.

Lethbridge-Stewart and Chorley emerged from the fields onto a cobblestone road. At the end a was an impressive building, built of thick white stone and set with imposing stained glass windows portraying various saints and martyrs. Up above soared a bell tower surmounted by a pierced parapet. Lethbridge-Stewart's military mind noted that some of the building's design seemed to owe more to a fortress than a place of worship. The top of each wall was set with battlements, and the huge double doors were made of thick oak. Unlike a fortress however, these doors were wide open to welcome repentant sinners.

'That *looks* like the Church of St John the Baptist,' Chorley said, clearly confused. 'But that should be at the end of Keynsham High Street.'

'So you're telling me we're in Keynsham?' Lethbridge-Stewart asked, irritated. Trust Chorley to get his directions all muddled up. It would be a simple matter to check the map though, and put themselves on the right path.

'I could have sworn the church was on the other side of the road!'

'Can I borrow your map?'

'Of course.' Chorley searched his pockets, but it quickly became obvious that he had spoken too soon. He no longer had it. 'I'm sorry, Brigadier. I think I was holding it when we got dragged into the Triangle. It's probably on the other side of that barrier thing. Anyway, this *can't* be Keynsham! I've been before and it looks nothing like this. Cobblestones! There shouldn't be cobblestones! And another thing – if that is Keynsham Church, then Frys should be that way.' Chorley waved his arm back down the road they had been walking along. 'This should be the main route to the chocolate factory. Where are all the lorries?'

Lethbridge-Stewart looked down the road. It was deserted. If this was indeed Keynsham, even on a Sunday there would be traffic. He would have expected there to be some lorries shipping supplies of Fry's Chocolate Cream and Turkish Delight out to the adoring masses. But there were no lorries, or for that matter vehicles of any kind.

'Let's see if anybody's home,' he said.

Together, they went through a small side gate and into the church grounds. Looking down at his feet, Lethbridge-Stewart realised that the path was made up of gravestones – monuments to the remains of influential village ancestors. Their ornate carvings had been worn down by generations of passing feet.

His voice echoed around the church as they entered. 'Hello. Is anybody there?'

There was the sound of scuttling feet and the curious flabby head of a reverend popped out of a side door. On seeing them, he entered the main church and waddled towards them. There was something strange about his clerical clothing. It didn't seem quite right to Lethbridge-Stewart, not that he was an expert of course, but it seemed to him that the reverend's outfit was more than a little out of date.

'Afternoon to you,' he puffed when he was close enough for them to hear.

'Good afternoon,' Lethbridge-Stewart said curtly. 'I wonder if you could help us?'

'Wedding, is it?'

'Um... no actually,' Chorley said.

The round man squinted at the journalist. 'So sorry,' he said. 'Funeral then?'

'Actually, we wanted to find out a little about this place,' Lethbridge-Stewart said.

'Oh.' The reverend sighed with an air of disappointment. 'You are in the village of Keynsham. Reverend Cunningham at your service.'

Lethbridge-Stewart shared a look with Chorley. So it was Keynsham!

'You're not from around here, are you?' Without waiting for an answer, Cunningham carried on. 'We don't get strangers here very often."

'Surely with the chocolate factory, you have all sorts coming through?' Lethbridge-Stewart asked.

'*Chocolate* factory?' Reverend Cunningham considered as if the word was unfamiliar. 'No chocolate factories here. We do have a number of textile mills that the lasses work at, but they are all local girls.'

'You say you don't get many strangers,' Chorley said. 'Have there been any recently? Any others I mean.'

'Strangers, other than you?' Reverend Cunningham thought about it. 'There has been a trickle of people dropping by over the last few weeks I suppose. More than normal anyway. Soft in the head, the lot of them.'

'Soft in the head?'

'Mentally backwards, I mean. Imagine not knowing what the Year of Our Lord is. Come to think of it, all of them were dressed oddly – a bit like you two.'

'And just what year do *you* think it is?' Lethbridge-Stewart asked, a horrible suspicion creeping upon him.

Cunningham either ignored him, or simply didn't hear. He peered at their clothes suspiciously and added, 'You're not from a travelling circus are you?'

'Not at all. Pillars of society the both of us,' Chorley said, flashing as disarming a smile as he could muster. 'Is there anything else that you can tell us about these strangers?'

'I suppose we did have a rather grisly situation involving a stranger a few days back.'

'Go on, old man. Tell us all about it.'

The reverend looked at Chorley, clearly put out by his casual tone. He cleared his throat and explained. 'A few days ago, during the dead of night, local rascal Tom Sawkins dug up the grave of Edgar Wells – a good Christian who is sorely missed. Who knows what witchcraft the bounder wanted poor Mr Well's body for? But for his sins the good Lord struck him down. He was buried yesterday under the grace of the Almighty, but no forgiveness will be given forth. He will burn in Hell.'

'Surely the whole point of Christianity is that he can be granted forgiveness, whatever he has done?' Chorley said, slipping automatically into his talk show persona.

The reverend's already red face went redder. Lethbridge-Stewart cut in. 'You said there was a stranger involved in this nasty business?'

'Sawkins wasn't alone,' the reverend said, still glaring at Chorley. 'When we found his body the next day, there was also a heathen stranger with him; a Mr Harry Fenton. All raggedy, and very dead. Struck down by our mighty Lord. His sister turned up at the funeral. A very forthright woman.'

'Is she still around?' Lethbridge-Stewart asked.

'I believe she is,' Reverend Cunningham confirmed, with a small nod of his wide neck. 'Oddly dressed, too. Some kind of uniform, of all things! She walked past earlier, heading in the direction of *The Ship Inn*. You could always try there.'

Lethbridge-Stewart said thank you, and they excused themselves. As they walked away from the church, Chorley glanced back.

'What was all that about the year?'

Lethbridge-Stewart frowned. 'A suspicion. I don't think we're exactly where we think we are. Or when rather.'

Samson and Dovey returned from Keynsham an hour later, neither sure why they'd decided it was a good idea to check the town. If Lethbridge-Stewart and Chorley *had* been there, then they wouldn't be missing. Lethbridge-Stewart would have reported in.

'I've been thinking about that, sir,' Dovey said, as they

neared the police cordon along the train tack again.

'Go on,' Samson said, since he didn't have any ideas yet. Regardless of why they'd gone into Keynsham, it hadn't helped answer how a train could just vanish, along with its tracks, and neither did it explain why Lethbridge-Stewart had vanished too.

'Have you ever heard of the Keynsham Triangle?'

'Can't say I have, Sergeant.'

'Okay. Well, it's kind of like a land-based UK version of the Bermuda Triangle.'

Samson listened as Dovey explained, and the more he spoke about it, the more animated he became. Samson could see why Dovey had been selected for the Corps. He clearly had a bit of a passion for the unexplainable. The kind of mind that suited the strange things the Corps tended to deal with.

'You think this Triangle stole the train and the Brig?' Samson asked, once Dovey had finished.

'After the things I've seen since joining the Corps…'

Dovey didn't need to finish his sentence.

They reached the cordon again and Samson went to move it, but was stopped by an exclamation from Dovey. The sergeant was picking something up off the grass.

'What you got?' Samson asked.

'OS map for the area. Open.' Dovey looked at it for a moment, then handed it to Samson. 'Look at the way it's marked, sir.'

'A triangle,' Samson said, studying the lines on the paper. 'This isn't the Brig's writing. Chorley's…?' He folded the map, a decision made. 'I think we need to bring the big guns in. If Lethbridge-Stewart has fallen into this Keynsham

Triangle, whatever it actually is, then we need to find a way in too.'

'What do you suggest? Miss Travers?'

Anne was the only person Samson would expect to solve this, but she was having some personal time off, preparing for her father's funeral. Which left them with…

'Time to contact the Madhouse. Miss Travers isn't available, so let's hope at least one of her team is half as good as she is.'

Ruth Gamlin wiped up the spilt ale from the bar. The landlady's effort made little difference. The once-proud varnish was so stained with decades of slopped drinks and the yellowish hue of tobacco smoke, that it would have taken a great deal more than a damp cloth to make any marked improvement. However, since *The Ship Inn* served the best beer and cider in the area, the punters didn't tend to care too much about its appearance.

She swept her eyes across the room, attempting to ignore the presence of Jack Golby directly in front of her. Business was good for late afternoon. Mostly wasters and drunks, but who better to add to her profits? Drunks by their very nature bought more. They were her bread and butter. The only real problem was when they ran out of coins. Unfortunately, this was exactly the current state of Jack. The man's bloodshot eyes and rough stubble would have scared most people, but not Ruth. Although she was small and round, she hadn't run a public house for all her adult life without toughening up.

'I arst yur civil enough, didn't I?' Jack slurred.

With a sigh, Ruth explained yet again to the drunk,

trying her best to be polite and keep her famous temper from flaring. 'I'm sorry, Jack. No money, no draught. I'm not a charity.'

Jack's face flashed with anger. 'I'm no charity case, either,' he mumbled. 'Jus thought yur put a little sumthing on the slate, that's all.'

Gloomily Jack tottered towards the door and nearly collided with a strangely dressed woman as she entered the establishment. Ruth glared at him as he was grumbling his apologies, but to her dismay the woman uttered the worst words that she could possibly have done.

'May I offer you a drink?'

Staggering slightly, Jack raised himself to his full lanky height. Giving a curt nod of the head, he addressed his saviour. 'Yur an angel, that's for sure. Pint o' scrumpy would be grand.'

'It would be my pleasure. Allow me to introduce myself first. I'm Charlotte Bibby.'

'You can call me Jack. Everyone else does,' the drunk slurred, as Ruth watched his eyes sweep down the young woman's odd clothing to land on stockinged legs. He remained lost in thought for a second, before adding, 'Don't suppose yur know anything 'bout bunions? Been playing me up all summer. Gone black it has.'

'I'll get the drinks,' Bibby said quickly. 'Sit yourself down.'

The slim redhead approached the bar and flashed Ruth a beaming smile. Giving her the polite but frosty look she reserved for strangers, Ruth poured two pints of scrumpy for the immodestly dressed woman.

Careful not to spill anything onto her Wren's uniform,

Bibby carried the two glasses of cider to the bench where the dishevelled man sat with his face down on the table, apparently unconscious. Bibby sighed inwardly. She supposed it was her fault for choosing the first person she bumped into. The effect of alcohol on the human body loosened the tongue and could help prevent awkward questions. These were the very reasons she had chosen to talk to Jack. However, she had forgotten the other side to the demon drink. A comatose man would tell her nothing.

Setting the glasses down, Bibby scanned the dingy room searching for another interviewee. Suddenly, in one fluid movement, Jack's grubby hand grasped one of the pints and brought it to the lips of his newly righted head. One massive gulp later, a third of the drink had disappeared.

'Jest resting me eyes, darling,' Jack said. 'Ave I told ya, yur beautiful?'

Feeling unsure of whether it was wise or not, Bibby nevertheless sank down onto the seat opposite Jack. Aware that the drunk was waiting for her to also take a swig, she picked up her glass and swiftly downed half of the cloudy orange liquid. To Jack's obvious admiration, she didn't even flinch. Bibby took her new drinking partner's approval as her cue.

'I was wondering if you could tell me about Mr Sawkins.'

'Dead and buried old Tom is. 'E wasn't nice though, not like yur. 'E couldn't handle scrumpy like yur either.'

'Well, I am a Bristol lady after all,' Bibby said, her checks flushing slightly with the alcohol. 'May I ask what happened to him?'

'Attacked, but nobody knows what did it. Some say that

perhaps it was an animal, but what animal does that to people?' Pausing to collect his inebriated thoughts together, Jack took another noisy slurp of cider before continuing. He dropped his voice to a drunken whisper. It was the sort of whisper that everyone in the pub could hear. 'I heard Tom was found early one morning all ripped apart in the graveyard. The Devil killed 'im and claimed 'is soul. It's as clear as day that's what happened. They buried 'im fast afterwards an' all – just in case the Devil came back.'

'I'm sure it wasn't anything quite so supernatural,' Bibby said flippantly, before she could stop herself.

'Well, it's what I 'eard!' Jack snapped back. 'Pity really. Tom was a drinking buddy o' mine. Generous with the booze, but not lovely like yur, of course. Many a night we'd knock back gin and 'e would leer at the women. Especially at Rosie, but she didn't like 'im at all. Found 'im creepy, she did. But so long as the drink flowed, I didn't care.'

'Do you happen to know his employer?'

'Oh no. 'E 'ad no job. Same boat as me 'e was. No job an' no money,' Jack said, before adding as an afterthought, 'Sometimes wondered where 'e got 'is readies from though, but as 'e bought the drinks... who cares?'

'So you don't know why he was at the graveyard?'

'Nah!'

Jack abruptly raised himself to his feet. He waved his empty glass in the air and staggered towards the nearest group of drinkers. Hitting the glass heavily on their table, he pointed towards Bibby. His voice rose aggressively, making a demand.

'Buy this 'ere lady a drink, why don't yur? A lady that's what she is, so buy 'er a drink!'

44

Bibby cringed in embarrassment, but the drunk's behaviour was the least of her problems. She had been stuck in this godforsaken place for the best part of a week, with no idea how she had got there. The only explanation that she could think of was that somehow she had travelled back in time, much like one of those tales in the pulp fiction magazines that her brother loved so much.

As the locals gossiped about her presence, more than once Bibby had felt their gaze settle on her navy blue Wren's uniform. Recently the gossip had included Harry Fenton, an oddly dressed stranger who had met a terrible end with the despicable Tom Sawkins. The more she overheard, the more convinced Bibby became that Harry was, like her, an interloper from the future.

Posing as the grieving widow of Harry Fenton at the funeral of the two men had confirmed her suspicions. Judging by the hushed whispers at the wake, as she had suspected Tom was a grave robber, but there wasn't the slightest clue as to why Harry had been there at all.

For all her efforts, she was no closer to discovering who sanctioned the body snatching. But she wouldn't give up. If she unravelled the mystery of what had happened to Harry, maybe she would be a little closer to finding a way back home.

Bibby looked up when a glass of port was placed in front of her, but it wasn't Jack that had provided it. He was busy arguing with the drinkers at the next table. The man in front of her was well-dressed and held an air of pompousness. He moved close to whisper in her ear.

'I couldn't help overhearing your conversation. You were enquiring after the late Tom Sawkins' employers?'

Bibby simply nodded, and the well-dressed man's voice became almost inaudible. He was obviously anxious that nobody would overhear. 'I hesitate to mention this to a member of the fair sex, but I take it you know what he was doing at the graveyard?' Again, Bibby simply nodded. The well-dressed man smiled wearily and leaned in closer. 'My master may be able to offer you a job. Would you join him for breakfast tomorrow morning? The old manor house at seven o'clock sharp.'

Anne had left Samantha's number with Jean Maddox in the Madhouse, just in case either she or Bill were needed urgently. And, as it turned out, they were. Well, kind of.

Colonel Douglas had called, asking if she was available to assist Samson down near Bristol. Apparently Lethbridge-Stewart had gone missing, with his last known location just outside the town of Keynsham. To Anne's mind, it could mean only one thing – the Keynsham Triangle.

Anne hadn't thought about the Keynsham Triangle for a few years now. It had been one of her father's pet projects, and he had investigated it on and off for the best part of a decade. She had been tempted, but she was waiting on a call from Alun, and explained they had a lot to do, what with the funeral preparations. Douglas had said he understood, and Anne suggested he send Jeff Erickson down to Keynsham instead. Physics wasn't his field, but he had a good working knowledge of it, plus he had a very sharp mind. He was probably their best bet while Anne was otherwise engaged.

It was a shame in a way. Solving the mystery of the Keynsham Triangle would have been nice. Something to wrap up on her father's behalf.

'You have more important things to worry about,' Bill had said, once she had updated him on the call. 'Jeff's a good man, he'll cope.'

Anne had agreed, but she couldn't help but wish she were able to go anyway. Nursing a cold cup of tea in the kitchen, her mind wandered yet again to the missed opportunity. She hardly noticed when Bill joined her.

'You still thinking about Keynsham?'

Anne offered a smile. 'Unfinished business. I wonder what I'll leave unfinished when it's my time?'

Bill took her cup off her, and went over to the sink. 'Thoughts like that help nobody,' he said, emptying the cup and swilling it out. 'Besides, since when do you ever leave anything unfinished?'

Anne shrugged. 'Well, if it wasn't for Ruth up in Edinburgh, you might have been that one thing.'

Bill laughed. 'Well, thank God for Ruth, then.' He switched the kettle on. 'You would have got there eventually. And if you didn't, then I would have asked you. Eventually.'

Anne stood up and walked over to him. They kissed briefly and Bill wrapped his arms around her. 'Thank you,' she said, peering up at him.

'What for?'

'Everything really.'

As the kettle boiled behind Bill, the two of them remained in their embrace for a few minutes longer, simply enjoying the warmth of the moment. They were interrupted by the clicking off of the kettle and the ring of the phone in the hallway. Bill chose to make the tea while Anne picked up the call.

It was Alun.

'Took me most of yesterday,' he said. 'Can't find Uncle Vincent's sons, but I've managed to track down his daughter.'

'Debbie?' Anne asked. It had been a very long time since she'd seen her cousins, and she rarely thought of them. For all she knew her cousin's name might have been Gertrude. But Debbie sounded right somehow.

'Well, she goes by Deborah Walker now, but yeah, that's her. Apparently she married a well-to-do chap about fifteen years ago.'

'And no sign of Uncle Vincent?'

'If he's in the Yellow Pages, I can't find him.'

'Okay.' Anne thought for a moment. Calling ahead would probably have been the right thing to do, but she didn't know if Deborah had any ill will towards her and Alun. Who was to say whether Uncle Vincent had sown seeds of discord between his children and his brother? From what Anne remembered about him, she wouldn't have been surprised. 'I think we should just turn up.'

'I was thinking that too. She can only turn us away.' Alun laughed. 'Debbie. She was a spiteful child, as I recall.'

Anne laughed too. Alun may well be right, but it was so long ago it was hard to remember. 'Whatever Debbie did, you probably deserved it. You were always getting yourself into trouble.'

For a couple of minutes they shared remembrances. A sure sign of how little they saw each other. They agreed to fix that in the future. They owed it to their parents.

A shower of early evening rain splattered down onto the

cobblestones, and Lethbridge-Stewart pulled up the collar of his jacket to prevent the vagrant raindrops trickling down his back. As they walked down the road, he could see a faded sign of an elegant sailing ship up ahead. They had almost reached *The Ship Inn*, and not before time.

For somebody who said he knew the area, Chorley's directions had been abysmal.

'Horses!' Lethbridge-Stewart said, as a horse and trap clattered past them. 'No cars or electricity, cobblestones, old-fashioned clothes.'

'It seems your suspicions may be right after all, old boy,' Chorley said.

Lethbridge-Stewart smiled wryly. 'You're taking this well.'

'It's quite a scoop. First journalist to go back in time.'

Lethbridge-Stewart wished he could dismiss his suspicions, but as they entered the small village... And that it *was* a village, and not a town, rather added to all the evidence.

'Well, I *did* want to get away from it all I suppose,' he muttered.

'I *thought* you gave up your Sunday rather easily. What's up? Trouble with the little lady?'

At their approach, a young woman sitting on a wall nearby looked over at them. Lethbridge-Stewart cringed with embarrassment. Why did Chorley have to talk so loud? For one awful moment it looked as if Chorley wasn't going to let it go, but when he saw the look in Lethbridge-Stewart's eyes the journalist held his tongue. Lethbridge-Stewart had already begun to push open the pub's door when a female voice called over to them.

'Just a gentle warning, boys. I wouldn't go in there – unless you like looking at bunions that is.'

It was the young woman. She stood and approached them. Now that he was paying attention to her, he recognised the uniform she wore. Women's Royal Navy Service, 1940s. Clearly the woman they had come to see.

'You must be Mr Spencer's sister,' Lethbridge-Stewart said.

The Wren smiled slightly. 'Well, so I tell the locals, yes. Was the only way to get the information I required.' She held a hand out. 'I'm Petty Officer Wren Charlotte Bibby. I can tell by your bearing you're military too.'

Lethbridge-Stewart was impressed by the woman's forthrightness. He shook her hand. 'Quite so. Brigadier Alistair Lethbridge-Stewart, Scots Guards. And this here is Harold Chorley.'

'Pleasure to meet you, sir. What year are you from?'

'Um. 1970.'

Petty Officer Bibby nodded. And sighed. A moment later she smiled again. 'You know, I think you've hit the nail on the head there.'

'Pardon me?'

'I overheard you just now, and I agree with you. We've all travelled back in time. From your confused faces, I suspect that you have just got here. I was exactly the same. Maybe if we pool our resources we can find a way back home.'

'We'd be delighted,' Chorley replied before Lethbridge-Stewart had a chance to answer.

A broad smile flashed across the woman's delicate features. 'I've rented a room nearby. It's not much, but it's better than nothing. You can sleep on the floor until you get your own place.'

'Well, that's very kind of, Petty Officer, but I don't intend to be staying here that long.'

Miss Bibby smiled. 'Have you tried leaving?'

Lethbridge-Stewart and Chorley exchanged a glance.

'Well, there you go then.'

It seemed they had no choice. Miss Bibby suggested they follow her, and she set off, Chorley leaned in close to Lethbridge-Stewart and whispered. 'Charlotte Bibby. She's one of the people that vanished into the Keynsham Triangle. Disappeared without a trace in 1939.'

Lethbridge-Stewart had worked out at least part of that. 'And she never returned?'

Chorley shook his head. 'Nobody has ever returned. I'm afraid we better get settled in here.'

Lethbridge-Stewart remained where he stood for a moment longer, and watched Chorley join Miss Bibby. History may have recorded her as never having returned, but Lethbridge-Stewart was damned if he was going to join her fate. Whatever that was.

— CHAPTER THREE —

Back in Time

Samson climbed out of his Land Rover and joined Dovey, who had been left at the site to supervise things overnight. The small platoon of men had remained, split into four squads, each stationed at various points along the 'barrier' of the Triangle. Whatever the phenomena was, it appeared to have grown since the last time it was measured by a local boffin a number of years ago. Samson had spent the night at *The Ship Inn*, reading up on the Keynsham Triangle. The information was sparse, and often contradictory. Sightings of local historical figures, various people who had gone missing since 1815; so many, including a scientist and his entire household, the original owner of *The Ship Inn*, even a newly-commissioned WRNS rating who had vanished the day she was due to leave to join the war effort in London. And for his efforts, all Samson had managed to do was give himself a heavy head.

'Any joy?' he asked Dovey.

'Not according to Erickson, sir, no.'

Samson had never really worked with Jeff Erickson before, although he knew that Erickson was usually the field scientist that was sent out when Anne was busy elsewhere. After almost twenty-four hours, Samson wasn't quite sure why. The man didn't seem to know what he was doing.

Sure, he kept himself busy, setting up instruments, running tests, systematically working out the exact measurements of the Triangle. But no solid leads.

'Mind you, I think I have something interesting,' Dovey continued.

'Anything would be good at this point.'

Dovey offered a smile. 'Yes, sir. Well, when Erickson had the men measuring the Triangle perimeter, I spoke to Mr Bolan...'

'Bolan the Boffin they call him in Keynsham.'

'Yes, sir. He was telling me about some of the ghosts he'd seen in the area over the years. One in particular was of interest.'

Samson couldn't see how.

'He described this tall chap, modern sheepskin coat, black hair, clipped moustache.'

Samson blinked at Dovey. 'You think...?'

Dovey shrugged. 'Sounded a lot like the Brig. So I checked, showed Mr Bolan a picture of him. Bolan wasn't certain, but he said that it *might* have been the Brig.'

'How is that possible? He only disappeared two days ago. When did Mr Bolan see this *ghost*?'

'About three years ago.'

'Then it can't be him.' Even as he said it, Samson knew he couldn't be sure. The last time Lethbridge-Stewart disappeared, almost a year ago, he had been catapulted back in time. To a different version of Earth, in fact. Could that have happened again...? 'I think I need to speak to—'

'Sergeant Major!'

Samson turned to the interloper. It was Erickson, scrambling across the grass from the rail track. 'Don't tell me he's actually found something,' Samson mumbled.

'Here's hoping,' Dovey said, equally quiet.

Once the scientist had reached them, he began to ramble, but Samson held his hand up to stop him so the man could regain his breath.

'Sorry,' Erickson said, clearly still excited. He leaned against the Land Rover to catch his breath, then turned back to Samson and continued. 'Now, you have to understand, I'm primarily a geomorphologist, but it pays to dabble in other things, so I may totally be misunderstanding things here. But I think I'm close to something.'

'Well, don't keep us in suspense,' Samson said.

'Of course. Sorry. Thing is, I've been running tests, every test I can think of. I'm not Doctor Travers, you understand, and applied physics are not my strong suit, but I got to thinking and I...' Erickson paused, no doubt noticing the irritated look on Samson's face. 'Yes, to the point. Quite.' He took another pause. 'I ran tests on the rail track itself, at both points where it simply ends. Not an easy task, by the way. I kept thinking of other things to do. And not just me, but the men stationed at those points who were assisting me...'

'Yes,' Dovey said. 'Everybody's been experiencing this strange desire to turn away. Made measuring the perimeter difficult. A common thing, according to Mr Bolan.'

Samson nodded. 'Same thing that happened to us yesterday when we first arrived.'

'Exactly. Ellery told me about that effect at the Vault in January. The infrasound, I think he called it.'

'I remember,' Dovey said. He had been there at the Vault. Samson had read his report, heard stories about it

54

from both Lethbridge-Stewart and Owain, the Brig's nephew. 'But this isn't the same thing,' Dovey continued. 'That feeling was almost like a fear, as if somebody was watching. It almost made you anxious, made you want to run away.'

'Whereas this... phenomena,' Erickson said, 'seems to create a desire in you to be elsewhere, do anything but move forward. And it's damn hard to fight. You can only go so far before you develop physical symptoms. Nausea and the like.'

'So, similar, but not the same,' Samson said.

Erickson nodded. 'But it did get me thinking about the way the universe works. Vibrations, energy. Everything in the universe exists on a vibrational level, and so I've been running tests on the rail tracks. Measuring the natural vibrations of the metal.'

'Okay,' Samson said slowly, concerned things were about to get too technical for him. If Bill were here, he'd be able to translate. Bishop had a good head for science.

'The vibrational frequency changes at the point where the tracks cut off. As I said, physics are not my strong suit, but something about the readings...' Erickson shook his head. 'I'm not sure what it means, but these readings, the frequency of the vibration... feels off to me.'

'Okay. What do you need to work out why these readings are off?'

'Honestly? I need Doctor Travers. This is her field.'

Samson shook his head. 'If she was available, you wouldn't be here.'

Erickson agreed, taking no offence at the observation.

'So, we're just going to have to muddle through. There

must be someone else at the Madhouse who can help?'

'Well, I suppose if I can speak to...' Erickson's voice trailed off. 'Hey!' he shouted to someone over Samson's shoulder. 'Be careful with that! It's expensive equip— Oh.'

Samson turned in time to see what Erickson was looking at. A young private was carrying some of Erickson's equipment over to the perimeter barrier, when he lost his footing and stumbled forward.

Erickson's admonishment cut off abruptly as the private simply vanished into thin air.

One moment he was stumbling forward, and the next he was gone.

'The Keynsham Triangle claims another,' Dovey said.

Anne and Alun reached Aylesbury later that afternoon, and the sun was still shining as they climbed out of Alun's little Vauxhall. Bill had, of course, wanted to come with them, but Anne had dissuaded him. Bad enough that they were going to turn up at their cousin's door without prior warning, she didn't want to aggravate matters by turning up with a complete stranger.

Not that she and Alun were a fixed feature in the lives of the Walkers, of course. But they were, at least, family, and that had to count for something. Well, she hoped so at any rate.

Their cousin lived in a place called Stocklake, close to the edge of Aylesbury, perfect for a walk in the country. Anne had lived in many places over the years since leaving home, and didn't consider herself wedded to any particular locale; city, town, country, it was all much the same to her. But she had to admit, Debbie had chosen well with

Aylesbury. If you were going to raise a family anywhere, this close to the country was ideal.

Alun continued his bad habit of perpetual small talk as they walked up to the house, and Anne's mind drifted to Keynsham, wondering idly how Jeff was getting on over there. Although tracking down Uncle Vincent was very important, a large part of her wanted to be over at Keynsham. If her father was still alive, he would have wanted to be there too.

She sighed.

Alun glanced at her. 'What?'

'It's nothing,' she said, and offered her best faux-genuine smile. Which, she had been told, wasn't very convincing at all. 'Let's get this over with.'

Alun nodded and rang the bell. They stood there for a moment in silence, watching a shape draw closer through the frosted glass of the front door. A female shape by the look of it. As Alun had suggested, Debbie was a housewife. An assumption Anne had taken exception with; it wasn't the '60s anymore! Still, in this case, his slightly reductive mindset had proven accurate.

The woman who opened the door might as well have been a stranger; if Anne passed her in the street, she'd never look twice. But standing there in that brief moment before opening the door and the first word, there was a certain familiarity in her mannerisms. There was little doubt that she was a Travers, even down to the little squint of disapproval when she realised she didn't recognise these two people at her front door.

'Can I help you?' she asked, her London accent betraying her origins.

Alun went to speak, but Anne stepped forward a fraction to assert her own authority. Much more than Alun, Anne was also a Travers, and was used to taking lead in any given situation.

'Hi, Debbie, doubt you'll even recognise us. We haven't seen each other since we were, what, about eight? I'm Anne, and this is my brother, Alun.'

A faint glimmer of recognition at the names, but still Debbie wasn't quite sure.

'Travers,' Anne said, to reaffirm the recognition. 'Your cousins.'

And then it clicked in place. 'Bloody hell,' Debbie said. 'Little Annie and Alun? Blimey, it *has* been a long time. We must have been visiting grandad at the same time, right?'

'That's my recollection.' Anne glanced around, and then subtly peered over Debbie's shoulder. 'May we come in? If we're not disturbing you, that is.'

Debbie glanced back, surprised, as if the thought hadn't occurred to her. Or she was just not used to welcoming visitors. 'Um, of course. Frank is at work, so I was just preparing dinner. Likes it ready for him when he returns, does my Frank. But, yes, you're family, sure he won't mind.'

She led them through the hallway and into the large kitchen. She raised her wine glass, and asked if they'd care to join her. Both Anne and Alun said no, thank you. Anne rarely drank this early in the day, and Alun was driving. Debbie looked at Anne as if she'd made a judgement on her drinking habits. The moment passed and Debbie asked what brought them to Aylesbury so unexpectedly.

'Tragedy, sadly,' Anne began, making herself comfortable on a stool at the... breakfast bar, she believed it was called. 'Our father passed away a few weeks ago.'

'Oh.' Debbie turned from the vegetables she was chopping. 'I'm sorry to hear that. Never really knew your father, of course, but...'

Anne smiled. 'Thank you.'

Alun looked from one woman to the other. 'We're sorting out funeral details now, and we want to contact your dad.'

'Yes,' Anne agreed. 'Father would have wanted his brother there.'

'No he wouldn't,' Debbie said, abruptly.

Anne and Alun looked at each, both a bit taken aback by the comment.

'I'm sorry for being blunt, Anne,' Debbie said. 'But your dad and mine haven't seen each other in a good fifty years. Before any of us were born. If they wanted to reconcile, they would have done so.'

Anne supposed she could understand the bitterness in Debbie's tone, but... 'Okay, maybe you're right, but I know Father, and he always...'

Debbie held up a hand to stop her. 'I understand the need to canonise someone when they die, to make them appear to be a saint in life, but we all know that, for better or worse, our fathers never attempted reconciliation when they lived. I doubt death would change that.' She offered a small, sad smile. 'Besides which, Dad died a few years ago.'

That was unexpected. Anne took a moment to process this, sad that there would never be a chance to tie up that loose end.

'We're sorry,' Alun said, climbing off the stool. 'Looks like we've wasted our time, and yours.'

'Don't be silly.' Debbie put down her knife and approached them. 'Our fathers may have issues with each other, which probably kept us all apart, but whenever I think of those times at Grandad's house in London...' She shrugged. 'Well, they always make me smile, and I then wonder what happened to you both.'

Anne wanted to say the same, but the truth was she had been too busy since leaving home to wonder about vaguely remembered cousins.

'Why don't I contact Joe and Patrick?' Debbie continued, speaking of her brothers. 'I'm sure they'd love to see you both again.'

Anne stood, taking hold of Debbie's hands. 'We'd like that. Maybe some good can come of all this, after all? The family's been fractured for far too long.'

Perhaps this was better, Anne considered. Wasn't quite the plan, but it was at least something they could all do. Fix something that her father had broken a long time ago.

As Lethbridge-Stewart studied the imposing building before him, the early morning sunlight crept through the sky, turning it a bloody red. Grey stone soared above, strangled with interweaving ivy, and a number of stone steps led down to an arched porch.

'Are you certain this is the right address?' he asked.

'He said the manor house,' Miss Bibby replied. 'Can you see anything else on this street that looks like a manor house?'

Lethbridge-Stewart conceded the point. It was certainly what he would describe as a manor house, but he would have preferred a more succinct address than the one Miss Bibby had given him.

When she had mentioned her invitation for breakfast with the late Tom Sawkins' employers, he had decided they should accompany her. For all they knew it could be a trap, but it was too good of a lead to simply ignore. Chorley had agreed, after all it was the occupants of the manor who were the first to disappear in 1815.

'Perhaps we can find out why?' Chorley had said.

Miss Bibby had spent most of the night trying to get information out of Lethbridge-Stewart, notably how World War II ended, and what life was like in 1970. He did his best to keep his answers vague, often turning the conversation around to her life before she ended up in 1815; he thought it best to conceal from the young woman that she never returned to 1939, and fortunately Chorley had agreed.

Apprehensively, Lethbridge-Stewart raised the large brass door knocker and rapped it twice smartly. There was no immediate answer, and he was about to try again, when the unmistakable scrape of bolts being drawn came from within. The door juddered open to reveal a very snooty looking man, well dressed in a black suit with a high starched collar.

'Hello, what can I...? Oh, it's you,' the butler said, spotting Miss Bibby over Lethbridge-Stewart's shoulder. 'Who are your associates?'

'Friends of mine. They've just arrived in the village.' Miss Bibby toyed with a lock of her long red hair as she spoke. 'I was hoping they could join me for breakfast with your master, and maybe we could come to some sort of arrangement with the household as well. You see they have nowhere to stay, and well... I wondered if it would be possible to get a roof for the night too.' Spotting the unsure look on his face, she added, 'We'll pay our way of course.'

She looked over pleadingly at her companions. Her face fell as Chorley patted his pockets and shrugged. Knowing that it was up to him, Lethbridge-Stewart fumbled in his pockets for something that could be used as a bribe. Deep in the recess of his sheepskin jacket, his fingers brushed his engagement ring. It was an uncomfortable reminder of his broken relationship, but could he part with it in such a way? Unsure if it was something he would later come to regret, he handed the ring to Miss Bibby.

'Take this as a measure of our appreciation,' the young woman said, placing the precious ring in the palm of the man's hand.

The butler looked amazed, but Lethbridge-Stewart spotted a fleeting glint in his eyes that was quickly covered up with an air of pompous self-righteousness. It was a glint Lethbridge-Stewart had seen many times before – greed. He just needed a nudge in the right direction.

'I don't think—'

'It'll be your little nest egg,' Miss Bibby said, before lowering her voice and whispering, 'We won't breathe a word about it.'

'I suppose I *might* be able to put you up in the servant's quarters for a night...'

'Or two.'

'Or two,' the butler repeated, uncertainly. 'But I'll have to check. Please wait here.' The door slammed shut.

Lethbridge-Stewart had to admit he was impressed. A little bribery and a bit of flirting may have bought them access to the house, and hopefully closer to solving the mystery of the Triangle. Chorley fidgeted impatiently, as they waited an excruciating five minutes for the butler to return. When he finally did he eyed both Lethbridge-Stewart and Chorley suspiciously before he spoke.

'I assume your associates are discrete?'

'No need to worry,' Miss Bibby answered as disarmingly as she could. 'Mum's the word.'

The butler visibly relaxed as if a great burden had been lifted off his shoulders, and he turned towards the two men. 'In that case, I have a small job for you. The master asks if you would be so kind as to unload the cart at the back. You may join him for breakfast once you have finished. You will find a scullery first door on the right of the servant's entrance. Please unload the wares there.'

'Wares?' Chorley asked, looking more than a little put out.

Instead of answering, the man held out his hand to Miss Bibby. 'May I escort the lady inside?'

'Of course, but I don't even know your name,' Miss Bibby said, giving a wink to Chorley as she linked arms with the butler and strolled towards the door. 'I'm Charlotte Bibby, by the way.'

'Oscar. Oscar Whittle.'

'So, Oscar, you simply must tell me all about your master. Is he a scientist or a doctor?'

'Please don't get blood on the tiles,' Oscar called back to Lethbridge-Stewart, before disappearing with Miss Bibby into the manor house.

'Blood?' Chorley exclaimed in surprise. 'What on earth have we just got ourselves into?'

Once the door had closed behind them, Lethbridge-

Stewart and Chorley marched to the back of the building and into a small courtyard. There was a small cart, with a chestnut horse still tethered behind it. The animal hoofed the ground and snorted as they approached, causing Chorley to give the animal a wide berth. Inside the cart there were two large foul smelling sacks. Lethbridge-Stewart clambered into the back and paused when he saw the blood soaking through the coarse material.

'Is that...?' Chorley's words dried up, but Lethbridge-Stewart knew what he was asking.

'I do believe it is,' he said wearily. The sacks were makeshift body-bags. 'Come on, Chorley. Let's get this over with.'

He indicated for Chorley to take one end of the sack, and he grabbed the other. The journalist shivered when he realised that his hand was holding tightly onto a stiff foot. Without saying a word, together they manhandled the awkward load out of the cart and carried it inside.

'Still no sign of Private Armitage?' Samson asked.

'Nothing,' Dovey replied, and checked his watch. 'Almost twenty-one hours since he vanished.'

Samson regarded the patch of grass that was now cordoned off. Erickson had run his vibrational tests, with some difficulty as the scientist really wanted to return to the rail track tests. Samson wasn't sure if this distraction was natural, or a result of being near the Triangle perimeter. Either way, Erickson's test showed the same results as the rail tracks. Whatever the Triangle was, it seemed to vibrate at a different frequency to the rest of the world.

'Perhaps he's been sent back in time,' Samson said,

although he still wasn't quite convinced by the idea. But right now, it was the only theory they really had about where the missing people went. And it was a theory with holes. He'd asked about Keynsham, talked to locals whose family trees went back to Keynsham in the early 1800s. Like any small town, Keynsham had its fair share of strange people, tall tales, old wives' stories, but none which seemed to confirm the time travel aspect.

If the missing people did go back into the past, then surely they'd have some descendants living in present Keynsham?

Samson shook his head. Aliens he could get used to; time travel, not so much.

'Whatever's happened, if we don't get—'

He was cut off by the abrupt reappearance of Private Armitage. Just like yesterday, only this time in reverse, the young private appeared out of nowhere, stumbling backwards. He bumped into Samson, whose reflexes were thankfully quick enough to stop Erickson's equipment, which Armitage had lost his grip on, from falling to the ground.

'Steady on, Private,' Dovey said, grabbing Armitage by the arm, balancing him. 'Where've you been?'

'I...' Armitage looked around confused. 'Sorry, Sarge, but weren't you and the sergeant major over there a moment ago?'

'A moment ago? Private, you disappeared almost twenty-four hours ago. It's now Wednesday morning.'

'But that's... Where did that man go? And those kids?'

Samson glanced around. There hadn't been any kids in the area, to his knowledge, since the Corps secured the land two days ago. He called over the closest of his subordinates and asked him to take the equipment to Erickson. Afterwards he was to bring the scientist over to them. When he turned back to the puzzled private, Armitage was looking at the land beyond the perimeter fencing. Samson narrowed his eyes.

'Explain what you saw, Private.'

Armitage swallowed, and nodded. 'Yes, sir. Um. I must have lost my foot as I was carrying that device for Mr Erickson, and I almost fell. Found my balance, and when I looked up everything had... changed? It looked like the same place, but you and the rest of the men had vanished. And so had the train tracks, come to think of it. Not just those...' He pointed at the space beyond the cordon where the tracks used to be. 'But all of *them*,' he said, and pointed at the tracks which hadn't vanished. 'Like... I dunno, like the railway never even existed.' Armitage scratched his head. 'And there was this bloke. Red faced, like he'd been drinking... I think he threw a bottle at a group of kids. They ran off as soon as they saw me. The drunk man moved towards me, and I think I must have took a step back... then he was gone, and I was bumping into you, sir.'

Samson nodded and looked back at the perimeter. Armitage had obviously stepped into the Triangle somehow. And looking at him now, he was clearly feeling the effects of it. 'Go and see the field medic. I believe Corporal Fenn is around somewhere.'

'Yes, sir.' Armitage saluted, and was about to walk away, when he stopped and frowned.

'What is it, Private?' Dovey asked.

'Just... And this sounds nuts, but... I've heard rumour

about time travel, that Doctor Travers herself went back in time last year, but…'

'Go on,' Samson said.

'It sounds nuts, Sergeant Major, but I swear the clothes that drunk man was wearing, and those kids… They were old. I don't mean well-worn, I mean, like something out of the eighteenth century.'

Well, Samson thought, *perhaps it is time travel after all.*

'That's decided it then,' he said to Dovey, once Private Armitage had left them to find Jack Fenn. 'We need Anne now. She's the only one with any real experience with time travel.'

Stedman sat alone in the dining room. Long ago it had been used for lavish dinner parties with a multitude of guests, but it had been countless years since anybody had arranged such an event. Now, deprived of the hustle and bustle of the hearty toasts of the past, the room seemed cold and inhospitable. Instead the huge oak table had just a few places set, and even this small number was more than double the usual amount.

Paying little heed to the lonely surroundings, Stedman picked up a silver spoon and casually decapitated a boiled egg. An annoyed grunt uttered from his lips when he found no deliciously runny yolk inside. Stedman liked his eggs runny, and it was one thing that Miss Nash always got wrong. His irritation quickly disappeared when he smelled the delicious aroma of curried ham and kedgeree. He lifted the silver platter covering the food and added a large dollop of kedgeree to his plate. Then his eyes caught sight of the extra places set on the other side of the table. He hesitated.

It was bad manners to start breakfast before his guests had arrived. He was so used to beginning his meal before his partner that he hadn't even thought to wait. If he had to rely on Wallace's time keeping, the food would be stale before he had taken a single mouthful.

Stedman's gut growled, and the scientist fleetingly regretted his decision to invite strangers into the house. So immersed had he been in his work during the previous day, that it had been almost twenty-four hours since he had last eaten and now his body was rebelling. At least his attire was appropriate, he decided proudly. Dressed in a fine-cut suit with a fashionable wig, he was well prepared to entertain. There was one problem – he was starving. He hoped that there would be enough food to go around. When he had heard that there was a stranger enquiring about dear departed Tom Sawkins, he had wanted to meet her. She might be the answer to his prayers, and as an added bonus the men with her may be willing to fill the vacancy left by the untimely death of his former employee.

Before his stomach had a chance to bring forward a further complaint, Stedman heard voices outside. The double doors swung open, and Oscar entered. Stedman beamed. At last the guests had arrived, and he could eat to his heart's content.

'Good morning, sir. May I introduce Miss Bibby, Brigadier Lethbridge-Stewart and Mr Chorley.'

Stedman watched the tallest of the men, as Oscar showed the party to their places, before bowing stiffly and leaving. A brigadier, eh? He wondered which regiment... Stedman was about to ask, but Brigadier Lethbridge-Stewart spoke first.

'I must thank you for inviting us into your home, Mr Stedman. Most gracious of you.'

'And what a beautiful spread!' Miss Bibby added.

Much to Stedman's delight, Miss Bibby helped herself to a large pile of curried ham. Promptly the scientist began to devour his breakfast, half listening to his guest's appraisal of the quality of the food. When his gut quietened down, he decided it was time to get down to business.

'Miss Bibby, I suppose that you are wondering why I invited you here. Other than your pleasant company, of course.'

'I assume it has something to do with Tom Sawkins.'

'Quite right,' Stedman replied his face turning serious, and he looked at Lethbridge-Stewart. 'But I am curious as to your presence. Why would a man of your rank be interested?'

Lethbridge-Stewart's reply was quick. 'I'm off duty, and have agreed to accompany a friend. A young woman being invited to such a place…? What kind of friend would I be if I were to let her enter unchaperoned?' He smiled. 'I am here in no official capacity, I assure you.'

Stedman regarded him for a minute. And nodded. 'Very well. But, please, what I tell you has to be in the strictest of confidence.' When his guests nodded their heads in agreement, he continued. 'Oscar said that you are aware of the service Sawkins was performing for us, so you understand a little of what we do in this establishment. I require a lab assistant that is willing to keep quiet about the work done here. But I warn you, the work would only be for somebody with a strong stomach.'

'My father was a doctor,' Miss Bibby said proudly. 'I

think you'll find that my stomach is quite strong enough, thank you. Until I find a way home I would be happy to serve as your lab assistant.'

'Wonderful. So that's settled until you are able to go home,' Stedman said, beaming with delight. 'As for you two, with the death of Sawkins I find myself with another vacancy. Would either of you men be interested? The pay is seven pounds ten shillings per cadaver.'

'I'm afraid we will have to decline your offer,' Lethbridge-Stewart replied as he tried a mouthful of kedgeree. 'I must say, this is delicious.'

'What are the bodies for anyway?' Chorley asked, pausing as he cracked open a boiled egg. 'Pass the pepper, will you, old man?'

'Research of course.' Stedman sighed. He passed over a silver pepper pot, which Chorley promptly shook over his egg. 'How can we understand the body without dissecting it? The benefits far outweigh any so-called high moral values. It keeps us busy.'

'Us?' Lethbridge-Stewart asked.

'Myself and my fellow scientist, Wallace.'

'So, you are dissecting the bodies for medical research?' Chorley asked, rubbing stray crumbs from his mouth with the back of his hand.

'How else are we to learn?'

'It may sound barbaric, but that's how it was way back in the nineteenth century,' Miss Bibby said. 'Grave robbing was the only way to get fresh specimens for study.'

'The nineteenth century?' Stedman repeated the words slowly, letting their meaning sink in. 'You say that as if you are not from the ninetieth century yourself.'

'I'm not,' Miss Bibby replied, looking him directly in the eye as she spoke. She appeared to be challenging him. 'I know it's unbelievable, but I'm from 1939.'

'And the brigadier and I are from 1970,' Chorley added.

Lethbridge-Stewart coughed, and looked at his companions in surprise. Evidently this was not information he had expected to be shared.

Stedman's gaze flicked across to his guests. Their attire looked outlandish to his eyes, and reminded him of the other strangers that had turned up in the village over the last few weeks. Each one of them had seemed out of place, as if they didn't belong.

'That makes sense, I suppose,' he said thoughtfully. 'I thought this whole situation must have something to do with time.'

'This situation?' Lethbridge-Stewart prompted.

'I don't know how or why any of this happened, but a few weeks ago when I tried to leave the house, I couldn't. Try as I might I always ended up turning away from the door.'

'That sounds familiar, doesn't it, Brigadier,' Chorley said, giving Lethbridge-Stewart a knowing look.

'Wallace didn't believe me when I told him. He rarely leaves the confines of the manor anyway, but I had important work to do outside,' Stedman explained. 'Then, one day, I found I could leave. I rejoiced, but I had celebrated too soon. The village was there as normal, but all the people around me ignored my presence. It was almost as if they couldn't see me. Somehow I was out of sync with the outside world. I had almost given up hope when suddenly a woman apologised for almost walking into me.

Everything seemingly returned to normal. But it wasn't. When I tried to leave the village last weekend to ask the advice of my colleagues in the institute, I found that I couldn't. The phenomenon is affecting the whole village now.' He turned to Miss Bibby. 'That's what I thought you meant when you said you wanted to find a way home.'

'You've got no idea at all what caused it?' Lethbridge-Stewart pressed.

'None whatsoever,' Stedman replied apologetically. 'There are other things that I feel are connected somehow though. Recently there have been some rather bizarre cattle deaths, as well as the unexplained deaths of Tom Sawkins and Harry Fenton. And there's something else troubling me, but I can't quite pinpoint it. Something not quite right with this place. I must admit it's a relief to have somebody believe me. When I mentioned this to Wallace he thought I was crazy.'

'Perhaps the answer lies in your lab,' Lethbridge-Stewart said. 'We should check there first. Where's your colleague by the way? Isn't he hungry?'

Right on cue the dining room door opened and the short stocky frame of Wallace stumbled in. His clothes were crumpled and stained with chemicals that told of long hours toiling in the laboratory, and from the dishevelled state of his thick blond hair and unshaven face he looked as if he had been working non-stop for days. The scientist made his way to the table and lowered himself into a chair next to Chorley. Without a word, he began to pile his plate with food.

'Ah, Wallace,' Stedman said. 'We have guests for breakfast.'

The tired man seemed to register their presence for the first time, and he quickly studied them, his eyes lingering on Miss Bibby's figure.

'Apologies for my rudeness,' Wallace said. 'I've been working all night, and I'm completely exhausted. I must say that it is a pleasure to meet you. It's so rare for us to have visitors, especially someone of the fair sex.'

'These people are from the future,' Stedman said.

'Are they now?' Wallace scoffed, showering the tablecloth with egg as he did so. 'Don't you think it's time you stopped playing silly games, Stedman. First you tell me that it's impossible to leave the house, and when that was proved false you changed it to the village itself. And now you've roped your guests into this nonsense.'

'Have you actually tried to leave the village?' Lethbridge-Stewart asked.

'No need. I have everything I require right here.'

Before Lethbridge-Stewart had a chance to reply, they were disturbed by a timid knock on the door. Stedman's young slave girl, Zara, entered, holding a large silver tray in front of her.

'Have you finished breakfast, sirs?' she asked in a soft voice. 'Shall I clear away the dishes?'

'I don't know about you lot, but I couldn't eat another morsel,' Chorley said contentedly.

'Hardly surprising with the amount you were devouring,' Miss Bibby joked. 'Eat any more and you'll explode.'

There was gentle laughter, and the girl picked up the platters and stacked them on the tray. Lethbridge-Stewart passed his empty plate and was rewarded with a shy smile.

Soon there was just Wallace's plate left to collect. She reached across, but before her slim fingers touched it there was an almighty cracking sound. Her lungs forced an involuntary cry of pain from her lips.

Wallace had brought a large silver serving-spoon down on the young girl's knuckles. The flesh immediately began to redden.

'I haven't finished, and just think yourself lucky we have guests,' growled the scientist. 'Now go!'

The spoon was withdrawn and the girl hurriedly picked up the tray, fumbling with her injured hand. It had happened so fast and was so unexpected that everyone was too stunned to utter a word.

When the heavily loaded youngster staggered towards the door, Lethbridge-Stewart sprung to his feet and opened it for her. Their eyes briefly met, and then she was gone. The second she left, the room was in uproar.

'What on earth do you think you are doing?' Lethbridge-Stewart barked. 'She's only a child!'

When Wallace shrugged off his guests' objections, Lethbridge-Stewart's face grew grave at his reply.

'Don't be ridiculous. That's only the slave girl. They don't feel pain like we do.'

Stedman watched Lethbridge-Stewart closely, fascinated by the concern for the slave girl displayed by this man from the future.

— CHAPTER FOUR —

Dreams of Freedom

Since the argument at breakfast, an uneasy truce had fallen between Lethbridge-Stewart and Wallace. After the commotion had died down, Stedman insisted that their visitors should look at their work. Lethbridge-Stewart wanted to check the lab out anyway so he was happy to indulge his hosts.

The upstairs lab clearly used to be a library or study of some kind. Bookcases were now devoid of books and filled instead with numerous test tubes, medical instruments and a whole host of highly noxious smelling chemicals. One side of the room was lined with several heavy wooden desks. Here and there lay the evidence of recent spillages, eating away into the fine varnish. Dominating the middle of the room was a six-foot long slab, which was so ingrained with blood that it was obviously used for dissection. There appeared to be a body on the slab, but it was covered from prying eyes by a large white shroud.

All disagreements seemingly forgotten, Lethbridge-Stewart was shown reams of notes and formulae and countless slides of dissected organs, but most of it went over his head. Like a hyperactive child, Wallace jumped from one thread of research to another and then back again. All the while Stedman stood by, looking a little awkward, but also brimming with contagious excitement.

'You have a Bunsen burner!' Miss Bibby had said, clearly delighted.

'I beg your pardon?' Stedman had looked at her. 'You mean this? Why it's an invention of my own making. Bunsen?'

'Then this is amazing! You've created it forty years before Robert Bunsen.'

That had been, to Lethbridge-Stewart, further proof, to him, that something very bad was coming their way. There was no such thing as a Stedman burner in his time. To Lethbridge-Stewart's mind it was clear that Wallace was a genius with a skewed perspective on life and an arrogant disposition, while Stedman was quite a capable inventor with the money to fund their experiments.

Wallace had been particularly proud of his discovery of a chemical in the human body that he had named *Somnium Factorem*. He was sure that it was this very chemical that caused the human species to dream, and he was convinced that a large dose was flooded into the body at the point of death, causing a dream state to aid with the passing to the next world.

By the time Wallace had run out of steam and announced his intention to catch up on his missed night's sleep, Lethbridge-Stewart rejoiced. He couldn't take any more of the technical jargon and noted that Chorley was hiding his boredom very poorly indeed. The journalist had long since given up asking questions and instead appeared to be counting how many tiles surrounded the small wash basin in the corner of the room.

Miss Bibby gave the impression that she was itching to

say something, but she waited until Wallace had retired to bed before she finally spoke. 'I've been thinking. The *Somnium Factorem* that Wallace told us about – it could be Dimethyltryptamine.'

'Dimethewhat?' Chorley said, turning away from the basin. 'What on earth is that?

'Dimethyltryptamine,' Miss Bibby repeated. 'It was discovered when I was about fourteen. My father was fascinated by it. He used to give me a sweet every time I pronounced it correctly.'

'I wouldn't say that in front of Wallace!' Stedman exclaimed in alarm. 'It's his discovery, and we're planning to publish a paper for the Royal Society... Once we get out.'

'Calm down, Mr Stedman. Nobody's taking your discovery away from you,' Lethbridge-Stewart said. Stedman didn't appear convinced, but he didn't press any further. Lethbridge-Stewart turned his attention back to the young woman. 'Miss Bibby, could this chemical have anything to do with what has happened to us all?'

'I really don't see how,' Miss Bibby replied with a shrug. 'It causes very powerful hallucinations, but causing all of this?'

A dead end, Lethbridge-Stewart thought. He had hoped that they would find a clue in the laboratory, but so far nothing. As he pondered their next move, Chorley's journalistic nature got the better of him and he peeked under the shroud at the body underneath. The journalist almost gagged, and Lethbridge-Stewart was surprised when Chorley swept back the shroud, to reveal a young man with straggly long hair underneath.

'Brigadier, this guy was on the train.'

Lethbridge-Stewart studied the body on the mortuary slab. It was obvious that the deceased was not from 1815. He appeared to be a mod, dressed in a sharp suit, starched shirt and a polished pair of loafers on his feet.

'That's Harry Fenton,' Stedman said, joining Chorley's side. 'I had Oscar dig him up last night, along with Sawkins. You kindly brought in their bodies from the cart earlier. I thought their deaths needed further investigation. Did you know him?'

'Not personally,' Chorley replied, shaking his head. 'But his picture was plastered all over the local rags. And his name isn't Harry Fenton, it's...' He frowned. 'Lee something or other, I think.'

'Fascinating, I'm sure, but more importantly, any idea as to what happened to the poor chap?' Lethbridge-Stewart asked.

Guarding himself against the sickly-sweet stench, Stedman leaned over to examine the corpse. The lad's face and upper limbs were covered in small scratches and puncture marks. Picking up a scalpel he poked into the wounds, disturbing feasting worms and insects. Finally, Stedman held up the scalpel. On its tip was a small grey feather.

'I believe he was on his back when he was attacked, and he tried to protect his face,' Stedman said, pointing at the puncture marks on the lad's hands. 'If I had to hazard a guess, these wounds could be from being pecked by a large number of birds.'

'Killer mice and now killer birds!' exclaimed Chorley. 'What's next? Killer hamsters?'

'Do you mind if I take a look?' Miss Bibby asked

Stedman.

'Be my guest.'

As Stedman stepped aside, the young woman apprehensively approached the mortuary slab. Lethbridge-Stewart got the distinct impression that she wanted to prove her worth as a lab assistant. Pulling a face at the smell, Miss Bibby carefully rolled the corpse onto its side. Fishing in her pocket, she brought out a well-chewed pencil and used it to prise back the dead man's collar.

'That's where the name came from,' Miss Bibby said happily as she studied the label. 'Look.'

When Lethbridge-Stewart leaned in for a closer view, he immediately saw what she meant. The label should have read 'Harry Fenton. Dry Clean Only', but much of the writing had faded into obscurity.

As Miss Bibby respectfully covered the dead man's body again with the shroud and she handed Chorley her pencil. The journalist automatically accepted it, but his face turned pale when he saw blood covering the rubber end.

Dropping the blood encrusted pencil, Chorley fled spluttering from the laboratory. Miss Bibby swiftly followed after him, a look of concern splashed across her pretty features.

Lethbridge-Stewart shook his head, and raised an eyebrow at Chorley's retreating form.

Samson was reticent to do this, but he knew he no longer had any choice. He had mulled over Private Armitage's report, once the lad had calmed down enough to give it in a more succinct manner. He remembered much more after an hour, no doubt thanks to a clearer head after the paracetamol Fenn had given him. There was little doubt in Samson's mind now that Lethbridge-Stewart and Chorley had somehow been transported to the past.

And yet, the people of Keynsham had no stories of such strangers in the town's past. And, according to the reports Samson had seen, the amount of people who had disappeared in the last 155 years ranged in the upper fifties. If fifty plus people had ended up in Keynsham's past, how could there be no stories about them? And, if not them, then surely there'd be some old story about the train that had arrived in the past?

It made no sense to him.

'Makes no sense to me, either,' Dovey said, sitting beside him in the front of the Land Rover, once Samson had explained his thoughts. 'But what's the other option?'

Samson was about to answer when the voice on the other end of the RT came back to them.

'Message sent to the Madhouse. Over.'

Samson pressed the send button. 'Thanks, Loony Bin. Please advise us as soon as Doctor Moreau in en ro— Bloody hell!'

Samson jerked back in shock at the cow which appeared from nowhere before the Land Rover. It was running, startled. Samson's sudden movement clipped the break stick, and the Land Rover began rolling down the slight incline.

He dropped the RT and gripped the steering wheel, gunning the engine and shifted the Land Rover into gear. The vehicle ploughed forward, and Samson had to jerk the steering wheel to avoid the cow.

'We have to go back!' Dovey shouted.

Samson glanced at him, and for a brief moment he agreed with Dovey, but the thought quickly passed when he felt the impact of the Land Rover breaking down the perimeter fence.

He slammed his foot on the break, and the two officers jerked forward, arms reaching out to prevent them from going head first through the windscreen.

'What the hell just happened?' Dovey asked, and winced.

Samson felt it too. A feeling of nausea. 'I think we both know, we must have...' His voice trailed off. 'Um, when did it become night time?'

Outside the Land Rover, the countryside was pitch black.

'So,' Lethbridge-Stewart said, now that he was alone with Stedman, 'this attitude that Wallace has about the little black girl...'

'Attitude?' Stedman asked, clearly surprised by the non-sequitur.

'Yes. You know, that she is inferior. Tell me, do you also believe that she doesn't feel pain like everyone else?'

Stedman hesitated briefly before replying. 'Well, no, not really. I've seen her tears and I suppose that's an obvious sign that she does feel in the same way. The same nerves at least. I would be happier if Wallace wasn't so rough with Zara, but...'

Lethbridge-Stewart finished his sentence. '...You lack the courage to intervene.' Stedman nodded uncomfortably, but his host's embarrassment did not deter Lethbridge-Stewart. He had seen much racism in his life, ingrained in the culture of his own time. But here he was, in a time when it wasn't even considered racism. But Stedman struck

Lethbridge-Stewart as a reasonable man, and he couldn't understand how a man of reason could condone such violence on another living being. 'Has there been anything in your experiments that proves Zara really is inferior? A darker skin can hardly count.'

'All my research has shown that under the skin we are all the same.'

'So why do you have slaves if you think that they are the same as you?'

There was an uncomfortable silence, before Stedman attempted to explain. 'My family's fortune came from the transportation of slaves to cotton plantations in the Americas. Twenty-five years ago my father thought nothing of bringing a few slaves back to England to tend to his retirement. When he passed on, I carried the responsibility of ownership. Since Zara's mother died five years ago, I've only had the two to look after – Zara and her grandfather.' Stedman paused as he studied the look on Lethbridge-Stewart's face. 'I'm not sure why you are so upset, after all—'

'Who would care about a couple of slaves?' Lethbridge-Stewart took a deep breath. 'In my time slavery is a matter for the history books. Indeed, one of my closest friends is a black man. Not only that but he's an officer in the Armed Forces. Oh, there is still prejudice, mistreatment, and a continual struggle for black people to be treated as equals, but...' Lethbridge-Stewart paused and shook his head.

There was confusion and doubt on Stedman's face, but also some understanding. Fascinated by this future Lethbridge-Stewart spoke of.

'Correct me if I'm wrong, but hasn't the slave trade been

abolished by now?' he asked.

'It has,' Stedman said. 'A law was passed eight years ago to stop the slave ships,' Stedman reluctantly agreed. 'But that was just for the trade itself. And I supported the ban, even though Wallace was dead set against it.'

'So, you thought it was a good thing, yet you still have slaves? Do you not see a contradiction in your actions?'

'But I didn't buy them myself, they were already here,' Stedman said, trying to desperately explain his point of view. 'I keep them warm and fed. Without me they would be begging on the streets.'

'You don't know that for certain. But whatever happens, at least they would be free. If you offered them jobs, they may decide to stay and work for you. And if it means you have to spend less money on research to pay their wages, then so be it. No scientific advancement is worth anybody's freedom. You're just used to having slaves, that's all. Deep down you know it's not right. You should set them free.'

'But Wallace—'

The point had obviously got to Stedman, and Lethbridge-Stewart hammered home his advantage. 'They are your responsibly, not Wallace's, and you have already said that you thought the ban was a good thing. Can't you see it's wrong to treat another human being in this way?'

Stedman finally conceded defeat. 'Tomorrow. I'll set them free tomorrow.'

Sometime later, Lethbridge-Stewart sat on the hard bed, and surveyed the bedroom that Stedman had kindly provided for the night. After Stedman had made his promise, he had insisted Lethbridge-Stewart make himself comfortable. The room was dusty and clearly little used, but at least the bed had fresh linen, and the feather pillow was more than adequate. For all its faults, it was miles better than the floor of Miss Bibby's pokey little room where he had spent the previous night.

Sat alone in the silence of the room, Lethbridge-Stewart found his mind returning to his recent break-up with Sally. It had ended badly, and suddenly. In the long run he didn't doubt it was the right thing to do, but he also couldn't deny that he still cared for her. And she for him. And if he failed to find a way to return to 1970…

He fished into the pocket of his flannel trousers and brought out his wallet. He flipped it open. There was a Polaroid of his Sally inside. Sadly, he studied her pretty face.

He was so engrossed with his thoughts that he didn't hear the knock on the bedroom door or the creak as it opened. It was only when Chorley began to speak, that he realised that he was no longer alone.

'Brigadier, what do you think our next…?'

Desperately, Lethbridge-Stewart tried to hide Sally's picture from the journalist's prying eyes. It was too late.

'Ah, I know that look. Trouble with the little lady, as I thought.'

Lethbridge-Stewart felt the resentment building up inside him. He had left his mother's to get away from all her questions. The last thing he needed was for the same thing to happen with Chorley. There was no way he was going to air his dirty laundry to a member of the press.

'Chorley, I don't know what you're—'

'I notice you gave your engagement ring as payment.'

Lethbridge-Stewart's heart sank. He had hoped that

Chorley hadn't noticed that, but as ever the journalist was good at spotting all the little details others missed. 'I don't want to talk about it.'

'No. Whoever does? Brigadier... Alistair, I do understand. Loss is the one thing I do understand.'

Lethbridge-Stewart felt awkward. 'Ah yes, I did hear about all that business in John o Groats. I was sorry to hear about... Well, you know.'

'Thank you, but I that's not what I was referring to,' Chorley said, dismissing the apologies with a wave of his hand. 'My wife, Rosemary, and I... Well, we're getting a divorce. Not my choice, you understand, but... Well, we've not been together properly for some time now. Our marriage ended at least a year ago, although I didn't want to admit it. Shortly after the Underground.'

'You can't blame me for that. I didn't pick you to cover the evacuation of London.'

'That's not what I'm saying, Lethbridge-Stewart.' Chorley paused momentary, as if he was weighing up his next words carefully. 'However, you have had a hand in things since then.'

Lethbridge-Stewart felt as if he was back on familiar territory. This whole conversation had to be a ruse to delve for classified information while he was otherwise distracted. Well, it wouldn't work.

'Chorley, you were warned away from things before you asked me to help you investigate Dominex. So you can't—'

The journalist held up his hand, to cut him off. 'We can talk about Dominex later, if we ever get back to our time. If we don't, it won't matter anymore. Regardless, my point is, I understand what you're going through with Miss

Wright.'

Lethbridge-Stewart was dumbfounded. He could tell by the way Chorley avoided his gaze and his nervous smile that he meant every word. For several long moments, an awkward silence filled the room.

'Yes, well...' Lethbridge-Stewart began. He cleared his throat, buying himself more time to work out what to say and gave it another go. 'I appreciate the... you know. The thought. But, you know, plenty more fish in the sea and all that.'

'So I hear,' Chorley said, nodding in agreement. 'Doesn't make the separation any easier, though, does it?'

'No. No, it doesn't.' For a moment Lethbridge-Stewart let the silence sit between them, and then he asked, 'What was it you were after anyway?'

Chorley gave a reassuring smile, and allowed Lethbridge-Stewart to change the subject. 'I was wondering what our next move should be.'

Lethbridge-Stewart mulled it over. It was already mid-afternoon and he was determined to make the most of the rest of the day.

'I think a little reconnaissance is in order, don't you?'

As they neared the front door, Lethbridge-Stewart noticed that it was wide open, letting in the afternoon air. Sitting on the doorstep was an old black man. On their approach, he turned to look towards them and gingerly rose to his feet. He looked weary, and moved stiffly as if he had pain in his joints. It had to be Zara's grandfather.

There was a pail of water and a scrubbing brush in front of the door. The slave poured some of the water over the doorstep, and then stiffly bent over to pick up the brush. Lethbridge-Stewart raised a hand to stop him.

'Don't mind us, old chap. I'm sure you could do with a rest. We won't say a word to Stedman and Wallace.' The old man raised himself upright, and looked suspiciously towards him. 'I take it you're Zara's grandfather?'

'Yes, sir,' the slave replied automatically.

'Allow me to introduce myself. I'm Alistair Lethbridge-Stewart, and this is Harold Chorley. And you are…?'

'Toussaint, sir.'

Even though Toussaint stood obediently in front of them, Lethbridge-Stewart felt that they were being studied closely by the old man.

'You're not in trouble,' Chorley said.

'No, indeed,' Lethbridge-Stewart agreed. 'In fact, I've got some good news for you. I've been having a chat with Stedman, and he's agreed to set you free. Zara too.'

Despite the surprise on his face, Chorley chose to remain silent at the revelation.

'They're going to let me go home?' Toussaint said, a look of bafflement on his lined face.

'I'm afraid that might not be possible, but Stedman is hoping you'll both stay on as paid employees. That will be entirely up to you, of course.' Toussaint didn't reply, but Lethbridge-Stewart registered the distrust in the old slave's eyes. 'There are a few things that need to be sorted out first, but please be patient. You have my word. Tomorrow you and Zara will be free.'

'Thank you, sir.'

Toussaint lowered himself to the floor, picked up the brush and began to scrub the stone doorstep. As they left the manor, Lethbridge-Stewart felt the old slave's eyes boring into him.

'I'm not sure he believed you, old boy.'

Chorley may very well be right, Lethbridge-Stewart knew. But he had to try.

'Ger outahere!' Jack Golby growled over his shoulder at the unholy offspring following behind him. The children simply laughed, and Jack felt his heckles rising even further. 'I said ger outahere!'

This time, to show that he really meant business, the almost-empty bottle flew out of his hands. It landed several feet short of his tormenters, and green glass splintered on the cobblestones. It didn't do any good. If anything, it made the boys giggle even louder at his poor aim. They were daring each other to go closer, and Jack bared his teeth in defiance. The lot of them should be in the workhouse. Evil they were. Pure evil.

The children suddenly stopped laughing. Then they were squealing and running. When Jack turned around, his muddled mind took a moment to realise that it was not his gallant attempts that had scared them.

In a field, a short distance away, stood a man. He wore strange clothes. Green, slightly baggy, a uniform of some kind. And he was carrying something. A strange contraption the likes of which Jack had never seen before.

Jack ambled closer, to thank the fellow for his timely interruption. As Jack staggered towards the stranger, the man swung his head to look directly at him. He seemed unsteady on his feet, but Jack could relate to that. Perhaps he had been drinking at the wonderful *Ship Inn*.

Before Jack had a chance to reach him, the man finally lost his balance and tottered backwards. The man vanished. Jack's mouth fell open in surprise. It was a ghostly apparition, but it was obviously on his side. It had stood up for him and banished the evil children. Jack mulled it over, as best he could in his drunken haze.

The Patron Saint of Alcoholics always looked out for him, of that he was sure. Perhaps the apparition was Saint Monica, intervening on his behalf to save him from the nasty children of the village. Monica was the Patron Saint of Disappointing Children too, so it seemed likely. He frowned. The ghostly apparition couldn't have been Saint Monica, as there was no sign of a halo. Jack pondered for a moment. It had been a gent not a lady, so maybe Saint Monica had sent her husband in her place. Yes, that fit.

A thought hit him. Perhaps if the holy deity was willing to intervene on his behalf with those nasty urchins, then she might grant him another boon. It was worth a try.

'Dear Saint Monica, favourably 'ear my plea for… for free scrumpy at the 'old *Ship Inn.*' Jack paused. Did he say it right? He didn't want to insult the Saint by getting it wrong. Suddenly he knew what was missing. 'Amen,' he added.

They had walked a fair way up Durley Hill, keeping their eyes peeled for the turning off onto Durley Lane, when Chorley suddenly stopped dead, causing Lethbridge-Stewart to bump into him. It was as far as they could go. It didn't come as a surprise. Stedman had told them that they couldn't leave the village, and the fact that they couldn't go on was confirmation of that fact. It was proof that their problems were not confined to being thrown back in time. They were cut off for a reason, and he was determined to find out what that reason was.

The phenomenon, whatever it was, was the same in nature as the one that they had discovered by the railway tracks in their own time. Together, they followed the strange force-field as best they could around the outskirts of the village. As they walked, Lethbridge-Stewart found himself scrutinising every tree, bush and ditch, searching for any clue to their extraordinary predicament. He came up blank at every turn, but at least he was able to confirm that the entire village was cut off from the outside world.

Once they had waded through a field of wheat and clambered over a small fence, Lethbridge-Stewart and Chorley found themselves at the exact point where they had awoken the previous day. There were still a couple of cows grazing away on the grass nearby. Chorley turned to him, a concerned look on his waspish face.

'Brigadier, how on earth do you think we can get back to 1970?'

'No idea I'm afraid, Chorley.'

Silence. Then, 'And if we can't?'

'Perhaps I'll look up one of my ancestors. Fergus Lethbridge-Stewart, he was a major general in the British Army. He was at Waterloo in 1815.' Lethbridge-Stewart shook his head. It was a glib idea. What was he supposed to say, that he was a long-lost relative? If he stuck around long enough, Lethbridge-Stewart realised, he could even be there to see the birth of his grandfather in Scotland.

'No,' Lethbridge-Stewart said, more firmly. 'I'm determined to get back to 1970 somehow. But we can't just abandon Miss Bibby to this century. History doesn't record her returning, but that doesn't mean she can't return with us to 1970.'

Chorley nodded. 'Well, we may as well try and find a way. I mean, there has to be one.'

'Let's hope so.'

Chorley approached the spot from which they'd first arrived. 'Maybe, if I use a stick or something. If it looks as if it is going to work, I can let go. At least we will know if it works.'

Lethbridge-Stewart nodded. It was worth a try. Chorley picked up a sturdy looking stick from the grass, and walked forwards. He stopped dead after he had walked a few feet forwards. It was as far as he could go.

'No distractions, Harold,' Chorley whispered under his breath.

He swung his arm quickly in a round arc, but mere seconds later his fingers betrayed him and he automatically let go. The stick flew out of his hands and landed next to the grazing cows, causing them to panic. With a moo, one cow bolted towards the barrier and vanished into thin air. Lethbridge-Stewart and Chorley looked at each other in surprise. The animal had done what they had been unable to do.

'I felt so sure that would work, but I couldn't help it,' Chorley said. 'I *had* to let go. I *needed* to let go. But somehow that cow managed it.'

'It was scared and not looking where it was going,' Lethbridge-Stewart said, thinking out loud. 'Maybe you can only get through if you are not consciously trying to do so. By accident, I mean.'

'So, all we have to do is stay here and wait to accidently fall through,' Chorley scoffed. 'That's not a very good strategy, is it? We're stuck here!'

'Not necessarily,' Lethbridge-Stewart said confidently. 'My men are bound to be on the case. I'm sure that they can find a way to rescue us, given time.'

'Yes, and then they too can be trapped in the past.'

Lethbridge-Stewart said nothing. Mostly because he agreed with Chorley.

— CHAPTER FIVE —

Night of the Voles

'I think we'd better call it a day,' Lethbridge-Stewart said, wearily.

Night time had crept up on them, and with each passing moment it was getting harder and harder to see. Chilly winds had blown clouds across the moon, and with no houses close by there were no other sources of illumination to assist them in their fruitless search for clues.

'It's about time. This place is so creepy after dark,' Chorley said. 'And it's *so* quiet.'

He had a point. The deserted field seemed dead, with no movement or sound. And then, as they turned to leave, they both heard it. A noise cut the night air. A low, rumbling inhuman cry of distress. Lethbridge-Stewart spun towards the direction of the sound, but little could be seen in the tomb-like blackness. Making a snap decision, he plunged into the darkness. Chorley reluctantly followed.

The animalistic cry led them to a row of tall, spindly trees, dark and imposing in the gloom. Lethbridge-Stewart headed for a gap between the branches and carefully pushed through. Twigs snapped beneath his intruding body. Their slight sound was drowned out by the commotion beyond. The foliage gave way, and suddenly there was nothing in front except an open field. Turning his head, he beckoned to Chorley, before creeping into the field. The origin of the frantic cries was closer now. Lethbridge-Stewart put his finger to his mouth for quietness, and together they crept closer.

This time the darkness aided as well as hindered them. Hidden in the gloom, Lethbridge-Stewart and Chorley took in the sight before them. Less than ten feet away swayed a cow. Black dots swarmed over its black and white hide, already dark with blood. As they watched, the animal gave another unheeded cry for help, before crashing heavily to the ground. The black dots left its body and regrouped. The panic-stricken animal emitted one final moo, as the rodents descended for the killing blow.

Lethbridge-Stewart wrenched his gaze away.

The moon crawled from the clouds, showering its delicate illumination onto the field. He looked back, and for the first time he could clearly see them. Feeble light shone on matted fur and glinted off sharp teeth and claws, and Lethbridge-Stewart immediately had a flashback to being trapped in a phone box in New York.

The rodents varied in size and shape, from tiny mice to rats. They were not moving smoothly, Lethbridge-Stewart noted. Their heads lolled to the side, and they bumped into each other, as if their bodies were not working correctly. One scurried up the dead cow's back and was silhouetted against the sky. Lethbridge-Stewart was sure that it was a vole of some sort, with a short tail and flattened snout. It should have been herbivorous, but it clearly had an inexplicable and unnatural craving for blood. Soon, another rodent joined it – a large brown rat that dwarfed its comrade. Together they gnawed into the carcass, and were soon joined by multitudes of rodents of all shapes and sizes, all eager to fill their bellies with beef.

Chorley tapped on Lethbridge-Stewart's shoulder and pointed back towards safety, with a look of disgust and horror flashing across his waspish features. Silently, Lethbridge-Stewart nodded his approval. It was time to go. So far the rodents hadn't noticed their presence, and he didn't want to push fate. They retraced their steps back to the trees and quietly pushed through. They only had to cross a small field and they would be on the open road and safe.

'Didn't I tell you? Zombie field mice!' Chorley hissed, as they hurried away.

The journalist's voice cut the air, like a foghorn in the deathly silence of the night. In alarm, Lethbridge-Stewart paused to look back across the field, towards the trees. Had Chorley's words given them away? For one sweet moment, it looked as if the creatures hadn't heard, but then he caught a glimpse of the grass moving a little under the trees. They were being followed.

'Chorley,' Lethbridge-Stewart ordered. 'Run.'

With one panicked look back at the approaching rodents, the journalist swiftly obeyed. Not to be outdone, Lethbridge-Stewart hurtled after him. They had almost reached the road when Lethbridge-Stewart's left foot skidded on a patch of mud. His balance lost, he fell heavily on his back. He desperately attempted to right himself, but it was too late. Within seconds black shapes engulfed his body. Up close, the true horror of the rodents was apparent. One field mouse was little more than a skeleton – parchment thin skin stretched over tiny bones. Many had missing limbs, and maggot eaten eyes. One house mouse had a dent across its back, probably caused by a spring mousetrap. The impact had almost severed its spine, but it didn't appear to notice or care.

They bit and scratched at him, his thick sheepskin coat giving him some protection. Frantically, he sprung to his feet and wrenched undead rodents from his body. Stamping hard on the floor, he felt small bones break. And then he ran.

When Lethbridge-Stewart finally reached the road, Chorley was standing in the middle waving his arms frantically at an approaching coach. For one horrible moment he thought the horses were going to plough straight into him. To his relief, at the last minute the coachman pulled hard on the reins, and the coach ground to a halt. As an oil lamp was waved in Chorley's direction, the horses hoofed the cobblestones, sensing the danger behind them.

'What is it, Neville?' came a worried voice from inside the coach. 'Is something wrong?'

'I'm not sure, sir.'

The face of a grey-haired man popped his head out of the coach window, and peered at them.

'I don't suppose you can give us a lift?' Lethbridge-Stewart asked, still panting after his sprint. They needed to get out of there, and fast.

'Well, I don't know.'

'Just to Stedman's place,' Chorley added, giving Lethbridge-Stewart a wink. Trust Chorley to name drop. 'It's not far.'

'Oh, Stedman,' the man said, breaking into a smile. 'Friends of his, are you? In that case hop in. Mortimer Hartley at your service.'

Gratefully, they clambered in the coach and the horse trotted away. They were safe.

'Brigadier!' Chorley whispered urgently, indicating the arm of Lethbridge-Stewart's sheepskin jacket.

Lethbridge-Stewart looked down. There were two rodents clinging to his clothing, but they were lifeless, as if they had been dead for weeks. If he wasn't mistaken, it was a harvest mouse and a water vole. Mainly vegetarian and certainly never dangerous. It was a puzzle.

Chorley quickly turned his attention to Mr Hartley. 'Thank you so much for the lift. Most gracious of you.'

Lethbridge-Stewart made the most of Chorley's distraction, and threw the rodents out of the window before their rescuer noticed.

Stedman bent over the mortuary slab and swept back the shroud, exposing the torso of Tom Sawkins. He glanced over at Miss Bibby. The young woman swallowed hard and composed herself, but she didn't look away. He was pleased. With a little training, she could make a very capable assistant.

He turned his attention back to the matter in hand – a post mortem on the former grave robber. The young lad from the future had apparently died after being attacked by a flock of birds, so Stedman fully expected Sawkins to have met his end in the same way. Even so, Stedman would be failing in his duty as a scientist if he didn't test his theory in a methodical manner.

There was a gaping wound in the corpse's neck, and he carefully poked the hole with a scalpel. Soft tissue gave way, until the vertebrae abruptly stopped his intrusion. Furrowing his brow, Stedman studied the injury more closely. Casually he withdrew the scalpel and shook off a wriggling maggot with a flick of his wrist. Using its length as a rough ruler, he measured the width of the hole and tutted to himself.

'Miss Bibby. See these marks on his neck. What do they look like to you?'

She leaned in closer, and crinkled her nose at the smell of decomposition. It was a natural reaction. By now Stedman had grown used to it and in time so would Miss Bibby.

'Bites?' she ventured.

'From the size and pattern, I would say human bite marks.'

'Human?' Miss Bibby said, surprised. 'Are you sure?'

Stedman nodded grimly, and turned his attention to Sawkins' chest. He poked the gooey tangle of splintered bone and congealed blood with the scalpel. The instrument slipped easily through the ribs. Where there should have been a mass of tissue, the scalpel simply found air. The organs were missing, and only the ribcage held the body together.

Stedman paused, unsure of his findings. He had a hard time believing that there was both a murderous flock of birds and a cannibal on the loose. Perhaps Lethbridge-Stewart would be able to shed some light on the matter when he returned. In the meantime, Stedman's real work could begin.

He was determined to discover something by his own merit, without Wallace's aid. Something he could use to prove that he was not simply the financer of the research, but an integral part of it. First though, he had something on his mind and he couldn't ignore it any longer.

'Miss Bibby, Lethbridge-Stewart informed me that in the future slavery is a thing of the past. Tell me, are negros seen as equal in your time? What was it? 1938?'

'1939,' Miss Bibby said, correcting him. 'Well, no. I'm sorry to say they are not. But they *are* free.'

Stedman nodded. Lethbridge-Stewart had exposed the hypocritical nature of his position. He had supported the ban on the slave ships, but it was true that he was used to having slaves in his life. Just ending slavery was not enough, but it was a start. To many negros would still be seen as inferior but, perhaps, over time, attitudes would change. Lethbridge-Stewart was from even further in the future. Maybe the situation had improved by his time.

'It's a little bit like after women got the vote, I suppose,' Miss Bibby continued. 'If you're not both white and male, somehow you don't count.'

'Women vote in your time!' Stedman said, dumbfounded.

'Oh yes, for a while now. But it has been an uphill battle to be treated truly equal.'

'Thank you, Miss Bibby,' Stedman said, turning back to the body on the mortuary slab.

Miss Bibby's words had confirmed that what he was about to do was right. He should embrace this brave new future. Granting Toussaint and Zara their freedom was the first step. He wasn't so sure about women getting the vote though. That was taking things too far.

Wallace would resist the change, of course, but a breakthrough would prove a useful distraction when Stedman told him that he was setting the slaves free. The chemical Wallace had discovered in the cerebrospinal fluid was the key. The exact source of the compound had eluded his partner. If he filled this gap in Wallace's theory, his fellow scientist would have to listen on equal terms.

Stedman picked up the scalpel and made the first incision. The blade cut deep. The putrefied flesh gave in easily, and soon the spinal cord at the base of the neck was on display. He selected a syringe and pierced the exposed spine. Pulling back the plunger, it filled with a clear, colourless liquid. He carried it over to an old microscope near the window and settled down to work with his back to the mortuary slab. He carefully let a drop slash onto a glass slide.

'Miss Bibby, would you be so kind as to turn up the oil lamp.'

He was aware of movement behind him and a strange soft crack, but the oil lamp wasn't turned up. What was the woman doing? He shouldn't need to repeat himself. Stedman turned around, disappointed by his new assistant's lack of concentration.

'Miss Bibby...'

The words dried up in his throat. To the side of the mortuary slab stood Tom Sawkins, the young woman held almost lovingly in his arms. If it wasn't for the scarlet blood spurting from Miss Bibby's neck and the decaying features of Sawkins, the sight would have had the air of a romantic couple entwined in passion.

Slowly the dead body of Tom Sawkins turned its head. The lifeless eyes, partly eaten by members of the insect world, fixed their stare on Stedman. The corpse's blue bulbous tongue rolled out of the dead mouth, followed by a drool of sticky liquid. There was a soft yet sickening crack, as decaying muscles kick-started into action, and Tom shuffled forwards. Released from the embrace, the lifeless body of Miss Bibby collapsed to the floor.

Frozen to the spot in terror, Stedman's scream was little more than a whimper. Mr Tom Sawkins, recently deceased, closed his mouth over his former employer's neck, and teeth sank into flesh.

The warm glow of the oil lantern filtered under the laboratory door, and into the hallway beyond. The radiance was inviting and a stark contrast to the shadowy darkness of the sleeping household. Even so, when Chorley and he approached the door, Lethbridge-Stewart found himself hesitating. Years of experience told him that something was amiss. The light was on with the key still in the lock, indicating that either Wallace or Stedman was awake, but the room was deathly quiet. He pushed the door, and the hinges groaned as it swung open.

'What is that smell?' Chorley asked, his hand covering his nose and mouth.

Facedown in the middle of the room sprawled the body of a man, surrounded by a stagnant lake of blood. Further away, by the mortuary slab, lay Miss Bibby.

'Good Lord! Harold, remain here, keep the doorway clear. Just in case.'

'In case of what?'

'We need to make a quick escape.'

Chorley's face paled at the implication.

Even from the far end of the room, Lethbridge-Stewart could tell Miss Bibby was dead. What could have done this?

Certainly not mice, he thought grimly.

He moved closer, his footfalls ingraining the thick burgundy liquid further into the carpet. Chorley remained hovering by the door as requested. When Lethbridge-Stewart reached the prone man, he turned the body over.

'Stedman,' Lethbridge-Stewart told Chorley. 'Dead.'

The scientist's right arm had been wrenched off at the shoulder and was nowhere to be seen, while his face wore a mask of pure horror. Lethbridge-Stewart had seen similar expressions more times than he cared to remember, but the sight was always regrettable. Nobody should die with such terror in their minds.

Swiftly he moved to Miss Bibby's side. The Wren's throat had been ripped open. She had likely drowned in her own blood. Sadly, Lethbridge-Stewart pushed her eyes closed. Whoever, or whatever, had done this would pay, he vowed to himself.

He searched her person for her military ID, and pocketed it for safe keeping. If, *when*, he made it back, he'd make sure Petty Officer Wren Charlotte Bibby's death was registered and her living relatives informed.

His eyes searched the room for clues, and fell on a red leather covered door, camouflaged by a bookcase full of notes and journals. If it hadn't been slightly ajar, he probably wouldn't have known it was there. Tentatively, he pushed it fully open and stole through.

He found himself inside a narrow room. There were rows upon rows of thick pine shelves, containing numerous pickling jars of all shapes and sizes. Some held internal organs such as hearts, livers and kidneys. Several of the largest jars held complete heads, hideously discoloured by embalming fluid. Perhaps the room was used as a primitive mortuary. He passed them, approaching an alcove at the furthest end, from which a faint noise emanated; the sound of chewing and splintering bones.

Any thought of retreat was unthinkable. He had to see what was around the corner, however dangerous it may be.

Silently, Lethbridge-Stewart crept closer. Chorley was close on his heels, blocking his retreat.

'You're supposed to protecting our exit.'

'On my own?' Chorley asked, his face showing what he thought of that idea. 'No thanks, I'll stick with you. Safety in numbers and all that.'

'Or easy pickings for whatever did this.'

Together they turned the bend and froze at the sight before them. Tom Sawkins stood chewing the raw flesh from a human forearm as if it were a chicken wing. There was a gaping hole in the dead grave robber's chest, and as each mouthful of flesh was swallowed, more of the undigested meat was pushed out of the cavity and onto the floor. When the undead monster's eyes looked straight at them, its head lolled onto its side and, with a ghostly groaning, it shuffled forward.

Lethbridge-Stewart glanced at Chorley. 'Back. Quick as you can!'

First Lethbridge-Stewart and Chorley, and now Samson and Sergeant Dovey. When Douglas rang Anne last night to explain that Jeff had taken his investigation as far as he could without her, she'd been flattered, then oddly amused to learn that Samson had vanished while relaying his report to Imber. After two more days of contacting family and professional friends of her father, Anne was about ready to do something else, so Douglas' call came at the right time.

She'd called Alun straight away, explained things to him, and he agreed that she'd needed another distraction. He didn't say so, but she could tell he felt the loss of their father less than she did. It wasn't completely unexpected. After all, she had been around their father the most in recent years. It was Anne who lived with him in Edinburgh, tried to keep an eye on him. Alun was safely ensconced in his ecclesiastical life in Oxford. Not that Anne blamed him; it was her choice to return from America last year, and she chose to remain in the UK in order to keep an eye on their father.

And now, for the first time since last summer, she stood outside the family home in London. She hadn't been able to return to their house in Edinburgh since his death; the only memories she had of that place were of those she shared with her father. The family home, she had hoped, would be different. This was the house she had been raised in, that she'd spent many years in with both her father and grandfather. So many happy memories. So many summers and winters with family.

She glanced back at Bill, who sat in his parked car. He smiled and nodded.

Anne smiled back. She could do this. She set off up the steps to the front door.

It would be fine. It wasn't just her father that the house reminded her of, but her grandparents, her brother as a boy, and even visits from Debbie, Joseph and Patrick when they were all kids.

She had agreed to go to the Keynsham, to try and solve

the mystery there, but first she needed to pop over to the family home. Somewhere in her father's basement lab was all the work he had done on the Keynsham Triangle. He may not be with her any longer, but that didn't mean he couldn't help.

She opened the door, took the first step across the threshold. And was immediately assailed by the ghosts that lived there.

The wind taken out of her, she collapsed against the wall.

Bill was by her side in an instant.

'Anne,' he said, softly, holding her. 'It's okay. Let it out.'

'Oh, Bill,' she said, the sobs coming on violently. 'How do I do this without him?'

Chorley didn't need to be told twice; he immediately sprinted across the laboratory towards safety. Lethbridge-Stewart held the door shut to buy more time. The journalist was halfway across the room when something seized his foot, nearly causing him to fall headfirst onto the bloodstained carpet. Fighting to regain his balance, Chorley twisted his body to look back. Still sprawled across the floor, the reanimated corpse of Stedman held his ankle in a cast iron grip. With only one arm, the dead scientist was finding it difficult to stand up, so instead its remaining hand grew tighter to hold Chorley in place. Vacant eyes fixed on Chorley as a sticky stream of drool trickled down Stedman's chin, but the gaping mouth was too far away to be of any immediate threat. It was a small mercy. Chorley couldn't escape, and it was only a matter of time before the grave robber broke through into the lab.

Chorley became aware of a figure behind him, and he ducked out of the way just in time. Long fingernails missed him by millimetres. He craned his neck to look back. Behind him swayed the body of Charlotte Bibby. As the dead Wren lunged for Chorley once again, Lethbridge-Stewart abandoned the door and rushed to help.

He grabbed a cleaver from the mortuary slab and crashed it down upon Stedman's wrist, severing it completely. Chorley was at last free, but it was too late. Before he was able to make his escape, Bibby seized Chorley's collar and pulled him backwards towards her slobbering mouth.

'Get out, man!' Lethbridge-Stewart barked, taking careful aim and throwing the cleaver at Bibby's corpse.

It pierced the dead woman's shoulder before clattering uselessly to the floor. Lethbridge-Stewart's assault had only delayed Bibby by seconds, but Chorley made the most of them. He desperately wriggled out of his jacket, leaving it in the Wren's clammy hands, and bolted for the laboratory's exit. Lethbridge-Stewart swiftly followed, slamming the door behind them.

Wallace snapped awake. The din from the laboratory had invaded his dreams and prompted him into consciousness. He groped for a match and used it to light the candle stub that he kept at the side of his hard bed. The flickering flame pushed away the darkness of the night.

Although the manor had many empty luxurious bedrooms, Wallace's place of rest was small and modest. Originally meant for a high-ranking servant, he had chosen it simply because it was the closest to the lab. With his unorthodox and irregular hours of sleep, the arrangement meant he could continue his research with the minimum of disturbance to the household, and also cut down on wasted travel time into the bargain. It was very rare that he was woken, either during the day or night, as the servants kept well away from the area when they knew he was sleeping.

The scientist strained his ears, but now there was no noise to hear. Was the disturbance his imagination? His question was quickly answered when a crash shattered the night's silence. Wallace hopped out of bed and rummaged around in the dressing table. In the top drawer he found what he was looking for. Swiftly he loaded his flintlock pistol – a memento from his father's days in the English cavalry. Not bothering to change out of his nightshirt, he tiptoed out of the room. If there were burglars in the house, they would have to deal with his shot before they could escape with any valuables.

Noiselessly, he padded along the hallway. The commotion appeared to have died down, but in the gloom he could make out shapes outside the laboratory door; two figures whispering together. The pistol raised in front of him for support, Wallace edged closer so he could hear the conversation.

'That was my favourite jacket!'

The accent had a familiar ring, and suddenly he recognised it. The voice belonged to one of Stedman's guests. Just as Wallace was about to enquire what they were up to, the second voice startled him.

'I've locked the door, so we've got them trapped, but I don't know how we're going to explain this to Wallace.'

'See what you mean, old boy. How do you tell him that

he's got zombies in his lab?'

'You could start by explaining that remark,' Wallace said loudly, striding out of the shadows.

His unexpected booming voice caused them to jump like startled rabbits, but Lethbridge-Stewart recovered quickly. He motioned towards the raised flintlock.

'Would you mind lowering that? We're on your side, you know.'

Wallace began to feel a little foolish levelling his pistol at his colleague's guests. It was not the manner of a gentleman to threaten guests while wearing just your nightgown. He lowered the weapon and waited patiently for an explanation.

'I'm afraid I've got some bad news. And I'm afraid you will need an open mind to understand what's happening,' Lethbridge-Stewart said hesitantly. He said nothing more, apparently waiting for Wallace to say something. Wallace nodded. 'Stedman is dead,' Lethbridge-Stewart said.

It took Wallace a moment to find his voice. 'Dead? How?'

'That body we brought you; it's a zombie,' Chorley blurted out.

Wallace repeated the unfamiliar word. 'Zombie?'

'You know... a reanimated cadaver? It killed Stedman.'

'Superstitious rubbish!' Wallace scoffed. 'I have never heard such hogwash!'

'We have proof in the lab, but I wouldn't...'

Wallace cut Chorley off with a dismissive wave of the hand, and turned the key in the laboratory door. Boldly, he entered, knowing full well that the warning of the undead was utterly ridiculous. No doubt he was the butt of some childish joke, and inside the room all would be well. His confident air evaporated when his feet squished on the crimson soaked carpet, colouring his bare soles red. The mutilated body of his fallen associate lay before him; a death mask of horror on his chiselled features. Beside Stedman lay the partly dissected corpse of Tom Sawkins, as lifeless and unmoving as when he was brought in. Then he spotted Miss Bibby slumped against the mortuary slab. Was she also dead?

Wallace tried to move closer, but was halted by a gentle touch just above his elbow. Angrily, he shook off Lethbridge-Stewart's hand and glared at him. He quickly moved to the young woman's side and checked for a pulse. There was none. She was already gone. He gently laid Bibby's body on the floor and covered it with a sheet before turning his attention to his dead partner.

He knew there was no point in searching for signs of life, but couldn't leave Stedman lying on the floor in such an undignified way. Struggling with the body, he attempted to lift the remains onto the mortuary slab. Suddenly his burden became lighter, and he realised that Lethbridge-Stewart was aiding him in his task. His head still reeling with the shock of his loss, it took some time for Wallace to register that Lethbridge-Stewart and Chorley were binding the arms and legs of all three bodies. Anger flared up. Automatically his hand rose, levelling his pistol at the two men.

'What the dickens has happened, and why are you tying them up?' he demanded.

'He may have explained it badly, but what Chorley told you is the truth,' Lethbridge-Stewart said grimly, pulling tight on the final knot. 'We need to keep these bodies secure.'

'How can you persist with such utter rubbish?'

'There's something very wrong here,' Lethbridge-Stewart said. 'Believe it or not, earlier tonight we were attacked by a gang of dead mice, and when we returned, your dissection subject was running amok.'

'You don't seriously expect me to believe that. Attacked by dead mice!'

'Don't forget the dead voles,' Chorley said unhelpfully, as he picked up his crumpled jacket from the floor and checked it for blood stains.

'Your fanciful tales of reanimated cadavers are obviously drivel, to cover up your involvement no doubt,' Wallace said with barely concealed bile. 'You've murdered a helpless woman for God's sake, and as for Stedman... You deserve to hang for what you have done. The law should be called, but that can wait until its light. We are all going to bed, and God help you if you attempt to escape.'

— CHAPTER SIX —

Meat Attack

It was just before midday on Friday that Anne finally arrived at the temporary investigation site that had been set up outside Keynsham. Bill drove his car off the lane and onto the grass, pulling up by the military vehicles. They had visited the base at Imber en route so that Bill could change into uniform; not his, unfortunately, as his was up in Edinburgh, but the spare was a good enough fit. Just. The trousers were certainly a tighter fit than usual, not that Anne was complaining about that. They both climbed out and Bill walked around to the boot to remove the files they'd brought from London, while Anne admired the sight.

'What?' he asked, noticing her look.

'Just thinking you should keep those trousers.'

'Is that so?'

'It is.'

Anne smiled at him as he hefted the box in one arm, while attempting to close the boot with the other. She was tempted to help him, but decided there was no point in dating such a strapping man without taking advantage of his strength occasionally.

She turned at the sound of footfalls behind her. A man in his late thirties was approaching her. Ginger, thick moustache, and wearing the usual combat fatigues of the

Corps. She offered a hand, and introduced herself.

The officer shook the hand. 'I know who you are,' he said, with a smile. 'You're quite infamous at the Loony Bin.'

'I assume that's a good thing.'

He chuckled. 'One would hope so.'

Bill joined them, and offered the best salute he could manage with the box in his arms. 'Lieutenant Dashner, sir.'

'Lieutenant Bishop, good to see you again.'

Anne shook her head at the military protocol. It was one thing she'd never get used to. 'If you'll lead the way,' she said tersely, impatient to get on.

'Yes, ma'am,' Dashner said with a sharp nod, and set off across the field. Anne and Bill followed.

'Any news on Samson?' Bill asked.

'Nothing since he disappeared two days ago,' Dashner explained. 'Erickson is doing what he can, but mostly that entails moaning about how out of his depth he is. But, unfortunately, still no sign of Lethbridge-Stewart, Samson or Dovey.'

'And Chorley?' Anne asked.

'He hasn't turned up either.'

It seemed that Dashner didn't think Chorley was important enough to consider. Anne understood the sentiment. Chorley had caused more than enough problems for them all since the London Underground, but Samson insisted he'd seen a different side to Chorley back in October. Anne was yet to be convinced.

She turned her mind to the reports she'd read on the way from London. If they were true, then somehow Lethbridge-Stewart, Samson, Chorley and Dovey had all been spirited to the past. Anne wasn't sure what could be done about that.

Nobody had ever returned from the Triangle, except a young private two days ago. She'd have to talk to him.

On the last occasion she had dealt with time travel, she had been lucky to have on hand an alien substance and the help of an alien who had a time machine. Now she had none of those things. Had the situation not been so pressing, she would have tracked down Ruby Slant, the current human form of the shape-shifting alien Rutan that had helped her in the past and present. But Ruby tended to keep herself off the grid as much as possible. Anne didn't doubt she could find Ruby, if time wasn't an issue. But, alas, it was. Add to that, of course, she didn't want to bring Ruby to the attention of the Corps.

Which left her with her father's files, and whatever Jeff had discovered in the last few days. Which probably wasn't much.

And there was Jeff, coming out of the command tent the Corps had set up – one of the many tents that littered the field near the barrier. He spotted Anne immediately and began walking towards them.

'Lieutenant, would you be so kind as to show Bill to Jeff's tent?' she asked Dashner.

'Of course.'

'Thank you. And have that private report to the tent. I want to talk to him.'

'Armitage?'

Anne nodded.

'Right you are. This way, Bishop.'

'See you later,' Bill said to Anne, shifting the weight of the box in his arms, and the two officers walked off.

Anne met Jeff half way. He smiled at her, the relief very

clear.

'I think your theory is right,' she said, before he had the opportunity to get side-tracked; a bad habit of his. He looked at her, surprised, then nodded his head. 'I've brought the notes and files compiled by my father over the years. I think our first task will be to go through those thoroughly.'

'Just the two of us?'

'Lieutenant Bishop will help. He's got some scientific grounding.'

'Right, that sounds like a good idea,' Jeff said, glancing around.

Anne frowned. 'What is it, Jeff?'

He shrugged. 'I don't know how to explain it... This place gives me the heebie-jeebies.'

'Not a very scientific reaction.'

'I know. But there is something more than science at work here.'

Anne watched him for a moment. She didn't want to say she saw fear in his eyes, but he was obviously unsettled. Jeff had done his fair bit of field work in the last few months, but he clearly still wasn't used to the odd things they encountered. Anne knew that science didn't always explain everything – or, at the very least, not their kind of science. She had learned that there were many kinds of scientific principles at work in the universe, and humanity barely understood a fraction of them.

'Okay, do you want to take me to the end of the line, as it were?' she asked.

'Of course. This way.'

Anne followed him. 'Any further theories on how we can get through the barrier?' she asked, as they walked.

'After a fashion. I've been thinking about that Welsh physicist, Norma...' He frowned. 'Something or other. Anyway, do you remember you showed me a paper by her, about her experimental work on quantum harmonics?'

Anne recalled it vaguely. She had been impressed at the time, and Jeff happened to be in the mess hall when she'd been reading it, which is why she had showed it to him. But the details of the work escaped her right now. She admitted that she barely remembered. 'But obviously you do, so tell me what she said.'

Jeff grinned. 'Well, I've been thinking about these vibrations, and the idea that our people have gone back in time...'

Absentmindedly, Wallace stirred his tea with a silver spoon, but it had long ago become cold. His colleague... no, his friend, was dead. Murdered by two strangers that they had invited into their own home, and shown all courtesy to. And Miss Bibby too. Two murders under his roof.

Wallace almost dropped his cold tea. It was Stedman's roof, not his! Little by little the ramifications of the previous day sank into his brain. Stedman owned the manor and everything in it, and without his support Wallace would be little more than a vagabond. Stedman's sister, Maud, wouldn't tolerate Wallace's presence when she took up residence, and when she did, she would turf him out onto the streets. Although born from a well-to-do family, his father had frittered away all of his inheritance on high living. It seemed like several lifetimes since Wallace had seen any of his relatives. Without a shilling to call his own, he would never be able to publish his research. He was sure he was close to discovering the source of the dream chemical. The pituitary gland – that had to be the key. Yet with the current events, he might as well have never started.

He put down his cold tea and sank into one of the drawing room's luscious dark green armchairs. Slowly, a plan formed. For a while his face was one of indecision. He knew what he had to do, but it sat uncomfortably with him. Then, with a sigh, he walked over to the sideboard and poured himself a liberal serving of brandy from a crystal decanter. Swiftly, Wallace downed the liquor and refilled the glass. The alcohol warmed his throat and dulled the stress of the last day. He was ready. Composing himself, he reached for a tasselled bell-pull and yanked it three times. There was a momentary delay before the drawing room door swung open and Oscar entered, bowing stiffly. Wallace gave his orders, and, bowing once more, the servant left.

Ten uneasy minutes passed before Oscar returned, escorting Lethbridge-Stewart and Chorley before him. Quickly he glanced at the butler, locking the door as ordered. Once done, Oscar stood to the side of the door and waited. The knowledge that Oscar still had the pistol gave Wallace comfort.

'Good morning, gentlemen,' Wallace said in a manner that smacked of insincerity. 'I trust you slept well.'

'Mustn't grumble,' Lethbridge-Stewart replied. 'I've slept in far worse places.'

'But it would have been better if we weren't locked in like common criminals,' Chorley added.

'You can hardly blame him,' Lethbridge-Stewart said reasonably. 'Stedman's dead, and Miss Bibby too. We're obviously suspects.'

'But it was the zombies,' Chorley complained. 'It had nothing to do with us.'

Wallace found his antagonism rising. 'I wish you would forget these childish tales of the undead. It does not help your cause,' he snapped.

'Quiet, Chorley. Let's hear what the man has to say.'

Wallace took a swig of brandy to steady his nerves. At least Lethbridge-Stewart might listen to reason. 'Last night, the pair of you murdered my colleague and friend in the most brutal way imaginable. Even worse, you ripped out the throat of a defenceless young woman. You both deserve to hang.' He paused to make sure the threat had sunk in. 'Even so, I am prepared to overlook your crime. Believe me, it pains me to ask murderers for a favour, but I am a practical man. The servants know of Stedman's death, but no one outside these four walls does, and for now it must remain that way. In return, I will not turn you in.'

'Why all the secrecy?' Lethbridge-Stewart asked.

'I have a vested interest in delaying the discovery of my colleague's passing. Stedman owned this entire place; the house, the lab, everything.' Wallace hesitated briefly. Now he came to say it out loud, this plan sounded callous. He had to make them understand. 'His sister, Maud, will inherit it all, and I will find myself thrown out and destitute. If the word of Stedman's death gets out before I have a chance to publish my research, then all my work would be to no avail. That is why I must ask you to behave as if everything is normal. Play fair with me and you may avoid the noose.'

'If Maud lives outside the village, the chances of her ever coming here are non-existent,' Lethbridge-Stewart replied. 'There are much bigger problems than publishing your research. We have to work together.'

'Absolute balderdash!'

Wallace took another gulp of brandy. He knew where these excuses originated, but for Stedman's killers to use it in such a way was an insult to his deceased partner's memory. When Stedman had insisted that it was impossible to leave the house, he had scoffed. He did try once or twice, just to shut him up, and on each occasion he had rushed back to the laboratory with an idea for a new experiment. This added some validity to Stedman's theory, and Wallace found himself almost believing it. But when Sunday rolled around and they were able to leave for Reverend Cunningham's service he had felt foolish. Stedman then shifted the supposed mystery to the village itself, but Wallace wasn't going to fall for it again. Perhaps Stedman was researching the mind, and was using him as part of an experiment. At the time, Wallace had found the silly games irritating, but now to his great surprise he missed them.

'You must understand that nobody can leave this place,' Chorley said, breaking Wallace's line of thought. 'Let alone enter.'

'Well you did.'

'But—'

'Look, I'll tell you what is going to happen if you are to avoid the noose,' Wallace interrupted, his patience rapidly vanishing. 'I will let it be known that Stedman is researching overseas, whilst I look after the house. When he never returns, I will sadly inform his next of kin that he was lost at sea. The house will then pass onto his sibling, but by then my work will have been published for the benefit of mankind.'

'But nobody can leave the village, let alone leave the country!' Chorley said loudly. 'Haven't you been listening?'

Wallace blocked out the impassioned pleas of his imprisoned guests as best he could, aided by the alcohol. He tried to take another sip of brandy, but the glass was empty. He needed a further top up. Wallace was about to get one, when Lethbridge-Stewart caused him to look up sharply.

'And what of his body?'

The answer was obvious, but it was almost too grim to contemplate. The words had to be forced from his mouth. 'It will be of immense value to my studies; dissected and no longer recognisable. It is what he would have wanted.'

'You make it sound so noble!' Chorley said with a small shudder.

The reaction of disgust on his former guests' faces said it all, but it was really only course of action left open to him. It was necessary for the greater good.

'Would you rather you were hanged? If you do this, once everyone knows that Stedman is away, I will let you go. But be warned. I have given Oscar my pistol, and he will be ready to use it if you put a foot wrong.'

'Mr Wallace,' Lethbridge-Stewart said, looking him in the eye. 'Can Chorley and I have a private word to discuss your proposition?'

'If you must.'

Grudgingly Wallace moved away, but he kept his eyes trained on them at all times. The two murderers talked in hushed voices, and after a few minutes Lethbridge-Stewart turned to face him.

'We agree to your terms, but on one condition. You

have to promise to perform a post mortem on Mr Stedman.'

Taken aback, Wallace was stunned into silence. For all his bravado of dissection, he shuddered at the thought of cutting up his dead friend. But if this was the cost for silence, so be it. He took a deep breath, and sealed the deal.

They waited awkwardly for lunch, as Oscar loitered near the door blocking off their escape. The fine cut of Oscar's waistcoat was spoiled with the bulge of a pistol, and Lethbridge-Stewart noted with interest that it was a responsibility that Oscar looked uncomfortable with. Lethbridge-Stewart wondered if the fellow would be able to pull the trigger if it came to it. Still, there was no reason to force the issue just yet.

As they waited for the meal to be served, Wallace poured himself another generous portion of brandy from a cut crystal decanter set in the middle of the table. He didn't offer any to his guests.

The man was getting more drunk by the minute. To take their minds off the deaths, Lethbridge-Stewart broached another subject. One that should have been at least a little more palatable to Wallace.

'Did Stedman inform you that he was going to free Zara and Toussaint?'

'Rubbish!' Wallace snapped.

Okay, so maybe not that much more palatable.

'He wouldn't have decided to do that,' Wallace continued. 'Besides, why would they want freedom anyway?'

'Surely that's obvious. If the situation was reversed, wouldn't you want to be free?'

'That's different. I'm their better,' Wallace dismissed,

pompously. 'Here they are well fed and housed. What more could they need? If they were free they would just be two more beggars on the streets. They have been rescued from poverty and starvation.'

'How would you like waiting on others, far from home and without pay? Stedman was going to free them, I swear. He was going to talk to you about it.'

'It's out of the question. They're essential to the running of the household.' Wallace lowered his glass and peered at Lethbridge-Stewart in suspicion. 'Was this why you killed Stedman, some misplaced notion of liberation? Was poor Miss Bibby just in the wrong place at the wrong time?'

'Stedman's arm was ripped off and eaten,' Chorley injected, much to Lethbridge-Stewart's dismay. 'Do you really think we could have done that?'

'Eaten? Don't be ridiculous! If you're trying to put me off my food, it won't work. You know, this is quite splendid brandy.'

The argument was interrupted, when a waft of vegetable soup filled the room. Loaded down with trays, Zara conveyed the starting course to the table. Immediately she became a target.

'You idiot!' Wallace screamed at her, when a steaming bowl was placed in front of him. 'I asked for minestrone not vegetable!'

'I'm sorry, sir. This is what Miss Nash gave me.'

'It'll do, I suppose,' Wallace grumbled.

The starter was devoured in an awkward hush, and the uncomfortable silence continued until Zara returned with the main course. The delicious aroma of steak, roast potatoes and boiled vegetables filled Lethbridge-Stewart's nostrils, but when Wallace had his plate laid out in front of him the sound of a slap filled the room.

'I always have my steak rare! Bring another one!' Wallace roared at the slave girl, her face reddening from the blow he had given her. He poured himself a further generous helping of brandy, as she hurried away.

'There was no need to hit the girl!' Lethbridge-Stewart roared in anger. 'She's only a child.'

Drumming his fork on the table, Wallace ignored Lethbridge-Stewart. By the time Zara returned with another slab of steak, the atmosphere was thick with tension. This time, the steak was bloody and rare. At last Wallace was satisfied.

Picking up the gravy boat, he poured a liberal helping onto his meat and potatoes and motioned that everyone else should begin to eat. No longer hungry, Lethbridge-Stewart sat there impassively, watching Wallace's every move, as Chorley poked absentmindedly at his meal with a fork. It was several minutes before Wallace realised that Zara remained by his side, waiting to be excused. He studied the black girl's face and, wetting his finger, wiped off an imaginary speck of dirt from her cheek.

'You're happy here with us, aren't you my girl?'

'Yes, sir,' Zara said automatically.

'There you are!' Wallace exclaimed triumphantly. 'Proof straight from her own mouth. We are her family. You could say that I am her father. Isn't that so, Zara?'

'Yes, sir.'

'You wouldn't want to ever leave us, would you?'

'No, sir.'

'Is that what you really think, Zara?' asked Lethbridge-

Stewart gently. 'Would you like to be free?'

Wallace didn't give the girl a chance to answer. 'Don't pay him any heed. He's only jesting. I'm sure Miss Nash needs your help, so toddle on.'

Grinning like a Cheshire Cat, Wallace cut a piece of steak and popped it into his mouth. Zara slipped out of the dining room, just as her master coughed and spluttered.

The mouthful caught in the scientist's throat, and desperately he reached for his brandy and attempted to wash the obstruction away. The liquid gurgled in his gullet and overflowed out of his mouth. The sticky alcohol rolled down his chin, like a baby's dribble, but the steak stayed where it was.

Lethbridge-Stewart rushed to Wallace's aid, just as the brandy glass slipped from his fingers to smash into hundreds of tiny shards on the floor. He reached under the scientist's ribs and pushed into his belly, simultaneously pulling upwards. The steak refused to move, clinging on.

As Wallace began to turn blue, Lethbridge-Stewart realised with a sense of helplessness he was losing him. Refusing to give up, he prepared to try again. Before he had a chance, to his surprise the half-chewed mouthful inexplicably flew out of Wallace's throat to land on the carpet in front of them. Lethbridge-Stewart gave Wallace room as the scientist gasped the much-needed air into his lungs. When he glanced at his unfinished meal, Wallace's scream came out as a croak.

The partially eaten steak was flapping about on the fine Royal Crown Derby plate. Of all the things Lethbridge-Stewart had seen in the last year, that took the biscuit. Is that why Wallace had choked? Had the steak tried to kill him?

It was ludicrous. As if a slab of cooked meat was alive! And yet...

'I get the distinct impression that we are being taunted,' Lethbridge-Stewart said, unable to keep the mocking tone out of his voice.

Wallace abandoned the dinner table and fled.

Lethbridge-Stewart gave the pulsating steak an experimental poke with a fork. The steak thrashed about, resembling a grounded fish, frantically attempting to re-immerse itself in life-giving water. The meat grew weaker, until at last it gave one final flip and lay still.

'Taunted?' Chorley asked, looking suspiciously at the stake. 'That was obviously an attempt to kill him, surely?'

'I was unable to stop it. It leapt out of his mouth all by itself.'

'Leapt out of his mouth!' Chorley exclaimed in surprise. 'You think whatever is causing all of this, was showing off?'

'It could have killed Wallace, but it decided not to. This was a challenge, I'm sure of it.'

'But a challenge to who? Us or Wallace?'

A good question, thought Lethbridge-Stewart. Shame he didn't know the answer.

Miss Nash covered up the apple pie and put it back in the pantry. Oscar had briefly left his master's side to inform her that pudding would no longer be necessary. Apparently there had been an upset at the dinner table, and everyone had lost their appetite. She just hoped it had nothing to do with her cooking. Too often she mixed up her different employers' preferences. Stedman liked his eggs runny and steaks burned to a crisp, but Wallace preferred his eggs rock hard and steak bloody as hell – or was it the other way around?

Not that she ever paid for her mistakes. Stedman had always been too much of a gentleman to complain, and Zara took Wallace's rage on her slim shoulders. It made her life easy, but did make her feel guilty. Now things were going to change and not necessarily for the better.

Earlier, Oscar had broken the news that Stedman had passed away during the night. It must have been a particularly virulent disease, as he had been fit and healthy the previous day. It could have been a tragic accident, she supposed. She heard household rumours that Stedman played around with dangerous apparatus powered by gas in his secret laboratory. Miss Nash was an unyielding believer that some things were better left alone, and gas was certainly one of those things. It was only a matter of time before it exploded and took the whole manor with it.

Oscar had requested her not to tell anyone of the master's passing. Not even Toussaint and Zara were to know. Although she hadn't been told the reason, she assumed it had something to do with his Will – otherwise why all the secrecy? She felt in her gut that it wasn't right to delay his Christian burial, but she didn't want to lose her job, so she had resolved to follow instructions. She just hoped she was doing the right thing.

Ensuring that the pantry door was securely shut, she decided to have the leftovers collected from the dining room. If they were not having pudding, there was little point in delaying the task.

'Zara, can you...?'

Feeling foolish, Miss Nash stopped mid-sentence. The slave girl was nowhere to be seen. She was sure that she had been there moments earlier. Furrowing her brow, the cook wondered where she could have gone. There was a lot of work to do. It was then that she realised that she hadn't seen Toussaint all day either. He was supposed to scrub the oven and bring back some fresh milk and a slab of cheese for high-tea from the local shop. With all the drama of the day, nobody had noticed that the old slave was missing.

Inside Toussaint's bare and cramped room, the old man sat cross-legged. Once more his wrist flicked the roughly hewn drumstick onto the animal hide, continuing the dull beat. The relics of his sacrifice lay at his knees. Stolen from the kitchen earlier in the day, the small black rooster's throat was slit and blood drained into a bowl. A little had been smeared onto the slave's eyes and tongue. Clutched tightly in his spare hand was a wooden cross, the symbol of Christianity. No longer were the old ways pure. So long had he and his kind been in slavery that beliefs both ancient and new were mixed together.

The spitting wax of the burning candle hissed in anger and threatened to cut off its feeble light. The flame was not so easily dismissed and fought back. The wick kept smouldering for a little while longer, casting shadows onto the walls. They were the same shadows that used to remind Toussaint of the noble dancers from his homeland, but recently had become devils and tormenters. However, this time they meant nothing. In his trance, they remained unseen by his eyes, but seen by another.

— CHAPTER SEVEN —

The Trespasser

Taking special care to avoid Wallace and his butler, Lethbridge-Stewart and Chorley delved deeper into the forgotten parts of the manor. When the lonely rooms unearthed nothing of interest, Lethbridge-Stewart refused to give up. There had to be a clue somewhere in the building, and if he had to search every inch then so be it. Eventually, when they climbed a well-worn flight of stairs and emerged into a short attic corridor, he knew that he was getting close.

A steady drumbeat reverberated down the corridor, joined by a croaky, slurred voice. The words were practically unintelligible, as if the speaker wasn't used to speaking at all. In trepidation, they padded as silently as possible along the hall carpet and halted outside a door covered with faded navy paint. It had to be the place. He was sure of it.

'Do you really think this is a good idea?' Chorley whispered, predictably.

Knowing that they had little choice, Lethbridge-Stewart took a deep breath and pushed the door open. Chorley was compelled to follow. Abruptly the drumming ceased, as the door clicked shut behind them.

The bedroom was gloomy. Tatty red curtains swept over the window, blocking the afternoon's bright sunlight. A figure crouched at the end of the room, but whoever it was remained silent as they entered. Just as Lethbridge-Stewart's eyes began to get used to the darkness, a sudden stream of light rushed in as Chorley drew open one of the dank curtains.

Blinking away the spots swimming in his vision from the sudden brightness, Lethbridge-Stewart took the bizarre sight in. Scattered around were the remnants of what he assumed was some sort of barbaric ritual. A fallen candle had melted wax onto the feathers of a chicken carcass at the foot of the bed, and upturned on the floor was a wooden bowl. Whatever the bowl contained had formed an ugly dark patch on the threadbare carpet.

Half bathed by shadows in the far corner, Toussaint sat cross legged on the floor. As the remaining curtain was swept open, plunging the room into full daylight, the old slave viewed them with blazing eyes. There was a choking gurgling laugh, and in garbled jolted speech he spoke.

'Did you enjoy your meal so much that you came for its recipe?'

'What's wrong with his voice?' Chorley said under his breath.

Toussaint's head swung around like a ventriloquist dummy to look directly at the journalist. 'I will soon master these vocal cords,'

'You're not Toussaint, are you?' Lethbridge-Stewart asked, Toussaint's manner reminding him of the 'possessed' Staff Sergeant Arnold in the London Underground. 'You're just using him.'

'Ah, the one who my mice nearly devoured.' His head veered sharply towards Lethbridge-Stewart, as he pushed his bare feet against the floor and slowly rose. 'You are familiar to me.'

'I think you may be right.'

Chorley pulled him aside. 'You don't mean...?' he asked, his voice lowered.

'The Great Intelligence?' Lethbridge-Stewart nodded. 'Perhaps.'

'It is rude to whisper,' the presence in Toussaint said.

'Yes, but it's not exactly good manners to inhabit an old man's body, either.'

The entity laughed. 'Well, since you came all this way, I'll give you the recipe. First you kill a cow, then you cut a chunk off and burn it, but not too much. Then you consume it before it consumes you.'

'Who are you?' Lethbridge-Stewart asked, bravely taking a pace forward to put himself between Chorley and the possessed man.

'Don't you want to know what's for pudding first?'

'Couldn't eat another mouthful, myself,' Lethbridge-Stewart said, refusing to be side-tracked. 'Come on, who are you?'

'It's delicious; plump and fat. Are you ready to be... consumed?'

'If you are not going to tell me who you are, can you at least tell me where you come from?'

'Everywhere.'

'That's a rather large boast, isn't it?' Lethbridge-Stewart said, his mind turning to what Owain had told him about the source of the Great Intelligence. 'Everywhere is on the big side, don't you think?'

'Nowhere.'

'How can you be from everywhere and nowhere? That makes no sense,' Chorley said, backing up slowly towards the door.

'Everywhere and nowhere. The fabric of time itself. It's not my fault if you are too stupid to understand. You still want to know who I am?' Lethbridge-Stewart simply nodded. 'I am the Loa.'

Lethbridge-Stewart stepped back. 'I'm afraid that name means nothing to me. But I feel we have met before, after a fashion.'

The Loa seemed to stop to consider. 'If not yet, perhaps one day yet to come.'

'Doesn't sound like the Great Intelligence to me,' Chorley said, just behind Lethbridge-Stewart.

'There is much you don't know about,' Lethbridge-Stewart pointed out in a low voice.

'Let me tell you a story,' the Loa said, a low laugh again gurgling in the borrowed throat. 'There once was a carcass of a cat killed by a stray dog. Much to the doggie's surprise its victim arose and blinded with slashing claws.'

'Was that supposed to shock us?'

'Not at all. Just a gentle warning,' the Loa said. 'Both animals are on the way here now. Leave now if you want to live.'

'Don't you think we should get out of here?' Chorley said nervously.

'Empty threats,' Lethbridge-Stewart said confidently. 'It's trying to scare us.'

With surprising agility, Toussaint's hand swept out and grasped Lethbridge-Stewart's throat. Fingers dug into his windpipe, as his body was effortlessly lifted off the ground. His arms flailed wildly as he struggled to breathe, but his fingers only grasped air.

Chorley rushed to help, but was knocked to the floor when Lethbridge-Stewart was hurled at him. Together they landed in a tangle on the thread-worn carpet. Disentangling himself from Chorley, Lethbridge-Stewart drew in deep breaths and allowed his body to return to normal.

'Why do you oppose me?' the Loa asked. 'The hunger must be quenched. You should leave!'

'Leave?' Chorley's journalistic instinct temporarily deflected his fear. 'How would we do that?'

The Loa scowled at him. 'You're running out of time. *Tick-tock.*'

Without warning, the old slave dramatically collapsed onto the bed. Lethbridge-Stewart rushed to Toussaint's side and checked the old man's pulse. It was steady and strong. Behind them, the bedroom door inched open and Zara peered around the frame. She seemed disorientated at first, but on spotting her grandfather's prone body she rushed to his side.

'When he didn't turn up to clean the oven, I feared the worst,' Zara said. 'What's wrong with him? Is he ill?'

The gentle knock on the front door ripped through Jack's brain, so he tried to ignore it. Thirty seconds later the unwelcome noise returned, and this time it was louder and more persistent. Grudgingly, he rose from his bed and wobbled into the hallway of his untidy and inhospitable house. With no money forcing a withdrawal from alcohol, Jack's hands shook so much that it took him a while to draw the bolt securing the door. When fresh air finally invaded the house, he saw a man standing on the doorstep. Immediately he regretted opening it.

He had met the fellow on a number of occasions over the last week and a half, but still had no idea who he was or what he wanted. The man was unstable and probably should be in Bedlam Hospital. If he wasn't such a pain, Jack might have even felt sorry for him.

'Please don't shut the door,' the man pleaded. Jack ignored him, and tried to shut the door. Unfortunately, he wasn't successful as the stranger held it open with the palm of his hand. 'Look, you must know what's going on here.'

'Sorry, but I've no idea what you're gibbering about,' Jack mumbled as he did his best to stop his hands shaking. He didn't want the stranger to think he was scared.

'You must do. As I told you before, this is *my* house – 28 Dragon's Hill. I live here.'

Once again, Jack tried to shut the door, but this time the stranger pushed his boot in the gap to prevent him. Resignedly, the drunk opened the door fully and gave the man his most withering stare.

'Look, what the hell is going on?' the stranger said, ignoring the best stare that Jack had done in many years. 'I return for a few days leave from the war effort, and then everything goes barmy.'

It's you that's barmy, thought Jack. He wished he had the courage to tell the madman so, but instead he tried once again to shut the door. The stranger winced in pain at the attack on his foot, but his boot didn't budge an inch.

'I should have been back at the Somme by now. They probably think I've deserted. I'll be shot for sure. Look, you must know what's going on.'

Jack slowly reopened the door and peered out at the uninvited caller. Was this man really a soldier on leave from the war against Napoleon? If he had deserted, they might come looking for him. If so, he needed to be careful.

'Is that supposed to be a uniform?' he asked, looking dubiously down at the man's clothes.

'What the hell else could it be?'

Jack pondered for a few seconds. It was important to know what soldiers looked like. If you saw one you needed to leg it. He knew that they wore red coats, white shirts and some sort of ridiculous hat. The man who rudely interrupted his day wore nothing of the sort. Instead he was wearing a woollen khaki green jacket topped off with a peak cap. This fellow wasn't a soldier. Wearing weird clothes certainly, mad most definitely, but he was not a soldier.

'So, you're fighting Boney then?' Jack said just to be on the safe side. The man looked confused, so he generously helped him out 'Napoleon…'

'Don't be daft. That was a hundred years ago,' the stranger replied removing his foot from the doorstep in surprise. 'You know… The Great War.'

If Jack needed another reason to dislike the man, he had it. Who in the world would ever think a war was great? He realised that the boot was no longer blocking the door. Taking full advantage, he slammed it shut in the uninvited guest's face.

For five long minutes, the man hammered on the door. Jack's brain ached more with each blow, so he busied himself routing through the piles of junk strewn across the smelly carpet. There was always a chance, however small, that there were a few drops of alcohol hidden away from his hungry eyes. When he lifted a rank pair of ripped breeches, all thoughts of the strange man were banished.

Underneath was a dusty bottle of gin. The heavenly fluid had been long lost and forgotten, but it was welcomed as if it was pure gold.

Toussaint's eyes fluttered open. For several seconds he just lay there, but when his gaze settled on Lethbridge-Stewart he sprung upright in alarm. Frantically the old man dug under the bed and grabbed his boots, all sign of the trespasser seemingly gone.

'I'm sorry, sirs,' Toussaint said, pulling on his footwear. 'I have overslept. I will work extra hard this morning to make up for my lateness.'

'Actually, it's afternoon, not morning,' Chorley said, causing Lethbridge-Stewart to give the journalist a sharp look.

'Afternoon! Oh, my dear God!' Realising his blasphemy, dread spread across Toussaint's face, and hastily he attempted to rectify the mistake. 'My sincere apologies. I meant not to take the Lord's name in vain. I don't know what came over me, but I beg you, it has nothing to do with my young granddaughter. She is blameless. I will take whatever punishment you see fit. I deserve it, but I implore you, please leave my granddaughter alone.'

'Don't worry,' Lethbridge-Stewart reassured the old man. 'We're not here to punish you or your granddaughter. I think you'll find that Wallace has other things on his mind right now, what with Stedman's death and everything.'

'What do you mean? The master's dead?'

'I'm afraid so,' Lethbridge-Stewart confirmed sadly. 'Do you remember anything since last night? Anything at all?'

'I cannot, sir. I must have been asleep. I did not touch

the master, I swear. I truly cannot remember anything of last night, or of this morning.'

'What's all this stuff for anyway?' Chorley asked, waving his hands towards the sacrificed chicken on the threadbare carpet.

There was an awkward pause before Toussaint replied. *'La Lament du Reveur.'*

Lethbridge-Stewart looked from the old man to Chorley.

'My French is a little rusty,' Chorley said, 'but I think it's something to do with dreams.'

'In your language, it means the Dreamer's Lament,' Toussaint said quietly. 'It is just a... song. Nothing more.'

'Like a hymn?' Chorley asked.

When Toussaint nodded, Lethbridge-Stewart studied the old slave closely. There was no hint of the Loa to be seen within him, but Lethbridge-Stewart knew the look all too well. The old man was holding something back. He decided to try a different tack.

'I'm sorry to tell you this, but when we entered your bedroom earlier, you were possessed.'

'Possessed?'

Toussaint sounded puzzled, so Lethbridge-Stewart attempted to put it a different way. 'A... a spirt had taken over your body. It called itself the Loa.'

Toussaint swung his head to Zara, who was perched on the end of his bed. 'Is this true child?'

'When I came in you were just lying on the bed,' the little girl replied. 'I thought you might be ill.'

'Zara wasn't here at the time, but I was and it happened,' Lethbridge-Stewart stated firmly. He had to make the man understand the reality of the situation. Toussaint remained silent, seemingly afraid to answer back, but his eyes betrayed his distrust. 'Whatever possessed you has been killing people in the village. Last night it murdered your master. If he had lived he would have set you free.'

Toussaint was clearly still sceptical.

'I had his word,' Lethbridge-Stewart said. 'If he hadn't died, you would be free right now.' He saw the cynicism on the old slave's face, and recklessly made a promise that he didn't know he could keep. 'I will make sure Wallace carries out Stedman's last wishes. You will have your freedom.'

'I pray you are truthful, and time will tell if you are,' Toussaint said, surveying Lethbridge-Stewart with suspicion. Brushing the dust from his work clothes, he grasped hold of Zara's hand and led her to the door of his crowded bedroom. He turned and addressed Lethbridge-Stewart one final time. 'Now I will conduct my duties, farewell.'

Once Toussaint had departed, they checked out as many of the other rooms as they could, but all they unearthed were stale odours and dust. Their luck ran out when they rounded a corner and bumped straight into Oscar. Lethbridge-Stewart could have sworn he saw the butler jump away from a keyhole as they approached.

Oscar greeted them in his usual stiff manner, and Lethbridge-Stewart held the strong impression that the snobbish man had only just remembered that he was supposed to be keeping an eye on them. Obviously flustered, he kept fingering the pistol in his waistcoat pocket.

When Lethbridge-Stewart politely asked him where they could wait for Wallace, Oscar's relief was plain to see. He escorted them to the drawing room, and once Lethbridge-Stewart had given his word that they would remain there, the butler rushed off once again to keep a dutiful eye on his master.

Like much of the manor, the drawing room was rarely used. It was lavishly decorated, no doubt utilised in the distant past to entertain local dignitaries. Positioned at the far end of the room stood a grand piano. It was unlikely to have been used as a musical instrument for many years. Oscar gave the impression that he was far too pompous to play in front of his masters, and it was likely neither scientist ever found the time. Set near an impressive bay window were two luscious dark green armchairs, and Lethbridge-Stewart sank down into one of them.

Chorley lowered himself to the very edge of the chair opposite, and leaned towards him. 'So, you think this Loa thing might really be the Great Intelligence then? And if it is, how would that explain us being shot backwards in time?'

'Possibly. From what I can gather, the Intelligence is able to travel through time.'

Chorley frowned. 'As I recall, from the Underground, the Great Intelligence is just a sort of formless, shapeless thing floating about in space, isn't it?'

'It's far more complicated than that,' Lethbridge-Stewart replied, casting his mind back to Owain's explanations. 'It could be another version of Sunyata, I suppose.'

'Shuun-yata?' Chorley sounded out the unusual word. 'Who or what is Sunyata?'

'It's a bit tricky to explain.' Lethbridge-Stewart was unsure where to even begin. He gathered his thoughts for a moment, before giving it a try. 'Sunyata is the source of the

Great Intelligence. A creature that exists in the space between realities. As Owain explained it, it is pure instinct, driven by a need to consume everything. And the Great Intelligence is like its hand print on reality.'

'I see,' Chorley said, although he clearly didn't. 'So, the Loa could be another *hand print* of Sunyata?'

Lethbridge-Stewart let out a breath of air. 'Between you and me, Harold, I have no idea. I barely understood most of what Owain told me about Sunyata.'

Chorley nodded. 'Yes, well, I can see why.'

'Quite.' Lethbridge-Stewart cleared his throat and stood up. 'At least the Loa appears to have left Toussaint's body for now.'

'For now?'

'Yes, I think it's safe to assume it will return.'

'And then?'

Lethbridge-Stewart didn't really want to say. But if it really was like the Intelligence, then they would have to sever the link between the Loa and Toussaint. Which would, in Lethbridge-Stewart's experience, mean Toussaint's death.

The wire brush scraped the final remains of burned and blackened grease out of the oven. Straightening his aching back, Toussaint wiped the small beads of sweat from his forehead. The arthritis in his legs started its usual throb, so the old man rose to his full height as delicately as possible. He hobbled across to a storage cupboard, replaced the brush inside, and then deposited the dirt in the rubbish bin. He thought intently for a moment, before pushing the kitchen door open a crack. The groceries had already been collected from the village, and with all the upset in the household he hadn't yet been given any more chores to do. If he was careful, he could snatch some time to himself.

Warily he peeked outside. There was no one there, and no sounds of activity close by. Toussaint breathed a sigh of happiness, and silently pulled the door shut. Gratefully he lowered himself onto a chair set by the kitchen table. As the old slave rested, the pain in his legs subsided.

To Toussaint's surprise, the strangers had been as good as their word. There had been no punishment awaiting him for his absence. Oscar hadn't realised he was missing at all, although Toussaint did have some peculiar looks aimed in his direction from Miss Nash. Mr Lethbridge-Stewart was an honourable man after all; if he hadn't lied about this then maybe Toussaint's freedom was indeed in sight – his freedom, and that of his granddaughter.

And if Lethbridge-Stewart's promise proved hollow, then Toussaint had faith that Gran Met, the creator of the world, would guide him in his quest.

He hoped that it was not the Loa that had caused the death of his master, but he didn't grieve his passing. To his mind it was because of men like Stedman, and his father before him, that slavery existed. The white man believed in their superiority over the black. However hard he tried, he could not believe that Mr Wallace was simply going to let him and Zara walk free. It was far more likely that Mr Lethbridge-Stewart would smuggle them out of the house and take them in his sailing ship back to their homeland.

No doubt he had his own motive to perform this good deed; maybe to atone under the gaze of the Gran Met for previous wrongdoings. The white man would never change.

All through his life, Toussaint had been shown time and

time again that nothing that he ever had was his and his alone. The French slavers in Hispaniola had even changed his African name to something more acceptable to their European tastes. There was probably nobody alive who knew his real name. Toussaint had been so young when it was changed that after all these years of bondage even he couldn't recall it. They had taken from him his birth-right and identity.

Toussaint felt his mood changing. The more the old slave thought about his life of servitude, the angrier he became. He should have spent his life in freedom. It shouldn't be given to him when he was old and being slowly crippled from arthritis. He should have had it always. It was his right. His life had been stolen from him, and he could never reclaim it.

Toussaint's eyes glazed over as footsteps trampled outside. He gave a brisk acknowledgement to Miss Nash as she entered, and he strode out of the kitchen with legs that were miraculously free of all symptoms of arthritis.

The Loa had returned.

— CHAPTER EIGHT —

Cat Chases Dog

Wallace moped around the laboratory, his head aching with the persistent thump of a hangover. He hated being awake as he sobered up, but sleep was a luxury that his consciousness refused to give him.

After his traumatic mid-day meal, he had been violently sick in the bathroom's small washbasin. For ages he simply stared at the remains of his dinner, willing it not to move. Fortunately, there hadn't been even the smallest flicker of life. It was only when Oscar wiped his chin that Wallace had realised that he was not alone. Partly glad for the comfort, but embarrassed at being found in such a comprising position by a servant, Wallace had shaken himself free and stormed off. His butler had cleared up the mess, before following at a discrete distance.

Most of the day had been frittered away in his bedroom, demolishing a bottle of the finest wine that the late Stedman's cellar had to offer. The alcohol hadn't helped as it pumped around his bloodstream, stubbornly refusing to allow his brain to shut down. It forced him to think about the writhing, wriggling steak. He knew it was impossible, but he had seen it. Could he believe the evidence of his own eyes?

Then, as those very same eyes began to see double, the

solution presented itself. He knew for a fact that there were not two overlapping doorways in his room. The drink had caused his eyes to become dysfunctional. In short, he could no longer believe what they showed him. If he did, then he may well walk into a wall or, at the very least, the doorframe. It was conclusive proof that the sense of vision could lie.

He had hypothesized that a large dose of *Somnium Factorem* was released at the point of death. He had almost died while eating, so it followed that he must have been dreaming while being wide awake. It's a pity that what he dreamed was a nightmare, but it proved that he had been right all along.

With his excitement building, Wallace had set aside the demon drink. Instead, he went to hunt for Oscar.

His search only lasted seconds.

The butler had sprung up from his knees, as soon as the drunken scientist had opened his bedroom door. Wallace had decided to disregard the misdemeanour. There were more pressing matters. If Oscar was there, who had been watching the guests? They could have fled the manor, which would have been disaster for his research. He needed time to publish. The last thing he required was for Stedman's witch of a sister to make him homeless.

In a slurred voice, he had informed his faithful servant to track them down. He was both surprised and delighted to be told that it was Lethbridge-Stewart who had saved his life, and they had no intention of running. It was due to his deal naturally. If they ran, they would be caught and hung. If they remained, then they would escape the noose. To be safe, he had dispatched Oscar to keep an eye on them. He didn't want any more murders on his hands, and Oscar still had his pistol if there was any trouble.

Now hours later, the alcohol was having its revenge, but he tried his best to snub the throb inside his head. The sun had already deserted the sky, so Wallace drew the heavy laboratory curtains shut to keep the darkness away. Lifting the glass cover of an oil lamp, he lit its wick and the room was bathed in gentle light. He glanced at the sheets that covered the bodies of Miss Bibby and the two dissection subjects. He had to remember to have Oscar put them in the mortuary later.

Rubbing his aching forehead tenderly, Wallace strode to the mortuary slab where the body of Stedman rested. His guests were fulfilling their part of the bargain so he must do his, however hard that may be. With a heavy heart, he cut the tight bonds on the arms and legs of his deceased friend and began the post mortem.

Jack Golby was already half-cut. The empty bottle of gin slipped from his inebriated fingers and fell to the cobblestones, smashing into vicious shards of glass. Jack paid it no heed. He continued his journey down the road, heading in the general direction of *The Ship Inn*. Occasionally his legs would wobble, and one foot would almost trip over the other. Against all odds he managed to keep his balance. Like so many other occasions in his life, his body was on autopilot. The path to the pub was burned into his memory. So long as he could walk, he could always find his way there. Getting back home posed more of a problem, but usually the alcohol would blot out any embarrassments of rattling on the door of the wrong house or sleeping in the gutter.

Discovering the gin had been a godsend. Now it had been consumed, the alcohol was working wonders to his state of happiness. It had banished the shakes from his body, but had fuelled the craving even more. It was always possible that Saint Monica had heard his plea and, if not, somebody might shout a round anyway. Jack swayed ever closer to his destination. Happily, he burst into an old rebel song, taught to him by somebody who he couldn't quite remember many moons ago.

'Gainst lawyers and gainst priests, stand up now, stand up now. Gainst lawyers and gainst priests, stand up now.'

His words, half sung and half shouted, cut the evening air. Jack had always liked the prose. Lawyers and priests were both money-grabbing gits. They both got rich off the backs of the honest workingman's hard graft. One wrote laws that would destroy peoples' livelihood. The other sold to the highest bidder the word of God for a place in heaven. The world would be better off if they had never existed. Shame the song didn't mention politicians. Jack would happily string all of them up by their scrawny necks himself.

In the gloom, he almost tripped over a loose cobble. Seemingly realising for the first time that it was dark, Jack's singing became a mumble. He hoped that Ruth was still serving drinks. Of course she would, he thought. It was only early evening after all. Evicting the unwelcome thought swiftly away, the mumble again became words.

'For tyrants they are both, even flat against their oath. To grant us they are loathe, free meat and drink and cloth. Stand up...'

When Jack Golby saw the green luminous eyes, the song petered out. Light spilled from a window close by, to reflect off an animal lurking in the undergrowth. The drunk came to an abrupt halt to gaze at the cat's eyes. Suddenly they disappeared. With their departure, Jack Golby unexpectedly felt lonely. Wishing for company, he knelt down by the shrubbery.

'Don't run awa' puss. Ol' Jack 'as a fishy for yur.'

The drunk held out an imaginary piece of cod. The animal seemed unimpressed with the blatant lie, and didn't come back. Nevertheless, the pang of loneliness rapidly passed. There would be people in the pub that could keep him company.

He was about to give up his half-hearted search for the cat, when he saw a faint glimmer of metallic brown at the root of the bush. A farthing! Eagerly, Jack scrambled towards the filthy coin. In triumph, he scooped it off the ground and kissed it as if it was his bride. Perhaps there was another one? In high-spirits, he rummaged around among the dandelions and grass. Finally, his fingers touched another round object. Still kneeling on the ground, he brought it up to eye level. A shilling! Certainly it was his lucky day!

He was about to put his prize in his pocket, when two shadows lumbered out of the undergrowth and caused him to fall heavily on his back in surprise. The first shadow was large and dog shaped. The light from the window glistened off its mottled black fur. Jack lay in the dirt and stared up at the animal as it moved towards him. It appeared to be unwell. Its movements were laboured, and its head rolled from side to side. Then its massive head pivoted in Jack's direction, and the drunk gasped in fright. The dog had no eyes! The sockets were empty, and congealed blood oozed from vicious abrasions across its muzzle. The mess of blood and fur continued its lopsided saunter past Jack's prone body. He breathed a heavy sigh of relief. Miraculously the hound from hell didn't appear to have sensed his presence.

Then the luminous green eyes returned. The cat that had turned its nose up at Jack's imaginary cod, bounded towards him in a most peculiar way. Out of its blood-encrusted fur dangled a sticky jumble of entrails. The cat didn't seem to mind that half its internal digestive system was hanging out of its body. It stared at Jack, boring into him with dead green eyes. *Later*, it seemed to say, *later*. Then it was gone, after the canine. The cat chasing the dog.

Jack rested on the floor for a few minutes, letting his heart rate return to its usual routine. Slowly he sat up. Everything was normal once more. There was no sign of the creatures from the bowels of the earth. The coins lay by his side, and he quickly clutched them tightly in his palm. Previously he would have sold his soul for just one more precious drink, but now he was not so sure... He uncurled his fingers from around the coins and looked at them. Maybe it was no coincidence that he discovered the money at the same moment the Devil's own cat and dog appeared. Old Nick could be offering him a deal. If he was given all the scrumpy he desired and would never again have the shakes, Jack was tempted to sign away his soul. Sitting on clouds playing the harp with fat and bloated bishops wasn't Jack's idea of fun anyway. Hell might not be as bad as he was led to believe, but was it worth the risk?

Jack scratched his chin, deep in inebriated thoughts. Surely a contract would need to be signed with a fiery pen if it was indeed a deal from Old Nick? He felt sure that all lawyers would end up in hell, so they were certain to draw up the contract. They had clearly messed up this time. If the Devil had left the coins without bringing forth an agreement, then it was finders keepers. Jack would spend the money, but refuse to make his mark on the dotted line. The Devil wouldn't have a hoof to stand on!

Smiling at his joke, Jack struggled to his feet and continued his expedition to *The Ship Inn*. Whatever had happened, it did make a change to seeing pink elephants.

In his usual meticulous fashion, Wallace studied Stedman's corpse. The hangover helped him shove all emotional feelings into an empty void in his mind. His partner's left hand had been severed and lay on the corner of the mortuary slab as if it was little more than a paperweight, but the right arm was missing. Removed violently and... misplaced somehow. Or perhaps eaten, if Chorley's ridiculous stories were to be believed.

Reaching for a scalpel, Wallace cut the clothing around the right shoulder blade to expose the full extent of the injury. The ball and socket joint had been splintered. The scientist scowled. Whoever had inflicted this wound on poor Stedman was very powerful indeed. He doubted very much that either Lethbridge-Stewart or Chorley possessed such brutal strength. Which left him with the questions; what had happened, and who had done it? Despite the *incident* at dinner, he couldn't accept that a reanimated cadaver was to blame.

In full grip of the hangover, Wallace's throat felt dry and parched. He longed for a steaming cup of tea. He was about to yank the bell-pull to summon Oscar, when his sobering

147

brain produced a wave of embarrassment. His servant had seen him screaming at a plate of steak, potatoes and boiled veg as if it was a tiger. Instead, the scientist turned a small wheel on his gas burner. There was a hissing through its pipes, and an angry flame burst forth when a match was offered to its end. He placed a beaker full of water above the flame. A tray containing a small silver teapot, milk jug, tea caddy, and one bone china cup with saucer was whipped from a cupboard and set on the workbench. Tea making in the lab was a normal state of affairs during his long nights of experimentation. Indeed, it was often his only activity unrelated to work.

While the water boiled softly away, scrutiny returned to his departed partner. This time, his inspection focused on the vicious gash in Stedman's neck. It was here that he found something unexpected. Hurriedly, he went to his medical instruments and grabbed a pair of long tweezers. With practiced skill, he plucked a small white object from deep within the lesion. Taking a few steps towards the oil lamp, he held it up in the light. He took a deep involuntary breath – it was a human incisor. The tooth was decayed with blackened enamel at the root, but it was definitely a human tooth.

Only a lunatic would bite into a neck like this, but Wallace found that conclusion hard to countenance. To believe that a human being, however mad, would stoop so low as to attack a gentleman and a woman in such a manner? Maybe the uncivilised natives in far off Africa would be so barbarous, but such things certainly would never happen in Great Britain.

Unsure of his conclusions, Wallace turned and stared

at the bound body of the former body snatcher lying on the floor. On impulse, he bent down and angled the face of Tom Sawkins towards him. Using one hand, he forced the lower jaw open. The man hadn't looked after his teeth during life, and many of them were rotten. Even so, only one tooth was missing – an incisor.

Slightly shaking, with the pain in his head forgotten, Wallace leaned forward. The tooth he had found embedded in Stedman's neck was an exact fit. Jerking upright in alarm, Wallace turned away from the body. It had to be a coincidence, he told himself repeatedly. The dead did not walk. He was a man of science, who knew such superstitious tales had no basis in reality.

He felt something snap under his foot, and his eyes flicked down. They rested on Stedman's missing arm, plucked free of white flesh and hidden partially underneath the mortuary slab, until his clumsy foot had disturbed it.

Feeling physically sick for the second time that day, he took an involuntarily step backwards. A gentle tug at his trousers caused him to freeze in fright. A tiny rip of cloth accompanied by a cold sensation sent goose bumps over his body. He craned his neck to look behind him. Tom Sawkins was still tightly bound and immovable on the floor, but the corpse's mouth was opening and shutting. The chomping blackened teeth nibbled the back of Wallace's well-tailored trouser leg, only a hair's breadth from his ankle. Decayed eyeballs rolled to stare towards him, and a hideous dead tongue slithered against Wallace's well-polished shoes.

He panicked and bolted for the door. With his heart beating at an alarming rate, he nearly ran straight into the obstruction before he realised it was there.

Blocking the way out stood Stedman, but this was no reunion of lost friends and colleagues. It was a nightmare given form. His dead partner's features no longer reflected the kind but shy person he was in life, but were instead a ghastly parody, with only one handless arm and a cold evil stare behind the lifeless eyes. The bloodstained and ragged remains of Stedman's shirtsleeve flapped as the corpse lunged at him.

Life preserving instinct pumped adrenaline into Wallace's body, giving him the energy to fling himself out of reach just in time. The impact of the leap knocked the breath out of him, and he lay on the floor panting for air. While he fought to gain some kind of composure, his eyes grew wide in horror. On the periphery of his vision, Miss Bibby had sat up. As the sheet fell from her dead face, she turned to look straight at him with cold unnatural eyes.

Wallace scrambled to his feet, but before he could flee, Stedman's slow-moving corpse lunged for him yet again. This time it was more successful. A blooded stump of an arm hooked around the scientist's neck and attempted to pull him towards waiting teeth. Desperately Wallace struggled, and again fortune smiled upon him. Without a hand to grip firmly to its meal, the corpse was unable to hold him in place. Shaking himself free, Wallace took flight.

Arms flailing in desperation, he leaped over desks and apparatus in his haste to escape. He was so intent on reaching the sanctuary of the laboratory door that he failed to notice the still lit gas burner fall to the floor. It landed on a pile of anatomy notes, and they quickly blackened and shrivelled under the intense heat until all that was left was charcoal. The flame rapidly spread to the carpet, bringing forth choking fumes. Wallace did not linger to observe the infant fire.

After talking to Private Armitage about his brief time travel experience, Anne, Bill and Jeff had taken to working through her father's files. She took a pile for herself, leaving Bill and Jeff to gossip and read while she sat on the grass outside.

She'd spent most of the night awake, even though Bill had arranged a room for her at *The Ship Inn*, reading by torchlight in the field. Bill had offered to remain with her, but she had pointed out the soldiers still guarding the rails and the fencing, and shooed him away to Keynsham. He didn't go, instead electing to sleep in Jeff's tent. Jeff eagerly took up the offer of the comfortable bed at *The Ship Inn*.

Anne's late-night reading led her to an interesting piece of paper, part of an interview with Mr Jeremy Harris, a man claiming to have visited the Triangle. It wasn't very concise, lots of rambling, barely eligible scribbles in her father's hand, but one thing it did contain that was of use, were contact details. At first light, she borrowed Bill's car and entered Keynsham. There she'd freshened up at *The Ship Inn* and visited Jeremy Harris, who lived in nearby Kingswood. He was old now, but despite this he remembered with perfect clarity his visit to the 'Mirror Keynsham', as he called it.

'An interesting term. Why do you call it that?' Anne asked.

'Because, young woman, that's what it was. I know my history, and I know Keynsham. Lived there my whole life. Well, until I moved here five years back that is.'

Anne nodded, and leaned forward in her seat. She pulled

out a notepad. 'And you've never told anybody about this?'

'Just one man. About ten years ago. Nobody else believed me, so I opted for silence. Bolan mocked me, and dismissed my story out of hand. Apparently, an altered state of mind isn't permissible.'

'Mr Bolan,' Anne said, the name sounding familiar. 'Keynsham's expert on the Triangle?'

'That's the one. Expert my eye! He has a closed mind, didn't want to hear what I had to say.'

'I do. Tell me, what happened? How did you enter the Triangle, and, more importantly, how did you return?'

Mr Harris regarded her closely, and narrowed his eyes. 'Have you read Aldous Huxley, my dear?'

'Not extensively.'

'Well, in 1953 he suggested that the brain is primarily eliminative, not productive.'

'Yes,' Anne said with a nod. She may not have read Huxley, but she knew of this principle. 'The brain, like our other senses, our nervous system, operates as a reducing valve, protecting us from that which would otherwise overwhelm us.'

Mr Harris seemed impressed. He offered her a custard cream. 'Huxley came by this conclusion after ingesting all kinds of hallucinogens.'

Anne had heard of many such experiences, of increased perception and altered states as a result of a various hallucinogens. Once she would have dismissed these stories, but... 'Okay. I've seen enough in recent months to accept that,' she said, her mind turning to the last time she had seen her father – on the astral plane. 'What does this have to do with the Triangle?'

'Well, in my younger days I experimented with mescaline, LSD, all the usual suspects. Haven't done so in ten years, mind, as.... Well, going into the Triangle changed me. Put me off such things.'

Anne let the silence sit between them a moment, before she said, 'Go on, Mr Harris. I'm listening.'

'It was during one such experiment that I happened upon the Triangle. I'd heard all the stories, of course; everybody in Keynsham has. But I never believed them. A bit of local colour for visitors. But this day, my mind working on a different level to everyone else, I saw the Triangle for what it was. Within that invisible barrier Keynsham is duplicated, reflected in fact. From the old manor house outwards. Only not the Keynsham of today, but back when it was a village.'

'The early 1800s, I'm guessing. When the first people reportedly disappeared?'

'Quite so. In this altered state of mind, I was able to cross the invisible threshold, oblivious to the instincts that would normally warn me against such an action. I walked around the town, spoke to a few of the people there. They told me that many strangers had arrived in the village in the last couple of weeks, and every single one of them remained there.'

'The missing people,' Anne mused.

'Yes. I didn't stay for long. There was a fire, an old manor house, and these... *creatures* in the streets. I'm sure you've heard of zombies?'

'*Heard* of, of course, but not really the kind of stories that interest me.'

'Stories...' Mr Harris chuckled lightly. 'I wish that's all

they were. These creatures... Dead men walking. Reanimated corpses. And, I'm sure, I even saw people from the present day there.'

'What makes you say that? Their clothing?'

'That,' Mr Harris said, nodding. 'And the colour of skin. Now I'm no expert on military history, but I saw this coloured fellow in military uniform heading towards the old manor. Not period-specific either. More like the uniforms they wear now.'

Samson, it had to be. Only... 'That was ten years ago, Mr Harris. This man, he's a friend, one of the team investigating the Triangle. He only disappeared a few days ago.'

'Time moves differently there, young woman. As Hugh Everett once wrote, "there are simple moments in time when it becomes possible to jump from one reality to another by creating a quantum bridge between two already existing possibilities." I believe that the Keynsham Triangle exists in one such moment of time, stretched from 1815 to now, yet always 1815 there.'

Anne had listened some more, thinking about Lethbridge-Stewart's visit to a parallel Earth last year and wondered if this was the same thing. But the more Mr Harris spoke, the more she understood. Lethbridge-Stewart was stuck in the past, the past of their world, only *not* their world. A discrete pocket of time, preserved like pickles in a jar.

After enquiring about the particular concoction of drugs he'd used ten years ago, and learning that he couldn't remember ('wouldn't be as much fun if I made notes,' he'd explained), she gave Mr Harris her thanks, explained that the man who had interviewed him ten years earlier was her father, and that she was hopeful the new information Mr Harris had given her would enable her to finish her father's research. This had pleased Mr Harris, glad that finally Mr Bolan's credentials would be shot down.

Before leaving Kingswood, Anne had put a call through to Douglas up in Edinburgh. She would need some specific equipment if they were to act on Jeff's theory, one confirmed by Mr Harris' story. Douglas had taken down the list and promised to have the equipment, and mobile lab, to the site by 2pm at the latest.

She now walked across the field, sipping the coffee from the polystyrene cup Private Armitage had given her, and spotted Bill waving at her.

'Fancy taking another trip?' she asked, once he had joined her.

'Where are we going?'

She smiled at him. 'If I'm right, 1815.'

'Oh, that kind of trip. Wasn't once enough?' he asked, obviously thinking of their respective travels into the past of Fang Rock.

'You should know better than that, Bill. Once is never enough.'

Lethbridge-Stewart thumbed through the pages of *The Life and Strange Surprising Adventures of Robinson Crusoe*. He had found it on top of the grand piano, and being a first edition, it was in all probability worth a pretty penny. More importantly, when his nose was buried in the book it was easier to ignore the precious time ticking away.

Once more his eyes flicked over to the grandfather clock. His patience was wearing thin. The Loa was bound to return, but they couldn't have Wallace on their backs if they were to find a way of defeating it. The reanimated meal should have been proof enough that they were telling the truth. It was imperative that Lethbridge-Stewart made Wallace understand the danger that they were all in. A close eye had to be kept on Toussaint, and that couldn't be done when they were being held at gunpoint. He had to speak to the scientist before they all ran out of time.

Now he knew what needed to done, there was only one obstacle. Ever since late afternoon, Oscar had stood by the drawing room door as if he was a guard at Buckingham Place. For all his bravado, years of experience told Lethbridge-Stewart that Oscar was uneasy in the role he had been given. He felt sure that the butler wouldn't shoot them down, but it was prudent not to press the issue until absolutely necessary. Now though, that time had come. He was ready to make his move.

Lethbridge-Stewart placed the novel down on the coffee table and rose to his feet. Much to Chorley's obvious amusement, Lethbridge-Stewart simply marched straight past Oscar and out of the door. Glancing back over his shoulder, he beckoned to Chorley to follow. The surprised butler looked gob-smacked, seemingly unsure if he should follow or stay guarding Chorley. Taking advantage of Oscar's hesitation, the journalist revelled in cheekily striding past him in exactly the same way, this time giving a cheery wave as he did so.

For a moment Oscar stood alone, unsure of his next move. The look on his face was priceless. The pompousness had vanished, to be replaced by a guise of abject dismay. With all airs and graces evaporated, the butler turned on his heels and rushed after them, ordering them in no uncertain terms to return to the drawing room.

Disregarding him, Lethbridge-Stewart instead strode to the bottom of the stairs. He was about to go up them when he paused. The smell of burning had invaded his nostrils. Something was seriously amiss.

'Can you smell that?'

'Smells like... like burning,' Chorley said, the worry sounding in his voice. 'Oh my God, you don't think the house is on fire, do you?'

At Chorley's words, alarm spread rapidly across Oscar's face. For one awkward moment he just stared at them with his mouth hanging open. He took a deep sniff himself, and without a word, he bolted up the stairs. As his boots thumped up the wooden stairway, he turned and called back down to them.

'I need to warn the master. He's in the laboratory. Would you be so kind as to warn Miss Nash?'

'Chorley, can you see if you can find her?' Lethbridge-Stewart said, as the butler disappeared from view. 'Try the kitchens first, and then check out the other rooms on this floor. Don't take any risks.'

'Of course. What about Zara and Toussaint?'

Predictably, Oscar hadn't thought about the wellbeing of the slaves, he thought. 'I'll check the slave quarters, and meet you back here,' Lethbridge-Stewart said.

The fire had become an inferno. Every surface in the laboratory was ablaze, and the fire spread happily to the adjoining storeroom. The high temperature caused the jars to shatter, showering splintered glass and body parts into the fire to be cremated by its flames. It smelled of countless summer barbecues and bonfire nights rolled into one.

Flames licked around the bound bodies on the laboratory floor. The coarse rope blackened and blistered in the heat. Dead hands strained against them, and at last the weakened ropes gave way.

In the midst of the inferno, the three corpses unsteadily rose. Their clothes and hair caught fire, but they didn't cry out as the blaze singed skin and burned lips. Miss Bibby and the unknown mod lumbered straight into the blaze and immediately erupted into flames. Only a few steps were taken before both bodies collapsed to the floor, as the now useless cadavers were abandoned. Smouldering like human candle, Sawkins stepped over Bibby's burning corpse and shuffled out of the room. Like a faithful pet, the flames followed.

Lethbridge-Stewart's search of the slave quarters had been unfruitful, so he hurried down the hallway on the second floor, checking out each room as he went. Hopefully Oscar and Chorley had better luck, but they needed to be quick. As far as he could tell, the fire was on the top floor of the manor – most probably in the laboratory. He was all too aware that the fire would soon spread to the lower floors.

The unmistakable aroma of burned wood and furnishings was stronger now. Slowing his pace, Lethbridge-Stewart turned the corner. A wave of heat hit him. Flames engulfed the majority of the hallway, eating away at the fine decor. Expensive wallpaper peeled off the walls, to be cremated in the blaze. A delicate watercolour of the Bristol docks shrivelled under the fire's condemnation. The expensive mounting cracked and splintered, giving the flames even greater access to the work of art. Soon it was nothing more than black flakes in a charred frame. As if this wanton destruction wasn't enough, the lush carpet heaved forth choking fumes. An item developed for comfort had been turned into a killer. It was the final humiliation for the aristocratic dwelling.

Before Lethbridge-Stewart had the chance to retrace his path, there was an almighty rumble. Just in time, he threw himself clear as the roof above collapsed and burning timbers and masonry plummeted to the carpet below. Lightly, Lethbridge-Stewart sprung to his feet. Patting himself down to dispel flecks of fine white ash from his clothes, he surveyed the situation. The cave-in had spread the inferno, and retreat was now impossible. The only way was forward.

Shielding himself from the intense heat, he tried the handle of the only door within reach. The metal was hot, forcing him to snatch away his singed fingers. Pulling a handkerchief from his breast pocket, he wrapped it around his hand and gripped the handle once again. This time the material protected him from the worse of the heat. He opened the door and slipped through, pushing it shut behind him.

Lethbridge-Stewart found himself inside a small square study. Apart from an uncomfortable warmth and a smell of burning wafting under the wooden door, it could have been any normal day. However, it wouldn't be long before the heavy oak would also succumb to the might of the fire. When that time came, the study would prove just as inhospitable as the hall. Unlike many of the manor's rooms, the room held signs that it was undoubtedly used a great deal. Dominating the room was a huge desk, littered with stacks of notes. Forgetting for an instant the immediate threat of the fire, Lethbridge-Stewart picked one of the papers at random. It was a detailed method of dissection procedures and meant little to him. He dropped it back onto the table, and the impact caused an inkwell to spill over, covering the notes with thick black globules. The ink was speedily absorbed by the paper, wiping out months of painstaking work in an instant.

There was another door at the far end of the room, and Lethbridge-Stewart strode towards it. He had already gripped the knob, when something caught his eye at the foot of the door. Ground into the beige carpet were sooty footprints – small, child-size footprints. He followed the sooty trail, and it guided him back towards the desk. Stooping down, he looked under the furniture. Deep in the shadows lay the prone form of a girl.

'Zara, are you all right?'

The young slave stirred, peering towards him with suspicious eyes. Her clothes were streaked with smoke, and her hair had little bits of white plaster embedded in the close curls. Lethbridge-Stewart realised that she must have been terrified and hidden from the fire, but the shadows underneath the desk would not provide sanctuary for much longer. Very soon the fire would make its deadly presence known.

'Don't worry. It's only me,' Lethbridge-Stewart said, as reassuringly as he could muster in the circumstances. He held out his hand towards the child. 'I'm sorry, but it's not safe here. We must move quickly before the fire spreads.'

But Zara didn't move. Aware that there was little time left, he reached under the desk and gripped the slave girl's wrist. Gently, Lethbridge-Stewart led her protesting body into the open. The youngster's face was dull and ashen, and she appeared unsteady on her feet. She opened her mouth as if to speak, and then suddenly collapsed to the floor. Tenderly he scooped her into his arms. She was so small and thin that her weight was easy to bear. Her eyes flickered. She was still conscious, but barely. Indubitably her condition was due to the noxious fumes creeping from the fire in the hall. The child desperately needed fresh air.

Beads of sweat cascaded down Lethbridge-Stewart's forehead. The study was becoming a sauna. The oak door to the hallway buckled and warped, as the wood turned to charcoal. The final barrier to the raging fire was almost gone. Anxious to leave at the earliest opportunity, he hurried back to the far end of the room. The door swung open, and a glorious wash of cool air swept across his face. He was halfway through when there was a dull thump behind him. The hall door burst inwards, smashed by burning fists. Framed in the doorway shuffled Tom Sawkins, his flesh peeling under the extreme temperature. Gripping Zara tightly in his arms, Lethbridge-Stewart fled the study. Through the heat haze, the deceased grave robber followed at a leisurely pace.

Lethbridge-Stewart wasted no time in navigating through the next few rooms. If his calculations were correct, he should be near the stairway leading back to the drawing room. Before long he emerged back into the main hallway, and the stairs were in sight. The tell-tale signs of fire filled the corridor, but to his relief there were no flames – just clouds of thick smoke. Knowing that Tom was unlikely to be far behind, he carried the small child down the hall and bounded down the steps. Through the billowing smoke he saw a figure hovering at the foot of the stairs. He hesitated. It was likely that the Loa had reanimated the bodies of Stedman and Miss Bibby as well. Was it safe?

'Brigadier? Is that you?'

Lethbridge-Stewart had never been so happy to hear Chorley's voice. He sped down the final two stairs and into the ground floor hallway. On seeing Zara curled up in his arms, Chorley hurried to his side.

'I wasn't able to find anyone, I'm afraid. How is she?'

'Inhaled too much smoke I think,' Lethbridge-Stewart croaked, coughing up the noxious fumes from his own lungs.

'Any sign of Wallace or Toussaint?'

'I'm afraid not, but we've got bigger problems,' Lethbridge-Stewart said grimly. 'I've just had a run in with that dead grave robber. The Loa's back. I wouldn't be surprised if Stedman and Miss Bibby are walking around this place as well. We need to get out of here immediately.'

'Just my luck,' Chorley moaned, as he followed Lethbridge-Stewart towards the backdoor. 'The house is on fire and zombies are on the loose!'

When they arrived at the rear exit, the backdoor was already hanging open. Carefully, Lethbridge-Stewart peered around the frame into the courtyard beyond. All was still, but bathed in shadow. The fresh air eased the burning sensation in his lungs as he apprehensively walked out into the dark. The child lay limply in his arms, but he didn't have time to rally her. Quickly, Chorley followed.

A sudden intake of breath caused Lethbridge-Stewart to look immediately to his left. Flattened against the grey stoned wall was the outline of a man. The form shivered in fear. He spoke. The voice was Wallace's.

'I... I don't believe in monsters and demons. They're just stories. So why... why won't they go away?'

'Because they're not stories. Surely you've got that by now?' Chorley said rudely.

'Chorley, he's not our enemy,' Lethbridge-Stewart said in a hushed voice. 'However, I do believe that is.'

All eyes swivelled, following his gaze. A gigantic hound blocked the pathway from the manor. Trails of thick saliva, intermingled with blood, trickled between sharp canine teeth to land in a pool by its shredded paws. The eyeless head lolled to one side as it padded slowly closer. Between its powerful legs came a once lithely cat. Its undead green eyes fixed its stare on the group. Immediately, the dog's empty sockets swung in the same direction.

Slowly, Lethbridge-Stewart backed away, and the others followed suit. An unpleasant aroma of burned hair caused him to look back. Tom, still smouldering from the fire, shuffled into view to block their retreat.

There was no way forward or back. The cat and dog moved as one animal.

Together the former foes advanced on their prey.

CHAPTER NINE

Gathering Reinforcements

'What the hell just happened?' Dovey asked, and winced.

Samson felt it too. A feeling of nausea. 'I think we both know, we must have...' His voice trailed off. 'Um, when did it become night time?'

Outside the Land Rover, the countryside was pitch black.

'Time travel,' Dovey said. 'Heard about it... Never thought I'd be part of it.'

Samson rubbed his head. 'Pays to keep an open mind, Sergeant. Come on, let's get some air and take a look around.'

Cautiously, he clambered out of the vehicle. They appeared to be in the middle of a field, presumably the same field as they'd left in the future, but he could only see as far as the Land Rover's headlights would allow. Everything was eerily quiet.

Samson looked around, thinking about Lethbridge-Stewart and Chorley. Well, he wanted to find them... No point wasting time standing in a field when they could be out looking for them.

'Right, Dovey, this is what... What is it?'

Dovey was pointing. 'What's that over there?'

In the distance, a red glow lit up the sky. It was a fire, although in the dark it was impossible to know what was burning. Instinct and experience told Samson that Lethbridge-Stewart wouldn't be too far from the heart of the action.

'Let's find out.'

The smoke swirled all around Oscar as he fruitlessly fought the flames, obscuring his vision and assaulting his throat. His bloodshot eyes streamed, and he coughed up black bile from his lungs. He covered his mouth once more with the wetted handkerchief. His breathing became easier. Less laboured. Less painful.

The fire was too fierce, preventing him from reaching the laboratory to warn his master. Instead, foolishly, Oscar had attempted to put it out. Picking up the pan of water lying at his feet, Oscar had thrown it into the billowing smoke with the vague hope that it would hit the flames. All that had happened was a faint fizzle.

Dropping the pail to the floor, Oscar staggered through the smoke and away from the extreme heat. The thought of locating his master nagged at his mind, but the instinct of self-preservation overwhelmed it. With Stedman dead and the manor burned to the ground, there would be no employment left for him anyway. He would be out of a job soon, and that was a fact that he had to accept. Yet loyalty to his master was second nature. Even now he would still help him if he could, but there was nothing Oscar Whittle could do apart from preserve his own skin. The manor was in flames, and Wallace had either perished or had flown.

Fighting down the urge to panic, he felt his way through the blinding smoke. After what seemed like an eternity, the servant's entrance loomed up in the gloom. Relief flooded through him. It was a way out at last. He abandoned the soot-stained handkerchief to the ground and sped up. With his escape at hand, the simmering panic was dispelled and instead he began to wonder how on earth the blaze had started in the first place. He couldn't help thinking that Miss Nash may have been right in her apprehension towards the gas that Stedman had experimented with. As if on cue, a small explosion rocked the foundations, causing him to stagger in the hallway. He struggled to regain his balance, and the pistol rocked back and forth in his waistcoat, reminding him of its unpleasant presence.

Oscar pulled the servant's entrance open, and made his escape from the burning building. Once he had his fill of the heavenly clean air, the first thing the surprised butler noticed were the guests standing near the back door with clouds of smoke billowing behind them. Were there other figures in the smoke? It was hard to tell. His eyes still watered from the fumes, so his vision remained blurred. He squinted and looked harder, but it was no use. He gave up. However, the slave girl was certainly there, held in the arms of Lethbridge-Stewart. Then he saw the master, cowering against the wall in obvious terror. What were the guests doing to him?

Clumsily Oscar took the loaded pistol from his pocket, nearly dropping it in the process. He pointed it towards the group and attempted a demand for surrender. The demand came out sounding like a toad's mating call. His lungs had taken more of a beating than he had thought. In spite of this, it was enough to make them aware of his presence. They turned towards him, the master included. Much to his amazement they hollered for him to run. It made no sense. He was safe from the fire. Why should he run?

A curious gargling growl caused him to look to his side. Too late he realised why. Even through his hazy vision, the sight was appalling. It was clear now what his master was scared of. He was scared of the hound from hell. It was less than ten feet away from where Oscar stood, and it was not alone.

Winding between its legs, slinked a cat from the butler's worst nightmares. He had always hated cats, but this one looked like Lucifer's own pet. Panic at last took a grip on Oscar.

His arm sprung up, with his index finger automatically squeezing the pistol's trigger. The shot went wide, and the ball of lead hammered uselessly into the ground. Gibbering uncontrollably, the usually calm and collected servant searched in his pockets for the spare ammunition. As he brought out the horn that contained the gunpowder, the lead shot slipped through his shaking fingers onto the ground.

Desperately, he stooped for the precious balls of metal before they rolled away. It was too late. The cat landed on his back, razor sharp claws puncturing his expensive waistcoat. In panic, he dropped the flintlock and swung himself rapidly upright. The hated cat clung on and climbed higher, until the butler could feel its whiskers tickle his naked neck. He tried to follow the master's instructions. He tried to run, but his legs were taken from under him. The canine had joined its feline friend in the attack.

Oscar stared into the empty sockets of the undead dog and screamed. The cat on his neck was no longer tickling.

Lethbridge-Stewart looked on in horror as Oscar lay helpless on the ground. Every fibre of his being wanted to spring to his assistance, but Zara was still in his arms and he couldn't abandon her with the corpse of Sawkins almost upon them.

He tried desperately to think of a way to help, when a loud cracking sound unexpectedly split the night air. It was a noise that he was all too familiar with. It was the sound of a gunshot from a modern weapon.

The shock of the bullet threw the lunging dog off balance, but it recovered quickly and turned snarling towards the courtyard's exit. To Lethbridge-Stewart's surprise, Samson stood in the doorway.

'Good Lord!' Lethbridge-Stewart exclaimed.

'Just me, Al!' Samson grinned. 'Can't leave you alone for five minutes, can we?' He squeezed the trigger once more.

Another bullet ripped into the canine's dead flesh. It did little to stop the creature, but it had now abandoned its pray. Oscar struggled to right himself, and the dead cat sprung off his back and scuttled away. The dog followed, but as it retreated its empty sockets glared at them with unseeing eyes. The deceased pets didn't retreat far.

'Quick, this way!' Samson shouted, and he let loose two more shots at the undead beasts.

Making the most of the distraction, Chorley immediately skirted around the animals to the safety of the road and Oscar stumbled with him. Lethbridge-Stewart was about to follow when he realised that Wallace remained motionless, quivering against the thick stone wall. The burned corpse of Tom Sawkins had continued his advance and raised a blistered arm towards the quaking man.

Holding Zara with one arm, Lethbridge-Stewart reached out for Wallace and yanked hard on his hand. He was just in time. The scientist tumbled to the floor, away from the grasping fingers. The sudden pain of hitting the gravel spurred Wallace into action and, scrambling to his feet, he fled. Samson fired off a final round, keeping the duo of undead pets at bay as Lethbridge-Stewart made his escape. The little slave girl hung limply in his arms, her gaze transfixed on the dead animals as they went.

They ran together onto the main road, their ringing footsteps intermingling with the crackle of the burning building behind them, and they didn't stop until the manor was only a fiery dot in the distance. When the Loa's puppets had been left far behind, Lethbridge-Stewart carefully set Zara down onto the cobblestone road. The young girl stood there, looking bewildered as the adults around her took a precious moment to recover from their ordeal.

'How are you holding up, Mr Whittle?' Lethbridge-Stewart asked, turning to the butler.

Oscar looked awkward at his concern. No doubt he was not used to people taking an interest in the wellbeing of a servant. Refusing to be put off, Lethbridge-Stewart insisted on checking his injuries. The butler had a number of nasty scratches down his neck, but fortunately his wounds were only superficial. The back of Oscar's fine waist coat had been shredded by the cat's claws, but it had protected him from the worst of the attack. The man had been lucky.

'Please tell me you're not alone,' Chorley said to Samson in-between breaths. He wiped the sweat from his forehead, leaving a sooty smudge instead.

'Sergeant Dovey is with me. I left him with the Land Rover. What's going on anyway? My bullets didn't have much of an effect on those animals.'

'There's an entity here calling itself the Loa,' Lethbridge-Stewart tried to explain. 'It's reanimating the dead – cats, dogs, mice, even humans.'

'Don't forget the steak dinner,' Chorley added unhelpfully.

'Steak dinner. That figures,' Samson said, with an unbelieving laugh. 'Seems like I arrived just in the nick of time.'

'Yes,' Lethbridge-Stewart said. 'Your timing is impeccable, Sergeant Major. I take it this means we have a way back to our time?'

Samson shook his head. 'Afraid not, sir. Dovey and I kind of ended up here by accident. Which, it seems, is the only way to cross the barrier into the Triangle.'

Chorley nodded. 'We came to the same conclusion.'

'Presumably Miss Travers is on the case then?' Lethbridge-Stewart asked.

'Hopefully. Up to now it's been down to Jeff Erickson, but I was requesting her help when that cow came at us.'

'Cow?'

Lethbridge-Stewart listened as Samson explained how a cow appeared out of nowhere, and suddenly he and Dovey were in the past.

'Must have been that cow you frightened near the edge of the Triangle, Harold,' Lethbridge-Stewart said turning to Chorley. 'We saw it disappear, but that was hours ago, long before the fire started.'

'Well, we've been here less than an hour...' Samson said. 'Guess people don't arrive here in sequential order.'

'It would seem not.' Lethbridge-Stewart nodded, his mind dismissing the conversation for now, returning to more pressing matters. 'What about the Land Rover? Is it far?'

'It's in the middle of a field, a little way behind that burning building.' Samson said, waving his hand back towards the manor. 'I'm afraid we won't be able to get through with those undead things in the way. We'd be sitting ducks.'

It was not the news that Chorley wanted to hear. He started pacing restlessly around the road, all the time staring worriedly back down the cobblestones for any sign of pursuit.

'Chorley, pull yourself together, man,' Lethbridge-Stewart barked, causing the journalist to start with surprise. 'Samson, I can give you a full debriefing when we are moving. It's far too dangerous to stay in the open. We need shelter, and fast. It's likely that the Loa is already on our trail. Any ideas?'

'How about the Church of St John the Baptist?' Oscar suggested, his face still ashen from his ordeal. 'It's not very far from here.'

'Good thinking,' Lethbridge-Stewart said, adding his weight firmly behind the butler's idea. Dovey would have to fend for himself until they were able to rendezvous with him. 'It's got thick walls and a solid door. The windows are high up too. It should be easy to defend.'

'Wouldn't there be more of those zombie things there?' Chorley said dubiously. 'With the graveyard and all?'

'Oh, I shouldn't think so,' Lethbridge-Stewart said, stifling the journalist's objections. 'They'll all be buried. I doubt that even the Loa would be able to break out of a coffin and dig through six feet of soil. It's got all it needs above ground anyway.'

'I suppose so…'

'Splendid,' Lethbridge-Stewart said, firmly enough to ensure that his point was non-negotiable. 'It's the church then.'

Before Chorley was able to raise any more doubts, Lethbridge-Stewart started off up the road, forcing the others to do likewise.

As they hiked up the road, Lethbridge-Stewart was true to his word and filled Samson in on the situation. A creature possibly connected to the Great Intelligence, reanimating the dead… He'd heard about what happened with Staff Sergeant Arnold back in March last year, but this seemed quite different. The word Chorley used was *zombies*… Samson shuddered at the thought. His latest 'girlfriend', Rhona, had a thing for watching horror movies – it was all she seemed to do when not serving behind the bar at *Maggie Dickson's Pub*. She'd love this, he decided, but for himself, Samson preferred their enemies to be a bit less gruesome.

'There's something wrong about this village,' he said, and Chorley looked at him.

'What do you mean?'

'The geography is wrong. I visited Keynsham a few times in the last couple of days, and I know it's changed since 1815, but…' Samson shook his head. 'This is all wrong.'

'I thought so, too. It's like north and south have been swapped.'

With a shake of his head, Chorley moved ahead of the small group, and Samson returned to his thoughts about their current situation. They couldn't just return to their time, which left them in a strange land where the dead walked. How did one kill something that was already dead?

A fair distance behind them all, stumbled the man that Lethbridge-Stewart had introduced as Wallace. He walked with his face down at his feet, refusing to talk to anyone. It was as if he was on autopilot, and his mind had hidden away from the world.

Samson turned to the little girl Lethbridge-Stewart had introduced as Zara. She followed behind him and smiled encouragingly. He held out his hand, but the offered appendage wasn't taken. Instead the youngster turned and looked behind her, back at the blazing manor in the distance. Zara halted her walk and stared transfixed at the sight.

Aware of her standstill, Lethbridge-Stewart and Samson paused quietly by her side. The flames illuminated the night sky, as if the burning building was a warning beacon lit to herald the great danger within. There was no sign of any danger in the night, so the two soldiers decided that a minute could be spared to allow the scientist to catch up. Not noticing that they had stopped, Chorley and Oscar trudged onwards down the road.

'I believe I know what's on your mind,' Lethbridge-Stewart said gently. The young girl turned and looked at him, with a quizzical expression in her intelligent brown eyes. 'You're thinking of your grandfather, aren't you? You must be very worried.'

Zara nodded, and then looked imploringly him. 'Can't I go back?'

'I'm sorry. I'm afraid it's too dangerous. But I do know that your grandfather loves you greatly, and he would want you to be safe.'

Once more, the young girl gazed back down the road at the red glow on the horizon. Samson's heart went out to her. The whole situation must be difficult for her to comprehend. From what he could gather, the burning building had been her home, as well as the last known location of her grandfather. Soon all that would be left would be a burned out stone hulk, scarred with soot. A part of her life had come to a dramatic end – burned away from existence.

'You're missing him already, aren't you?' Samson said, stooping down on one knee to the little girl's level.

The child turned back to them. 'I can't bear to be parted,' she admitted, averting her eyes from his worried face.

Samson was about to give more words of encouragement, when Wallace suddenly barged his shoulder into the child as he walked past. He paused for a moment, looking blankly into the features of Zara as if she wasn't there. The child shrank back, and her expression hardened.

Samson felt a flash of anger well up inside. 'Oi, you, apologise to the girl.'

A glimmer of acknowledgement flickered across Wallace's face, and suddenly he swung around to look at Samson directly in the eye. 'What, apologise to the likes of *her*?' Samson felt the man's eyes sweep over him. 'And you're hardly any better.'

'Please show some respect, man,' Lethbridge-Stewart barked. 'Sergeant Major Ware is an essential part of my command staff.'

'Is he indeed? A negro, an officer in the British Army? That's not a future I'm interested in seeing,' Wallace said,

174

giving a humourless laugh. He turned his back on them and trudged after Chorley and Oscar.

Samson bit his lip. He'd been the butt of racism throughout his life, but rarely had he heard such anger and disgust directed at a little black girl.

He looked down at Zara. 'Don't you worry about him. He's just jealous.'

'Quite so, my dear,' Lethbridge-Stewart agreed. 'You're quite safe from Wallace now. He will never harm you again, I promise. Come, we can't let Chorley get too far ahead.'

It was likely that it wouldn't be long before they felt the pursuit of the entity's minions, so they couldn't waste any more time by dawdling. This time, Samson insisted Zara took hold of his hand, and the young girl complied.

There were raised voices in *The Ship Inn*.

Jack Golby was far from happy at the premature closing of the tavern. What did it matter that Ruth had a headache? She had a service to perform, and she should pull him a pint. For once he actually had the money. She shouldn't complain, just serve. Unfortunately, Ruth didn't see it his way. The landlady's voice roared throughout the tobacco-smoke filled room, as she brought out the heavy artillery.

'Have you seen the time? It may not be late, but it certainly ain't early!' she screeched, loud enough to wake the dead. 'I can close when I wish, and as I've already told you I don't feel well. It's quiet anyhow, so I'm shutting! So off with you!'

'After all the pounds that I've put in yur pocket for yur terrible cider, and this is 'ow ya treat me,' Jack bellowed.

'Pounds, hah!' Ruth scoffed. 'More like farthings and

175

earache, and I've never seen you leave a drop of that so-called terrible cider!'

'Yur usually open longer than this. Come on. Just one gin fer the road?'

'If you don't leave now, Jack Golby, by God I'll have you barred!'

'Don't need this place anyhow!' Jack said rebelliously.

Grumbling, he scuffed his feet along the beer-stained carpet and ambled through the door. He crashed it shut behind him, using the final drops of his mutiny in the petty act. Ruth's threat held far more weight with the alcoholic than he let on. Without the refuge of the tavern, his life would be unbearable. He staggered halfway up the street and looked back at his favourite place. It had no right to shut early. If he had his way it should never shut at all. It was its God given duty to soften the blow of living by the administration of intoxicating liquors. Medicine of the gods, it was, and that witch of a landlady refused to keep the hospital permanently open. Curse her!

As if to taunt him, Ruth opened the door and scowled in his direction. It was then slammed closed and heavy bolts drawn to hammer home that no more booze would be obtained from the premises. To Jack, outside felt like a prison cell, with tantalising glimpses of freedom being snatched through the bars. Everything Jack wanted was on the other side of a locked door, but just like a prisoner it was denied him. Loitering for a few minutes, he at last gave up and decided to set out on the depressing journey home.

Then from across the cobblestones, a black shifting mass caught his eye – a devilish seething mass. A look of concern crept onto Jack's face. Had Satan's lawyers realised their mistake and come to rectify it? They'd have an argument on their hands if they had. He hadn't spent all the money yet anyhow, so some deal could surely be reached.

He realised what the black shapes were – they were mice. He always thought lawyers were more like slugs than mice so it probably wasn't them, and there wasn't even the faintest sign of a fiery pen. No, this was something else. Since the cat had bounded after the dog earlier, then maybe they were supposed to be chasing the cat. A courageous thought struck him. If he helped the mice, they might put in a good word for him when the lawyers turned up. His voice rang clear in the evening air.

'Hey yur! They went thataway!'

The rodents ignored him and continued their journey across the cobblestones. They obviously didn't need his help. To Jack's surprise, they began to squeeze through the small gap under the thick door of *The Ship Inn*. For a fleeting moment Jack wished he was a mouse. Before long they had vanished into the heavenly tavern. No place for devils and demons, Jack mused. He scratched his head in bafflement at the puzzle. They had certainly looked evil, but surely the Almighty wouldn't allow the defilement of such a worthy place as *The Ship Inn*. They probably wanted a drink, that's all. After all, who doesn't want a drink every now and then?

As they trudged up the road, the silhouette of the church's bell tower could be seen against the dark sky. With the odd glimpse of a battlement through the trees, it was almost as if they were treading across the wilderness towards the safety of a castle, not a place of worship. Even so, either was preferable to their vulnerable position in the open.

Lethbridge-Stewart was pleased to see that Samson had taken the young lady under his wing, and as they walked Samson was attempting to distract the youngster's mind by teaching her the nursery rhyme *Goosy Goosy Gander*. Since their little chat, Zara appeared more relaxed in their company, although she kept wistfully looking back to the glowing building in the distance.

Presently Lethbridge-Stewart became aware of a person walking by his side. Looking up, he saw that it was Wallace. He put aside his personal feelings regarding Wallace's treatment of Samson and Zara; the last thing they needed was to get into a heated argument when they were in the open and vulnerable. There would be time for recriminations later.

Fortunately, Wallace no longer looked as if he was in a state of denial and shock. If he had remained that way, he would have been a liability and could have got them all killed. The difference in his manner was remarkable. In spite of everything, he was now bright and alert. He put his hand on Lethbridge-Stewart's shoulder and spoke.

'I owe you my gratitude. If it hadn't been for your quick thinking, I would have been... someone's supper. My sincere apologies for not having faith in you earlier. I don't believe in monsters, but I do believe my own experiences. Even though I cannot understand why, these creatures obviously exist.'

'Yes, they obviously do, don't they?' Lethbridge-Stewart said shortly, but Wallace appeared to take his words as an acceptance of his apology.

Together they rounded the top of the hill, and at last the church was in plain view. Lethbridge-Stewart took over from Chorley in spearheading the group, encouraging everyone to speed up the final few paces.

However, as they entered the church grounds his concern grew. The building was in pitch blackness and the door pulled shut. Hurrying ahead of the others, Lethbridge-Stewart tried the door. It was firmly locked.

'Reverend Cunningham lives over there,' Wallace said, waving his arm towards a small cottage a short distance away. 'He should be able to let us in.'

Changing direction, they trudged wearily towards the homely looking dwelling. To Lethbridge-Stewart's relief light bled through the curtains into the dark evening, indicating that the reverend was still up. They had almost reached the front door, when a scream cut the night air. It was faint, so it was some distance off.

Abruptly the cry stopped.

'The entity is gathering reinforcements,' Lethbridge-Stewart said darkly. 'We haven't got much time.'

— CHAPTER TEN —

A Toast to Saint Monica

'It's been a week since anybody saw him,' Sally said, her voice laced with worry.

'I know,' Anne said, trying her best to be soothing.

It was true that Sally and Lethbridge-Stewart were no longer engaged, and that their split had created a few issues for them both, including a reassignment to Imber for Sally: administration duties. But Anne knew that deep down Sally hadn't wanted it to end. Of course, in Anne's view, she thought it had been a good decision on Sally's behalf, or Lethbridge-Stewart's as it turned out... Sally had planned on ending things, but Lethbridge-Stewart had beaten her to the post. A fact Sally resented. And yet, despite all this, her concern for Lethbridge-Stewart was still very real.

'This is the second time he's disappeared,' Sally continued, as if Anne hadn't spoken. 'And look what happened last time.'

The last time in question was when he'd disappeared for three weeks in April last year, although, for him, it had been four months spent in an alternative version of Earth (which, Anne now realised, made him over three months older than his legal age!). Based on Mr Harris' recollection, and what she had gleaned from her father's notes, Anne didn't think it was the same thing. She didn't know how much time had passed for Lethbridge-Stewart inside the Mirror Keynsham, but if Mr Harris was right, then it stood to reason that less time has passed for Lethbridge-Stewart than the rest of them. The reverse, in fact, to the 'last time' (which at least cut off some of his age discontinuity, Anne supposed).

'Sally, try not to worry,' she said. 'We'll be running our first test tomorrow, and if it's successful then we should be able to travel into the Triangle and bring him home.'

'And what if it isn't?'

'Then we shall refine things until we work it out. Based on all the information I've been given, and the facts as we know them, Jeff and I are confident we can do this. We just need a guinea pig,' Anne added with a sigh.

'So, there's a risk?'

'Always is in the initial stages of tests that involve a living subject.'

Sally was quiet for a moment. 'I volunteer,' she said finally. 'I'll be your guinea pig.'

'No,' Anne said quickly. She sighed again. 'Sal, I can't risk you. Lethbridge-Stewart won't forgive me if something happens to you.'

'Like he cares!' Sally snapped. 'If he cared so much, then he'd have fought to keep me stationed at...' A deep breath.

Anne shook her head and looked outside the phone box at the busy Keynsham High Street. 'He'll blame himself, and you know that as well I do.'

They had talked through all of this a lot in the last few weeks, but Anne knew that healing, loss, took much longer than a few weeks to work through. One day, both her and Sally would accept their respective losses as a normal part of their lives. Eventually the sting of hurt, the hole in them, would not occupy so much of their thoughts. At least Sally would, hopefully, find a new love one day. Anne would never find another father.

'You're right,' Sally said softly. 'I just don't know what I'd do without him in the world.'

Anne smiled sadly. 'I won't let that happen. Trust me, Sally, I will bring Alistair back.'

Reverend Cunningham let forth an annoyed grunt. In his expert opinion, callers should stick to Sunday services and pre-arranged dinners. Turning up in the late evening was neither polite nor wanted. The reverend's small piggy eyes glared at the motley crew standing on his doorstep. He recognised two of the unwanted guests as the strangers that had visited the church a few days ago. They were accompanied by Mr Wallace from the manor, his butler and two of his slaves. One of them was the little girl Zara, and the other appeared to be a recent addition to Wallace's household, dressed in strange clothes. A military uniform of some kind. Cunningham felt offence at the very sight of a slave disrespecting the British Army.

If it wasn't for the presence of a member of the aristocracy, he would have sent them away with a flea in their ears. Since Wallace held much respect in the village, the reverend thought it prudent to find out what they sought before dismissing them.

Not wishing the callers to believe they were welcome, he decided against inviting them in. He just scowled, and left a pause that, in the past, had served him well in unnerving the unsolicited. When he finally spoke, they would have no doubt that he was in firm control. The pause went smoothly, but before he had a chance to say a word, one of the strangers slipped past his large belly and into the warmth. Reverend Cunningham turned to face the intruder, his face turning red with rage at his arrogance.

'I say! How dare you burst into my home! I know we met before, but I can't seem to recall...'

'I'm Brigadier Lethbridge-Stewart, Royal Scots Guards. Now, be quiet and listen,' the man said, somewhat rudely Cunningham thought. 'We haven't got much time.'

Cunningham suddenly became aware that the rest of the group had used the distraction to also enter unbidden. Things were rapidly getting out of hand. Control needed to be seized at once.

He was halfway through informing the trespassers that they would fry in the very bowels of Lucifer's loins if they didn't leave forthwith, when Lethbridge-Stewart began talking over him. Not to be outdone, he raised his voice to compensate. Only the words 'sinners will be cast into the pit for all eternity' left his mouth, before he realised that nobody at all was listening. For the first time since being a novice, he found that he was no longer the centre of attention. His speech petered out, and he began to listen to Lethbridge-Stewart instead. If he couldn't persuade them to leave by his old and trusted methods, he would have to at least find out what they wanted.

'It may be difficult to grasp, but the dead are walking,' Lethbridge-Stewart said. 'We must take refuge in the church immediately.'

Reverend Cunningham smiled inwardly. During his time as an emissary of Our Lord, he had occasionally been called upon to deal with matters of the spectral world. It was

183

always in a creaky old building full of dry rot, rasping floorboards and owned by the over impressionable and over imaginative. All he had done on those occasions was to half-heartedly perform the exorcism ritual. After each incident, he was rewarded with a huge supper with much wine. Of course, the so-called ghost had never returned. More than likely they had never existed. If he quickly performed an exorcism in the manor, he could get rid of his unsolicited guests quickly and efficiently. Afterwards he could claim the usual recompense. Judging by the presence of Wallace from the manor, the supper would be good indeed.

'The bell, book and candle are what you need for this predicament,' he said gravely. 'I will collect the necessary implements.'

'Now listen to me. That will not do any good,' Lethbridge-Stewart insisted, much to the reverend's frustration. 'As I have told you, we need to take refuge in the church. Please get the key and hurry.'

'Nonsense!' Reverend Cunningham grunted, as he collected his Bible and a cross from the sideboard. He knew how to banish ghosts, real or imaginary, and nobody was going to tell him how to do it. Now where had he put the spare candles?

'Reverend Cunningham.' At the sound of his name, the reverend paused. It was Wallace that had spoken, but the aristocrat's voice was so different to his normally refined tone that Cunningham couldn't help but listen. 'I know it sounds insane, but it's true. The dead really *are* walking. Please, we must go to the church.'

Seeing the fear in Wallace's eyes, the reverend decided

on a change of tactics. Motioning the visitors to remain, he walked to the kitchen. A large iron loop containing the church keys hung from a hook beside the pantry. Idly, he plucked them from their resting place and slipped the keys into his pocket. It would do no harm to humour them for a while. When no ghouls came, he would then be able to diffuse the situation easily. They would be grateful for the service he had performed and embarrassed by their earlier panic. Within the confines of the church they would undoubtedly pray and listen to his sermons.

He would be in control once more.

As the stagecoach thundered down the road, the occasional pothole caused Mortimer Hartley to bang his head painfully on the roof. He looked out of the coach at the darting landscape, but it was simply a blur of darkened trees and bushes. They were going too fast. Hartley raised his walking stick, ready to give a rap to attract Neville's attention, but before he could, splintering wood and frightened whinnies filled his ears. Then there was blackness.

When he came to, Hartley sensed the sweet tang of blood taunting his taste buds, but to his relief nothing appeared to be broken. Indubitably, when he undressed there would be an attractive marbling of purple and green bruises all over his body.

Gingerly, he crawled out of the wooden box that had protected him from the worst of the crash. When his shoe kicked a smashed oil lamp, the noise brought him to his senses. Neville. What had happened to the lad? Before he could search the wreckage for his faithful employee, he became aware that he was not alone.

The mill owner swallowed hard. The crash may not have been an accident after all, but a deliberate ploy by highwaymen and footpads. Perhaps the notorious Cock Road Gang had waylaid him?

He backed away, as the shadowy figure moved closer. The man became bathed in the feeble light, and a belly laugh forced its way from Hartley's lips. It was James McGregor, one of his employees.

More figures moved out of the gloom. He recognised them all, but something was very wrong. Some were in their work clothes, but some were in nightshirts or dressing gowns. Several were barefoot, but it was their features that were the most striking. They were pasty and ashen, with streaks of crimson that could only have been blood caked onto their skin. Their movements too were abnormal. Jerky. Uncontrolled. Erratic.

Hooked hands swiped towards Hartley's head, and nails ripped into the skin of his cheek. In terror Hartley ran for his life, and the mad men shuffled after him.

Gradually the unnatural moans of his workforce faded into the distance and he slowed his pace. Had he outrun them?

Abruptly he stopped. In the road ahead moved a stumbling, erratic figure. Hartley stared at the pallid and bloodshot man, as he turned his head slowly towards Hartley. Panic-stricken, he took flight. Only one thought filled the turmoil of his mind. He needed sanctuary and the protection of the Almighty.

'What the hell was up with 'im?'

Jack Golby surveyed the fleeing mill owner with surprise. He was used to the toffs peering down their noses at him, but this was the first time that a member of the ruling classes had turned on their heels and ran from his presence. The silver spoon up the man's backside was probably itchy, thought the drunk. It obviously needed polishing, and that act certainly could not be performed in front of humble ol' Jack. Shaking his head in disbelief, the drunk staggered the final few steps to his tiny terraced house, and patted his pockets for his key. It wasn't there.

He beat his fists uselessly on the rickety door of his home. The warped wood whimpered in protest but stubbornly remained closed. Through his clouded mind, Jack realised that he had left his key back at *The Ship Inn*, and he had no choice but to return. Hollering and hammering on the door would be required until Ruth opened up. It would not be an easy task to rouse her from her warm and cosy bed, but he had little choice. Once she had wrenched the door open to bawl at him in her usual manner, he would politely explain that his door key was perched on top of an upturned glass in the middle of his usual table – just put there for safekeeping like any reasonably minded person would have done. He only needed a moment to locate said item, and he would be off. *Sorry to trouble you, ma'am, and if you ever need anything just yell.* With luck, she would allow him a cheap gin for the road. Given her earlier mood he knew that it was unlikely, but miracles sometimes happened.

With a snort, the drunk ambled back down the darkened street.

Jack's inebriated body made surprisingly swift work of

the return journey, and it wasn't long before the comforting sight of his home-from-home loomed ahead. The sign portraying a faded elegant sailing ship flapped back and forth in the night's breeze, and he looked at its gentle movement for an instant. Ruth had threatened to paint it over, but as with many of her schemes it had only been idle talk. He was trying to remember her exact words, when he realised that he was procrastinating. Annoyed with himself, Jack went to the tavern's entrance and raised his hand ready to strike. The elevated knuckle stopped abruptly in mid-air, inches from the wood of the door.

To his dismay all his carefully worked out speeches and polite soothing phrases had leaked out of his brain. He was scared to knock. What if she fulfilled her pledge to bar him? Jack's arm fell limply to his side and, instead of knocking, he started to count how many bricks were in the wall. It was a pointless exercise, but it allowed him to put off the inevitable.

After losing count for the third time, a small overlooked fact was at last noticed. Light bled from beneath the thick green curtains that hung in the bar's large window. The landlady would have extinguished the oil lamps if she had retired to bed, so obviously she was still up. This revelation brought back Jack's lost confidence. Before it slipped away again, he bounded forward, knocked politely and waited. The expected yell of disturbed protest never came. Jack scowled. He gave another polite rap, but again there was no reply. With his patience fast waning, he raised his fist and hammered loudly. Politeness had been substituted with rudeness.

'Oi, come on. Open up. I've left me key in yur.'

188

The force of Jack's final blow caused the door to edge open – it wasn't locked.

Extending several gnarled fingers, he pushed at the door until it was half open. Making a snap decision, he stole inside. Maybe he could get the key and be gone without disturbing anyone. Almost immediately, he regretted the rash decision. At any second he expected to be challenged by the angry red-faced landlady, demanding to know what he was doing sneaking into her pub.

Loudly, he tiptoed into the bar. It was empty. Jack inhaled the gorgeous fumes of ale, and immediately had the urge for a swift one. It took all his willpower to resist. If he was caught helping himself to the booze, then he would be barred for sure.

Somebody had spilt what appeared to be a large quantity of port on the floor, so he stepped carefully over it. It had soaked into the carpet, making a massive ugly red stain, and he didn't want to tread it in further. He quickly padded to his favourite table, but the glass that he saw so vividly in his mind's eye wasn't there. Confusion swept across him. What had happened to his key? He no longer had any choice. He would have to search the building for Ruth, to find out if she had seen it.

The hunt was brief and incomplete, but it didn't take long for even Jack's glazed eyes to tell that *The Ship Inn* was completely deserted. Both Ruth and her husband had vanished, and without them how was he going to get served? Turning the poser over in his mind, a big grin smeared onto his prematurely aged features. His prayer to Saint Monica had worked.

Jack slipped to the spot he had always ached to be –

behind the bar. It was as if it was his destiny. His bloodshot eyes darted across the racks of spirits and malts. One in particular caught his eye. Jack picked up a fine bottle of twelve-year-old whisky like a new-born baby, and cradled it in his arms. His hand felt for a glass, and swiftly a generous amount of brown liquid cascaded into it. There was a slight pause for thought, before it was topped up with an even larger dose. At long last he was where he had always dreamed of being, and he was going to make the most of the opportunity. Happily, he raised a toast to Saint Monica.

When Reverend Cunningham returned to the living room, he beckoned for the visitors to leave and declared that he would allow them to seek sanctuary. He sensed the relief that his words brought and congratulated himself at regaining control. The reverend glared as Wallace helped himself to a long carving knife stuck into a hulk of bread on the coffee table, but he didn't push his luck. Reverend Cunningham was of the firm opinion that you never argue with a man brandishing a knife. Holding his tongue, he followed the unwelcome guests as they filed back to the front door, but instead of continuing into the night the reverend was astonished to see them freeze in front of him.

Peering over Lethbridge-Stewart's shoulder, he saw a figure looming out of the darkness. He groaned. Just when he had got the situation under control, another unwanted visitor turned up. He should incorporate this problem into his next sermon. It would be unwise to tell the congregation that they would burn in hell if they interrupted him at ungodly hours, but he could make it a message to stand on your own two feet and embrace the Lord's tests willingly.

Curious to know who the approaching person was, Reverend Cunningham attempted to push past those in front of him. Much to his surprise, they didn't yield. The visitors tried to retreat back into the cottage, but his huge bulk prevented them. The figure was now close enough to be recognised. It was Gary Ludlow, the local blacksmith, and he looked ill. Through his clothes seeped a dark patch that could only be blood, and he obviously had trouble walking. His compassionate nature, which had been concealed for so many years under rich food and power, burst to the surface. A member of his congregation was in distress and needed his aid.

His view was suddenly cleared, as Lethbridge-Stewart rushed forward and lashed out at the distressed blacksmith. The blow landed square in the chest of the stumbling man. Gary fell to the floor with a sickening snap – surely it was the sound of the poor man's neck breaking on the cold stone of the pavement. The reverend stared at the unspeakable murder being committed in front of him. It was a breach of the Sacred Holy Commandments, right in front of his church.

'That was Gary Ludlow,' Cunningham said in a weak voice, as if mentioning the poor man's name would end the madness.

Nobody else appeared to be distressed at the cold-blooded murder, and he knew he had to say something. Unfortunately, for the first time in his life, he didn't know what to say.

The blacksmith rose unsteadily to his feet. He wasn't dead after all, and happiness leaped forward. The joy was short lived. Gary's head was set at an impossible angle, and the blood that seeped from under his clothes began to drip onto the stone beneath his feet. From his mouth uttered an unearthly moan, and drool soon joined the blood spatters on the floor. Behind him came other figures. They too moaned as their feet scuffed against the gravestones that made up the path. Screwing his eyes shut tight, the reverend screamed.

The first thing he thought, when his screams stopped ringing in his ears, was that judgement day had come. The second was whether he would be looked upon as a sinner with all the rest. He well knew the greed that had consumed the slim altar boy of his youth. Power and high living had corrupted him. He knew that the fear of damnation was the only reason people listened to his sermons. Regret washed over him, and at the same time he knew that this was not the end of the world. He wasn't sure how – he just knew. His faith enabled him to come to his senses. Gradually he opened his eyes.

Around him was pandemonium. He watched as the unwelcome visitors forced their way through the servants of Lucifer and sprinted to the church. As the demons approached him, he considered the Bible clutched tightly in his pudgy hands. He turned the Holy Book in his meaty palm and realised what needed to be done. He no longer wanted to be in control. He just wanted to live.

The demons took little notice of him as he fled, with only the closest lurching after him. They had other prey on their minds. Scarcely believing his luck and wheezing acutely from the short run, he joined the visitors huddled beside the church entrance.

'Quick,' Chorley cried out, his voice raising several

octaves in panic. 'The door! Unlock the door!'

'I noticed you left without the key,' the reverend said helpfully. 'So I thought I'd better come with you.'

He fumbled with the lock, and the thick door clicked open. Pushing it wide enough for his ample frame, Reverend Cunningham skulked into his place of work. The others slipped after him.

Lethbridge-Stewart stopped at the threshold and looked around, his dark eyebrow knitting in concern.

'Where's Oscar and Zara?'

CHAPTER ELEVEN

The Siege Begins

Mortimer Hartley's cracked ribs throbbed so much that he thought he would pass out. Each breath brought yet more searing pain, but the oxygen it provided was critical fuel for his frantic journey. The instinct of self-preservation kept him going. He knew that more of the madmen were on his trail. From time to time he caught their groans on the wind or spotted swaying silhouettes in the distance.

His desperate mind clung to the belief that they would not be allowed to befoul the church's sacred ground. The Almighty would surely prevent such a blasphemy. It was this blind faith that made the pain bearable and had enabled him to get within sight of the church bell tower. The heavenly sight spurred him onwards. If he was to die, he at least wanted a chance to pray for his sins and, who knew, he may live after all.

Before long, his footsteps reverberated on the church path. Hartley's head reeled with relief. He had made it. Forcing his tired legs to speed up, the mill owner ran straight into the midst of the madmen he had tried so hard to avoid. There were dozens of them.

Hartley froze and for once his luck held out. By a miracle, they hadn't noticed him. Something or someone a short distance away took their full attention.

Craning his dizzy head, Hartley peered past the madmen. On the floor lay the butler from the Stedman household. By him stood a black girl of around eight years old, staring at the advancing madmen. The mill owner's thoughts went out to her. If it wasn't for her colour, she could have been one of his employees. There were many of similar build and age in his mill, working away on his produce. Hartley willed her to flee, but her feet appeared to be rooted to the ground. To the mill owner's surprise there was a moan, but it was not from the disease-ridden. The man on the floor stirred. He was alive, but the crowd was almost upon him.

Forgetting his ills, Hartley rushed to help.

Haziness swamped Oscar's cranium. Why was he spread-eagled on the floor? A moan of protest left the butler's lips, as he brought his head upright to look at his surroundings. The world was out of focus, but he could sense movement. Something was moving in his direction, but what was it? Then, in a torrent of thoughts, it all rushed back. They had been fleeing to the church. He was at the back of the group because Zara's legs were so much shorter than everyone else's. He must have tripped and hit his head. How long had he been unconscious? It must have only been seconds, or surely he would be dead by now.

With supreme effort, Oscar pulled himself unsteadily to his feet. Immediately, his vision cleared, as if somebody had swept back a pair of curtains inside his head. Less than five feet away ran a bloody man with ragged clothes. A corpse was heading straight for him, and behind him shuffled many more. Unable to contain himself, Oscar let forth a cry of fright.

'It's all right, Mr Whittle. Come with me,' said the corpse. 'We must hurry.'

'Who?' Oscar stammered in surprise, his head spinning.

He stared at its eyes, and saw the friendly gaze of the living. It took a moment for him to realise it was Mortimer Hartley, the owner of the textile mill on the far side of the village. But the shuffling figures behind him were definitely corpses, and they were almost upon them. Gratefully, he took the offered arm of support.

'Zara! Where's Zara?'

The thought barged into his brain like a disgruntled bull. Wildly Oscar looked around and saw that the child was only a few feet away. Hartley offered her his other hand, but Zara shrank away. With his terrifying appearance it was little wonder that she didn't trust him. Knowing that every split second was essential, Oscar abandoned the support and scooped the girl up into his arms.

Before he had a chance to escape, he felt his fine waistcoat clamped by a vice-like grip, almost knocking him off balance. Gritting his teeth, Oscar tried to yank himself clear, but it was no good. Little by little, he felt himself being dragged backwards. Pain sheared through his body, as hungry teeth clamped into his flesh. The first mouth was soon joined by another diner, and then another.

Desperately trying to protect Zara from the ravenous corpses, Oscar fought back violently, using his nails to gouge at flesh that felt no discomfort.

Against all odds, suddenly he was free. The butler bolted for the church with his precious cargo in his arms.

Panting with the sudden effort, he stole a glance behind

him and the reason he was free became clear. Hartley had knocked his attackers to the ground, but it had come at a price. The courageous man was now swamped by the undead. The landlady from *The Ship Inn* bit down onto his back, and in triumph a mouthful of cloth and white flesh was torn free. Then the rest of the undead joined the feast.

A hand on his shoulder caused Oscar to start, but to his relief it was only Lethbridge-Stewart. To the butler's surprise, his master rushed past him into the night, brandishing the reverend's carving knife with a grim look of determination set in his eyes.

'Get them inside, Sergeant Major,' Lethbridge-Stewart ordered before following after Wallace.

Oscar allowed Samson to escort him into the church. He set the little girl down on a pew, but he knew he couldn't remain in safety himself. He couldn't rest while his master needed his help in rescuing Hartley. If only he still had the pistol.

Samson tried to stop him as he groggily stepped once more into the cold night air, but it was already too late. Hartley was dead. While the mass of hungry corpses ate their meal, the small group of the living retreated to the church and the heavy door was locked behind them.

After a few minutes, the pound of undead fists began.

'Wasn't that the fellow who rescued us from the mice earlier?' Lethbridge-Stewart asked Chorley. 'What was his name? Monty Harvey or something?'

'Mortimer,' Oscar corrected him, before Chorley had a chance to reply. 'Mortimer Hartley. One of the master's friends.'

Lethbridge-Stewart noted with concern that the butler was pale and looked unsteady on his feet. He rushed to Oscar's side just in time, and caught him as his legs gave way. Reverend Cunningham busied himself lighting candles to banish away the gloom, and Lethbridge-Stewart and Samson half dragged, half carried Oscar to a pew.

'See what you can do for him,' Lethbridge-Stewart told Samson.

Without waiting for an answer, Samson unbuttoned the remains of Oscar's blood-soaked shirt. Oscar shifted in pain, but didn't attempt to push him away. The burgundy stained clothing was pulled back to reveal a mass of deep bite marks. Fat and muscle had been scooped out by sharp human teeth, leaving cavities filled with reservoirs of clotting blood. Much to Lethbridge-Stewart's discomfort, it reminded him of a half-eaten take-away smothered in tomato sauce. Pushing this macabre thought away, he helped Samson rip the shirt into makeshift bandages.

Samson wrapped the first bandage around a particularly nasty wound on the injured man's shoulder, and Lethbridge-Stewart used the moment to take stock.

Their position was dire, but the building was strong and defensible. The impressive stained-glass windows were out of reach of even the most imposing of the Loa's puppet corpses, and the main door was thick and strong. There was a side entrance further down the building, and he noted with interest that there was no hammering of hungry corpses on its heavy oak door. Perhaps the Loa was unaware of this alternative way in. They were safe for now, but it was clear that they couldn't remain holed up there forever. The unearthly groans of the living dead were a constant reminder of the gathering forces outside. The church was simply a stopgap – a place to think.

Samson pulled tight the final makeshift bandage, and together they shifted Oscar to a more comfortable position.

'I've done the best I can, but he's lost a lot of blood,' Samson said, just as Chorley joined them by Oscar's side. 'My field medic training only goes so far. Really he needs a hospital.'

'Not much chance of that,' Chorley said bitterly. 'What if he dies and tries to take a bite out of my leg or something?'

'We'll just have to hope he pulls through then, won't we?' Lethbridge-Stewart said, exasperated at Chorley's tactlessness.

Lethbridge-Stewart had to concede, to himself at least, that Chorley had a point. The last thing they needed was a ready-made pair of hands for the Loa to inhabit right inside the church. Oscar needed a close eye kept on him, just in case.

Beside him, Wallace began to pace restlessly along the aisle. He had been so calm just moments earlier. It was as if somebody had flicked a switch inside his head. Lethbridge-Stewart realised with sadness that the scientist's moods were fluctuating so rapidly, that he was surely on the brink of a nervous breakdown. The scientist's voice quivered, giving the impression that he was on the verge of hysterics.

'It's all very well barricading ourselves into the church, but surely we need to destroy those... those monsters out there! We can't hide forever!'

'One step at a time, Wallace,' Lethbridge-Stewart said calmly. 'One step at a time.'

'He is right though,' Chorley said. 'We're stuck in here

now. The Loa's got us well and truly penned in.'

'The Loa… You mentioned that just after we escaped the fire,' Wallace said, grasping at the unfamiliar name. 'It's what's making the dead walk, isn't it?'

'It certainly appears that way,' Lethbridge-Stewart confirmed.

'What about destroying this Loa thing? Then all these walking corpses would just… just stop, wouldn't they? I mean, they'd all become normal dead bodies.'

'I'm afraid that's impossible,' Lethbridge-Stewart said, shaking his head slowly. 'The Loa exists well beyond our reach. It's the void outside our universe. You can't kill it in any conventional way.'

'You're talking about Hell!' Cunningham snorted, fingering the Bible still clutched in his pudgy hand. 'An exorcism is what we need.'

'So there's nothing we can do?' said Chorley imploringly, causing a whine of protest from the reverend. 'What about Toussaint? It's using him as a medium, right?'

'Toussaint?' Wallace said in surprise. 'What on earth has he got to do with all of this?'

'The Loa has taken his body over and used it to raise the dead,' Lethbridge-Stewart explained wearily. 'Without him, there is a chance that the Loa would be catapulted safely back to its own domain. There are no guarantees though.'

'So, you're saying if Toussaint dies, this might end?'

From a nearby pew, a child's voice caused Lethbridge-Stewart to turn away from Wallace. He hadn't even noticed that Zara was there. Undoubtedly it was second nature to say very little in front of her master, but Wallace's casual disregard for her grandfather had broken the spell.

'My grandfather won't hurt you. I know he won't. I swear. You've got to let me go back.'

Samson sat next to her. 'I'm sorry. I know it's hard, but you must stay here with us.' He flashed her an encouraging smile. And, for the first time since leaving the manor, Zara smiled too.

He'll make a good dad one day, Lethbridge-Stewart thought, and returned his attention to the problem at hand.

Monday afternoon, and it was time. Anne glanced at Bill, who smiled at her, no indication of doubt whatsoever. Even Jeff looked confident; a rare thing indeed. Anne turned to their guinea pig, Private Armitage.

'Are you ready?' she asked.

Armitage nodded. 'As I'll ever be, ma'am.'

'Okay, then.'

Anne took the syringe and carefully stuck it into his arm.

'The solution should take effect quite quickly, so make sure you let me know when things look... different.'

Solution. Sounded so harmless. But really what she had just put in his system with a mixture of some of the most powerful hallucinogens around. She'd spoken to Mr Harris again, in the hope that he could provide them with some kind of guide for the right concoction. With a bit of prodding, and checking through lists of hallucinogens, he was finally able to offer up some names. It was then down to Anne to work out the most effective mixture, taking into account how certain hallucinogens reacted with others. It was dangerous science, one she was not confident of (chemistry was not her strong suit), but it was necessary. She had warned Armitage – Chris, as he insisted she call him – made him aware of the dangers in this. Such a concentrated mixture was bound to have adverse effects, and not all of them could be predicted. He said he understood, and now here they were.

Bill stood a short distance away, near the machine he had helped Jeff build, which was now connected to the rail tracks, barely a foot from where they ended. If Anne had the mix of hallucinogens right, then Armitage would see what Mr Harris had seen ten years ago. The village beyond the fencing, somehow hidden from the perception of normal human senses. And, if Armitage could, and was able to relay the appropriate information, then Bill had orders to activate the machine, which would then be calibrated to match the vibrational frequency of the Mirror Keynsham.

'Whoa,' Armitage said, eyes wide. 'Over there.' He pointed, just right of the rail tracks.

Anne looked. She saw nothing except the flat grass, curiously short despite nobody cutting it in over a hundred and fifty years. 'What do you see, Chris?'

'The sarge.' Armitage stood up and made to move forward. Jeff was about to stop him, but Anne shook her head. They followed closely. 'He's there with the Land Rover.'

'Any sign of Samson?' Anne asked.

'No. But… There's the brigadier.'

Two out of four. It was a good start.

'Bill, let's give this a go,' Anne said.

Bill nodded and activated the machine. Anne put a hand on Armitage's shoulder, to pause him. He may have been able to pass through the barrier, but the test would have been useless if they couldn't follow.

A steady hum filled the air. Bill jumped back from the machine. Anne frowned, and then realised what happened. His foot had been resting on a track. The change in vibration had shocked him. He smiled at her. Anne shook her head, and felt a sharp pain in her mouth.

Her teeth. The nerves in her gums were buzzing. And, it appeared, the same was true of Bill, Jeff and the guards standing near the tracks.

The humming of the track increased, turning into a groan, a shifting of molecules in the iron as the tracks heated up.

Bill returned to the machine and checked out the flickering needle. He looked over at Anne and gave her a thumbs-up.

'Okay, Chris, off you go,' she said.

Armitage turned so he was walking sideways, crab-like. Once he had reached the prearranged spot, indicated by a small square of metal, wires linking it to the tracks, he stopped. Half of him was missing, no doubt on the other side of the barrier. He didn't seem to notice, instead his head was turned away and he was watching whatever was happening on the other side.

'Whoa,' he said slowly. 'It's a bloody zombie cow!'

There was that word again. Which at least added further weight to Mr Harris' experience.

'Crank it up,' Anne said. They were so close.

Bill twisted the dial a few more notches, and apprehensively Anne waited. If the machine did the job she hoped, and thus proved Jeff's theory, then soon the rest of Armitage would be seen. They hoped to bring forth the village, match the vibrational frequency, just long enough so they could enter and find Lethbridge-Stewart and the others.

'Damn it!' Bill hissed.

Smoke started pouring from the machine.

A spark on the track, and a strange pulse surged along the wire towards Armitage.

'Chris!' Anne shouted. 'Private Armitage, step away now!'

Armitage looked at her, confused. 'I can feel it,' he said. 'The vibratio—'

His voice was cut off abruptly and his entire left half flopped on to the grass. His right half was, presumably, still inside the Mirror Keynsham.

The test had failed.

At first it was difficult to see out of the coloured glass, but as Lethbridge-Stewart's eyes became more accustomed to the dim light outside, his vision improved. The illumination from the open front door of the reverend's cottage aided his inspection of the surrounding area. It didn't look good. He watched a figure stumble up the path to join its comrades at the front of the church. From his vantage point Lethbridge-Stewart couldn't see the church door, but from the noise he knew that there were plenty of the Loa's puppets already there. The tell-tale inhuman moaning and thumping of hungry hands spoke volumes. There was no way that anybody could slip out by the main entrance, but that hardly came as a surprise. What he really needed to know was how many of the reanimated villagers were in the other parts of the church grounds.

Another figure slowly moved into view, dragging its

broken leg behind on the stone path. It too headed straight for the door. Lethbridge-Stewart swept his eyes to the far side of the church. As far as he could tell there were no corpses waiting in the shadows. That side at least appeared to be free of the Loa's undead army.

He had seen all he needed. He jumped down, surprised when Reverend Cunningham brushed past him to take his place. With unexpected agility, he clambered up and peered into the darkness.

'Oh, not my geraniums!'

The reverend tutted loudly at his putrid congregation, as if he was more concerned about the destruction of his flower beds than the fact that the dead were walking. Lethbridge-Stewart guessed that in reality the man was in shock, and was terrified under his brash exterior.

It was clear they couldn't hold out indefinitely, especially with the Loa's reinforcements continually adding their weight to the siege. Eventually the weight would become too much, and the door would give way. He needed to act now while he still could. If the Loa was indeed unaware of the side door, there was a slim chance that he might be able to slip out unnoticed.

'Reverend, can I have a quiet word?'

With a huff, Cunningham abandoned his position at the window. As he climbed down and the hammering on the door echoed throughout the church, Samson attempted to distract the young slave girl from the danger outside by singing the nursery rhyme again.

Wallace gave him an irritated look, but Samson continued relentlessly. Unfortunately, it didn't help matters much, as Zara didn't appear to be listening to the rhyme anyway.

'Reverend, follow me please,' Lethbridge-Stewart said, before walking towards the far side of the church. 'Wallace can you join us?'

Without complaint, Reverend Cunningham and Wallace followed him and Chorley tagged along too. Once they reached the altar, out of earshot of Zara, Lethbridge-Stewart got straight down to business.

'Wallace, do you think Toussaint knows about the side entrance? Has he ever been here?'

The scientist studied him quizzically before answering. 'Why do you ask?'

'Because if he is aware of it then it's a fair bet that the Loa is too.'

Wallace thought hard before he answered, and when he did he avoided Lethbridge-Stewart's gaze. 'Neither Toussaint nor Zara were allowed to come to the church services. They are unlikely to know about that door, but I wouldn't like to stake my life on it.'

'I've seen him doing errands about the village, but he's never been here,' Reverend Cunningham confirmed. 'Anyway, that entrance hasn't been used in years.'

'In that case, I think it may be worth the risk. Reverend, do you by any chance have the key? I need to find a way to slip out unnoticed.'

'If we take one step outside that door, we will all die!' Reverend Cunningham exclaimed in alarm. 'No, no. It's much better if we stay here. That door's solid as a rock. Once they find they can't get in...'

It was unbelievable. The reverend seemed to believe that the creatures would simply get bored and go away.

Lethbridge-Stewart needed to make the man see sense.

'There's no way I can stop the Loa whilst I'm trapped in here with all those things outside. But out there I can—'

'It's madness! Sheer madness! We're safe here, so—'

'That door won't stop them forever,' Chorley said, cutting Cunningham off. 'More of those things are arriving all the time. Eventually they will break in.'

'Chorley's right. If the Loa isn't dealt with, we won't have a chance,' Lethbridge-Stewart added. 'And if there's anybody else alive out there they won't either. Think of your congregation. All I'm asking is for you to let me try to sort this mess out.'

'I suppose I can let you out. The key's in the vestry,' Reverend Cunningham mumbled, looking down at his feet in embarrassment. Lethbridge-Stewart's carefully chosen words had finally got through to him. 'Do you think there are many left alive?'

'I hope so. I really do.'

Lethbridge-Stewart waited for the reverend to return with the key, while the others returned to the nave. The man was certainly taking his time. As he lingered, Lethbridge-Stewart listened at the side entrance for any sign of the undead beyond, but could hear nothing. Presently he became aware of somebody approaching, but to his irritation it wasn't Reverend Cunningham. Chorley had returned, and he had Samson in tow.

'Chorley tells me you're leaving the church, sir.'

'I'm returning to the manor, to take care of this once and for all,' Lethbridge-Stewart said firmly. 'I was going to inform you once I had the key.'

'Then I should go with you,' Samson said. 'You can't go alone. You'll need back up.'

'I'm planning to rendezvous with Dovey anyway, but an extra pair of eyes would be useful,' Lethbridge-Stewart agreed. 'You're needed here though. Chorley, I would like you to come with me.'

Chorley looked at him suspiciously. 'Me?'

'You said it yourself that these things will break in, sooner or later, and I could really do with your help. And since you're the reason we're all in this mess...'

'You can hardly blame me for what the Loa is doing.'

'No, but it was you that insisted we investigate the Keynsham Triangle.'

'Which in turn led me here,' Samson added with a slight smile.

'Anyway,' Lethbridge-Stewart said, ignoring the goading look on Samson's face, 'you can't let everyone else take the risks, can you?'

'I suppose not,' Chorley said dubiously.

'So that's settled.' Before Chorley had a chance to change his mind, Lethbridge-Stewart swiftly turned his attention back to Samson. 'I'd like you to remain to protect the civilians. Keep a guard on this door in case we return, and if Oscar fails to pull through, make sure you secure the body.'

'I don't think Wallace will take too kindly to me being in charge,' Samson said.

'I don't care what that man takes kindly to.'

'Good, neither do I.' Samson grinned. 'It would be my pleasure.' The smile faltered after only a few seconds. 'You're going to kill Toussaint, aren't you?'

Sadly, Lethbridge-Stewart nodded. 'I can't see any alternative. If only there was some other way.'

'You're probably right. We haven't any other option,' Samson agreed. 'That poor little girl. There should be some spare ammo in the Land Rover, if you're running low.'

'Right then. Let's get on with it,' Lethbridge-Stewart said. He looked around the church. 'Now where the blazes has that man got to? We need the key asap.'

As the men left to search for Reverend Cunningham, Zara darted behind a pillar and out of sight. Always a quiet child, nobody had noticed the slave girl listening in on their conversation.

CHAPTER TWELVE

Death by Cow

The doorway was obscured by a shrub; wandering ivy added its discrete camouflage to the neglected access point. All was still. Slowly, Lethbridge-Stewart opened the door wider and winced when the little used hinges squeaked in protest. He looked for movement beyond the shrub, but there was no sign that the noise had attracted any unwanted attention. He waited several long seconds to be sure, but it appeared that the corpses hadn't made their way to this part of the church and were concentrating all their efforts on the main entrance. His gamble that the Loa had no knowledge of the side entrance seemed to have paid off. It was unlikely to be watched, but it was vital that they were careful just in case.

He slipped through the gap to confirm that the coast was clear, and then beckoned to Chorley. The journalist swiftly followed his lead, and the door clunked closed behind them. The pair crept silently away from the church into the foreboding murkiness of the night.

Taking care to avoid the path, they headed towards the back of the church and into the graveyard. Lethbridge-Stewart felt certain that there would be none of the living dead to hinder them there. So long as the Loa thought that they were inside the besieged church, it would be of little value patrolling it.

Rarely read inscriptions to missed loved ones were passed by, as they picked their way through the mass of haphazard headstones. Occasionally Lethbridge-Stewart crushed underfoot a flower left for the dear departed, and the petals stuck to the mud on the underside of his boots. Their destruction caused small pangs of regret to prick at him, but he didn't dwell on it. Haste was more important. Stealthily they moved past the greying stone monuments, until the moaning of the Loa's minions disappeared into the distance.

Clambering over a stout wall, Lethbridge-Stewart found himself in an open field. Pausing for Chorley to follow suit, he peered up at the stars that poked through the cloud cover and swiftly found his bearings. It was essential that they reached their destination as soon as possible. He just hoped that it was not too late.

They circled around the fields, aiming to get to the manor without approaching it by road. He was positive that route would be guarded. Eventually they found a rough dirt path, and followed its course. All being well, the burned-out building would be in sight very soon, and behind it the Land Rover and Dovey.

Their footsteps crunched on the new surface, as they kept an eye out for any danger lurking in the darkness. There was no sign of the nocturnal animals that usually flourished in such places. The Loa had plainly killed or driven to ground all living things.

Their good fortune held out, and it wasn't long before Lethbridge-Stewart spotted the red glow of flames in the distance. Swapping the dirt and stone for mud and grass, they changed direction towards the still burning building.

A nauseating belch filled *The Ship Inn*, but for once there was nobody to condemn Jack for his gross lack of manners. He followed the almighty belch with a smaller cousin. It was less repellent, but almost as revolting. With shaky hands, Jack reached again for the whisky. The bottle was upturned over the glass for a full twenty seconds, before he realised that it was empty. Only a drop or two of the precious amber liquid drained into the waiting vessel. On any other occasion this would have been a heartbreaking event, but not today. Today he had a whole pub to himself. His eyes darted to the rows of liqueur bottles lined up behind the bar. He picked one at random, but as he began to open it the bottle slipped out of his fingers to smash by his feet. A strangled cry of anguish automatically left his lips. Even though there was plenty more, the loss of alcohol in such a way was a blow. Sadly, he stooped on one knee to study the label. *Merry Legs Gin*, it read. Jack breathed a sigh of relief. It was only cheap grog.

Returning to the bottles, the drunk chose another, but this time he was more careful. Selecting a strong rum, Jack tenderly took it to his favourite table. En route, his feet trod on the stain that he had earlier assumed to be port. A thick crimson liquid bubbled up over his shoe. Flicking a piece of raw meat off a chair in irritation, Jack sank down. For a moment he wondered what the meat was doing there, but he found he could no longer concentrate properly and didn't really care anyway. Even by his own standards, he was plastered. No matter, the rum would calm his reeling brain.

This time Jack dispensed with the glass and swigged

straight from the bottle. The alcohol burned his throat, but it was a welcome sensation. The event it caused was not so welcome. Another belch left his lips, and with it came the contents of his stomach. Wiping his mouth clean with the back of his hand, Jack wildly looked around for Ruth. If the landlady saw the mess he would be barred for sure. If he left quickly, Ruth wouldn't know it was him that had defiled her pub. She may blame it on others. Knowing that he had no time to lose, the drunk staggered to his feet. He made his way to the door, clutching the rum to his breast as he did so. He wouldn't abandon that prize.

Hardly believing that he had been forced to leave the pub by the stupidity of his own gut, Jack swayed up the road. The cobblestones made his drunken movement more awkward, so he subconsciously sought an easier path.

Before long he was striding along at great wobbly paces. The clean night air enabled the sickness to be banished, and now he was thinking with a tiny bit more clarity. Fumbling with the bottle of rum, that clarity was swiftly stamped down, but the nausea didn't return.

He had been walking for over half an hour, when suddenly he stopped dead.

'Whes the bleedin' hell are I?' he said loudly.

All Jack could make out was a field surrounded by a low hedgerow. For the first time in many years his autopilot had failed him and had taken him considerably off route. There was nothing for it. He would have to return the way he came. Jack set off, grumbling and knocking back rum as he went.

Ten minutes later, he became aware of the bubbling of running water. It was the river. If he followed its course, he knew that it would guide him back to within a stone's throw of *The Ship Inn*. All paths lead to the Promised Land, but should he really go that direction? What if he bumped into Ruth?

Then another thought hit him. His bloody key was still in the pub. Would it be too late to go back? With his hazy mind grasping that it was either that or sleep in a doorway, Jack decided a return to the messy crime scene was the best course of action. Even if Ruth was there he could deny all knowledge.

Traipsing across a muddy ditch, he soon found himself by the riverbank. It was here that the green eyes returned. The luminous orbs glowed from the other side of the river. They could have been from any cat, but Jack knew that it had to be the servant of Old Nick. The stare that bored into his skull was too familiar.

Jack looked for its canine companion, but it didn't appear to be present. Nevertheless, the sight that he did see caused a sinking feeling to sweep across him.

In the distance, a red glow of fire could plainly be seen. It could only mean one thing – the cat had brought the fiery pen with it and wanted his signature. He was a fool to think he could dupe Old Nick. For all his earlier bravado, the very idea of losing his soul now caused jabs of terror to invade Jack's inebriated body. The precious bottle of grog slipped from his fingers and fell onto the grass. The alcohol gurgled out of its uncorked top to join with the earth, but Jack paid it no regard. Instead he fumbled in his pocket and brought out the remainder of the money that Old Nick had given him.

'Hey, yur! I don't want it, yur see!' he cried across the

water at the staring eyes. 'Tell yur master I ain't signing nothing, yur hear!'

With all his strength he threw the coins towards the luminous green eyes, and they landed with a faint *plop* into the murky river. Slowly, the orbs moved closer. Jack wondered if Old Nick's cat could swim, and the thought brought forward further dread.

'It's not all there, but I'll get the rest for yur now,' he garbled, without the faintest idea of where he would indeed find more money. All he could think of was to run.

Turning quickly, Jack's already unsteady body stepped unexpectedly onto something round and hard. With his balance snatched away by the discarded bottle of rum, Jack tumbled sideways. In desperation he attempted to use his hands to break his fall, but they made contact only with water. The liquid slipped through his clutching fingers, offering all-encompassing saturation rather than the requested support. His clothes became weighted, dragging him down further into the muddy brown water. Then, as if waiting for this very moment, the raging currents took full advantage of the man floundering in their midst.

Handicapped by alcohol, Jack was unable to fight against the dragging power of the river. He opened his mouth to scream, but immediately dirty water invaded his lungs and choked the sound. Precious air bubbled away, starving his body of oxygen.

Before the white light beckoned him to the afterlife, the alcoholic rebel saw the best day of his life flash before his eyes. He had *The Ship Inn* to himself, and no damn river was going to take that away from him. His life's ambition was complete, and he had returned Old Nick's money without signing away his soul to boot. He was happy.

The final thing Jack Golby thought, as the water completed filling his lungs, was that he didn't mind drowning. In many ways it was just like being drunk, and being drunk had always been his closest friend.

Samson stared at the locked side entrance to the church, half expecting it to be prised open by undead hands. At least guard duty kept him away from Wallace for a while. When Samson had informed him that while Lethbridge-Stewart was away he was in charge, it hadn't gone down well. Wallace had been outraged that a *nigger* had been elevated above him, and Samson made a mental note to take the man down a peg or two at the earliest opportunity.

There was a creak as the door opened. Lethbridge-Stewart and Chorley must have returned. Hopefully they had sorted this mess out, and they could find a way to go home. As it inched open, another thought hit him. Wasn't the door locked? The reverend had told him that he had secured it. When a blood-encrusted hand slithered around the door, the reason for it being unlocked seemed unimportant. The others hadn't returned after all.

Samson fingered the pistol in its holster, but he knew he should save the few remaining bullets if at all possible. Urgently he searched for a weapon. He enviously thought of the carving knife that Wallace had purloined from the reverend's cottage, but he doubted the man would have handed it over even if he was close by. To his side, Samson spotted a waist high ornate candlestick. It was better than nothing, and at least had three sharp candle holders at its peak.

The undead creature groped blindly for him, and Samson thrust the candlestick with all his might towards the corpse's stomach. There was a sickening squelch and a flow of stagnant blood. The spikes of the candle holders crashed through skin into a cavity that had until recently contained a kidney. Wrinkling his nose at the sickly sweet odour of decaying innards, Samson pushed harder until the candlestick was deeply embedded into the dead villager.

With all his strength, Samson shoved as hard as he could. With the stick still impaled in its stomach, the corpse lost its balance and collapsed backwards out of the doorway into a throng of its comrades. Leaping forward, he slammed the door shut.

And spotted the key on the floor, either knocked out of the lock, or deliberately put there in an attempt to hide it. *Which fool did that?* Samson wondered.

Once the door was locked, he removed the key and stashed it in his pocket. This time he wouldn't take any risks.

'Reverend,' Samson called out, as he strode back into the nave. 'I thought you said you had locked that damn door?'

After half hour traipsing across the countryside and dodging the resurrected dead, up ahead, the headlights of the Land Rover finally came into view. Lethbridge-Stewart spotted Dovey leaning against the bonnet.

It was only when Lethbridge-Stewart and Chorley stepped into the beams of light that he saw them. He straightened up immediately and saluted. 'Brigadier, sir.' He peered behind them. 'Where's Sergeant Major Ware? Did he not—?'

'He found me, Sergeant, but now's not the time for a debriefing.' Lethbridge-Stewart pointed to Chorley. 'Oh, this is Harold Chorley.'

'Yes, sir. Thought it might be.'

Chorley beamed at that, clearly taking the recognition as a compliment. Lethbridge-Stewart didn't bother to point out that a dossier on him had been circulated to all officers in the Corps, so they'd know him if he tried to approach and secure secret information by nefarious methods.

'Samson told me you've got some spare ammo.'

Dovey nodded. 'Yes, sir. There's some in the back. There's should be a few grenades as well.'

'Excellent news.' Lethbridge-Stewart doubted the Loa's reanimated corpses would survive a grenade being thrown in their midst. Their chances of survival had moved up a notch.

'By the way, congratulations on your promotion,' Lethbridge-Stewart said, as he moved towards the Land Rover. 'When Major Leopold recommended you for it, I was more than happy to app—' Abruptly, he paused.

In the darkness, a small sound reached his ears. Vegetation had been crushed underfoot by a great weight somewhere nearby. They were not alone.

Lethbridge-Stewart surveyed the field. In the gloom of night, little could be seen except various shades of black and grey shadows.

Several of these shadows lumbered forwards. They were great humps. Too big to be human, but there was so little light that it was impossible to tell what the stalking silhouettes actually were.

'Sergeant, do we have any night-vision goggles?'

'Yes, sir.' Dovey jumped into the back of the Land Rover and reappeared with a single pair. He handed them over to Lethbridge-Stewart.

He went to put them on, but something to their left caught his eye. A man, in the far distance, appeared to be watching them. Only... He put the goggles on and balked at what he saw. It was a man, all right, or at least one side of one. And, more importantly, it was a member of the Corps.

'Who the devil...?'

Dovey strained his eyes to see. 'I think that's Private Armitage, sir.'

'Blimey. You've good eyes,' Chorley said.

Dovey nodded. 'Useful when you're trained to be a sniper, Mr Chorley.'

'Right. Sergeant, find out what Armitage is doing, and see if he needs...' Lethbridge-Stewart's voice trailed off.

From behind the Land Rover lurched a black and white monstrosity, splattered with crimson. Ribs, scoured with tooth marks and liberated of flesh, protruded cruelly from the massive leathery belly. One lifeless eye swivelled towards them, and for a moment it seemed like their gazes met. A strangled, forlorn moo emerged from the beast, and was instantly replicated by the approaching silhouettes. With a sputter of fresh blood, the corpse of the cow charged towards them.

— CHAPTER THIRTEEN —

The Loa Gambit

Although slower and jerkier than the living animal, the Loa obviously found the dead cow simpler to control than the human body. Perhaps it was the animal's four legs that made it easier. Lethbridge-Stewart only had a split second to react.

Flinging himself to the floor, the bloodied bulk crashed past. A swift roll away from the Land Rover ensured that the hooves missed his head, but it was by a narrow margin. Immediately the cow turned to charge again. Lethbridge-Stewart once more rolled sideways, but this time he was not fast enough. A hoof caught his arm and pain seared through his body. Turning a blind eye to the wound, he clambered to his feet and looked wildly around for the others.

'Brigadier! Over here!'

Chorley had circled to the far side of the Land Rover, as far away from the marauding cow as he could. He wouldn't be safe there for long. The undead beast was having difficulty turning its bulk around, but soon the other two cows would be upon them. There was no way they could survive an onslaught from three of the undead beasts.

The cow charged for the third time, but on this occasion Lethbridge-Stewart didn't dive out of the way. Instead he ran straight at the Land Rover, and the creature thundered after him. At the very last minute, he flung himself sideways and onto the grass. It was too late for the undead cow to stop, and there was an almighty crash as it smacked its half-eaten head into the driver's side door, skewering itself cruelly on the bent metal. The Land Rover rocked alarmingly as the cow's corpse thrashed about, attempting to free itself.

A hideous unearthly moo caused Lethbridge-Stewart to tear his eyes away from the trapped animal. For a brief moment, his eyes alighted on a ghastly sight a short distance away. Half of Private Armitage lay on the grass – very clearly dead.

'Brigadier!' Sergeant Dovey yelled.

The second cow had almost reached them, but before Lethbridge-Stewart had a chance to move, Dovey ran straight past and threw something at the approaching beast.

The sergeant's shot was perfect. The grenade hit the leathery hide and bounced onto the grass in front of the dead cow. A split second later, there was an almighty explosion and a nauseating smell of burned beef. When the smoke cleared, the cow lay convulsing on the floor. Gradually the twitching stopped, as the Loa abandoned the useless carcass.

Dovey slipped the pin out of another grenade and aimed it at the third cow. There was a twisting of metal, and the first cow was suddenly free from the Land Rover.

'Dovey, look out!'

In shock, Dovey turned, but the warning had come too late. The dead animal crashed straight into the soldier, knocking him backwards. The shock of the impact caused the grenade to fly out of Dovey's hands, to land by the Land Rover's front wheel. In alarm, Lethbridge-Stewart threw himself to the ground, and Chorley followed suit.

There was a shearing heat, as the grenade went off. The Land Rover was catapulted into the air, and landed with a crash on its side, before bursting into flames. A few seconds later, another blast joined the first as the petrol tank exploded.

Expecting the undead cow's hooves to trample him at any moment, Lethbridge-Stewart sprung up. He needn't have worried. Both the animals had been knocked off their feet by the blast, and were desperately attempting to right themselves. Dovey lay face down in the grass, and taking full advantage of the cow's temporary incapacitation, Lethbridge-Stewart rushed to the sergeant's side.

Carefully, he turned the man over, and leaned down to check his pulse. There was no heartbeat. Dovey hadn't made it.

'Dammit,' Lethbridge-Stewart said.

'Sorry, old boy. Seemed to be a good man,' Chorley said behind him.

'He was. Saved my life once.'

Sadly, Lethbridge-Stewart straightened up. As he did so, he saw the dead man's fingers twitch. Lifeless eyes swivelled around to stare at him, and an earthly moan emitted from the deceased soldier's lungs.

'Run!' Lethbridge-Stewart shouted.

The corpse rose unsteadily. The two men bolted towards the smouldering manor house at the end of the field. Lethbridge-Stewart stole a glance behind him, and he realised with dismay that the dead cows were charging after them. They had a head start, but the beasts were gaining slowly on them.

At last a six-foot high stone wall loomed up out of the

gloom. Lethbridge-Stewart arrived first and bent down to offer his hands to help Chorley climb up. Without hesitation, the journalist set his foot in the makeshift step and he was lifted to the top. Quickly, Chorley scrambled over and disappeared from view.

Aware that the cows were close behind, Lethbridge-Stewart backed up and ran at full pelt towards the six-foot wall. His time on the army assault course served him well. He vaulted, and his fingertips grasped the solid stone edge. Immediately he swung his leg upwards with all his might. The momentum propelled him onto the top of the wall, but for one agonising second his right leg dangled on the wrong side. Hurriedly, he yanked it over and dropped down to the safety of the other side. He was just in time.

There was a multitude of crashes, as the wall was hit again and again by stampeding hooves. The stones rocked with the impacts, but held firm. The attacks on the wall subsided and then stopped altogether. Then there was silence.

Against the odds, they had made it to the manor in one piece.

Elsewhere in the manor, Toussaint sat in chair, the fire raging around him, but never touching him. He had his eyes closed, but the Loa saw clearly. It smiled through Toussaint's lips.

'Welcome back, Brigadier,' the Loa said.

Toussaint stood up and left the burning room, the fire parting before him.

Jeffrey Robert Erickson had always been fascinated by the

Earth, the way it was formed. Even as a child. It was the reason he had become a geomorphologist, much to the dismay of his father, who was a career solider. As the only son of Robert Geoffrey Erickson, Jeff had been expected to enter the army too, but he didn't have a military bone in his body.

Jeff wanted to understand the world, not help destroy it.

When Anne Travers first came to him, he had been excited to hear about the team she was building; a research team that would have access to the latest equipment, the latest theories, and the ability to explore and research things unheard of by the scientific community at large. She wanted him for his expertise in biogeomorphologic processes, the interaction between landforms and living organisms. He'd been flattered, and immediately signed up. It was only then, after he'd been read into the Official Secrets Act, that he learned the truth.

He would be working for the military.

And now here he was, surrounded by troops from a top secret regiment of the Scots Guards, unable to tell his father, since Commodore Erickson had not signed the OSA as they pertained to the existence of the Corps. His dad had never really been proud of him – his disdain for Jeff's work was abundantly clear. But, finally, he was doing something that would make his dad proud, and he couldn't say anything. Not that he was complaining. He had seen some amazing things in the last half a year; be it the ferocious Bandrils at the Argyll Highlands, or studying the unusual formation of the Mutalith and the fragments of that silicon-based lifeform that had possessed the gangster Hugh Godfrey last

December. On top of that, he worked alongside some of the top experts in their fields. Not least among them, Anne Travers herself. He had learned much from Anne since joining her team in September, but he was no replacement for her. He knew this, and if ever he needed confirmation, the last week would be enough.

Yet, despite this, his thoughts on how to bring the Keynsham Triangle back into phase with the rest of the world had been welcomed by Anne. She had come up with a few theories of her own, ways in which they could make it happen. And when their first test failed, and poor Private Armitage had died, she took it badly. Even Lieutenant Bishop proved little comfort to her. She left the site, and returned to her room at *The Ship Inn*. Bishop assured them all that Anne would return the next day, she just needed to process things a little first.

Jeff understood. He never knew her father, although he knew *of* him, of course, and it was clear his death had hit Anne hard. If the situation was reversed, he wasn't sure how well he'd handle the death of his parents. Worse than Anne, probably.

He had spent the entire night looking at what went wrong, discussing the problem with Bishop and Corporal Ken Leake, previously of the Royal Corps of Engineers. Anne hadn't returned the next day, and without waiting for permission, Jeff took himself to Keynsham to talk to her.

He found Anne sitting in the beer garden at the back of *The Ship Inn*. She had a cup of coffee before her, and looked up as he approached.

'Hi, Jeff,' she began, before he could take a seat. 'I think you're going to have to take over. I thought I was ready to go back to work, but...' She shook her head and lowered her eyes.

Jeff smiled sadly. He sat opposite her. 'Anne... I understand how you must feel; I feel just as responsible. But Armitage... *Chris* knew the risks that come with the job. Military men always do. They have no illusions about what they signed up for.'

Anne laughed. But it was not a nice sound. There was much bitterness there. 'I doubt Chris expected to die in a scientific experiment. He didn't sign up for that. And we, as scientists, didn't sign up to kill people.'

'We didn't...' Jeff stopped himself. Intentionally they may not have killed Chris Armitage, but he was still dead because of their experiment. One day, maybe, Jeff would come to terms with that. But not right now. 'It was an accident, Anne. A fault in the machine. Nobody is to blame.'

'Keep telling yourself that. I'll stick to the truth.' She looked up at him, tears in her eyes. 'Who's going to explain this to his family? Did you know he had a baby daughter? Just four months old.'

Jeff wanted to reach out, but she was his boss and they weren't that familiar. So, instead, he decided to be scientific about things. After all, science wasn't about emotion, it was about cause and effect, thinking things through logically.

'Doctor Travers, according to everything we've learned in the last couple of days, there appears to be a whole village of people in that Triangle, including our own people. We owe it to them, to all the families of those who have gone missing over the decades, to solve this problem.' Jeff paused, and then added, 'Finish your father's work.'

Anne looked at him for a moment, then ran her hands

over her face. 'Okay, Jeff,' she said. 'What do you have in mind?'

'Why don't I tell you on the way?'

Finally Anne smiled. 'Let me freshen up, and I'll meet you out the front.' She stood up. 'Are you married?'

'Only to my work.'

'Good to know. If you can talk me around like that, hate to think how easily you'd get your own way with a wife.'

Jeff watched her walk back into *The Ship Inn*, unsure whether he'd been complimented or insulted.

Shielding themselves from the final onslaught of the blaze, Lethbridge-Stewart and Chorley trod carefully through the manor's courtyard. Most of the readily available fuel had been consumed, so the fire was now subsiding, but it still bathed the area in an eerie flickering glow. The windows had burst outwards, and the remaining glass had melted and fused in the extreme heat.

As they crept across the courtyard, the devouring flames briefly glinted off something on the stone floor. Curiously, Lethbridge-Stewart kneeled down to investigate. It was Wallace's flintlock pistol. Oscar must have dropped it when he had been attacked.

Lethbridge-Stewart picked the old fashioned weapon up with his handkerchief and rubbed the soot from its wooden stock. It might look as if it belonged in a museum, but he needed a gun, and this was the only thing on offer.

'You're not seriously intending to use that thing?' Chorley whispered in surprise.

Lethbridge-Stewart nodded in reply. If he was going to take down Toussaint he had little choice.

'You need gunpowder and shot, as well you know,' Chorley said.

'I am perfectly aware of how it works, thank you.'

Lethbridge-Stewart was sure that the butler had dropped the ammo as well, but where was it? Quickly he scanned the paved floor for the powder horn and the lead shot. To his relief, he found the horn a few feet away hidden amongst a small patch of weeds, and Chorley helped him track down as many of the small round balls of metal as the poor light allowed.

He was about to load the pistol, when Chorley grabbed his arm.

'Not here! One spark from the fire and boom!'

'Good point,' Lethbridge-Stewart said, both grateful for the warning and surprised that it had come from Chorley, of all people.

'You need to half-cock the trigger first. Look, I'll show you how to do it,' Chorley said, much to Lethbridge-Stewart's astonishment. He watched gobsmacked as the journalist loaded the pistol, and handed it back to him with one of his trade mark showbiz smiles. 'I did a documentary about it for BBC 3. Amazing what sticks in your head. My memory has been like Swiss cheese since Dominex, but this seems to have stuck.'

Surprised and impressed by Chorley's practical skills in loading archaic weapons, Lethbridge-Stewart nodded his thanks and, together, they crept out of the courtyard.

There was no guarantee that Toussaint was still in the vicinity, but they had to start somewhere. Even if the old slave's hijacked body was nearby it was doubtful that he was alone.

For once, fortune seemed to be on their side. As they skirted around the gutted building, the dying flames briefly lit up a man-sized shape close to the manor's main entrance. The figure was partially obscured by smoke, but in the feeble glow of orange light a black man in slave's garb was just about visible. The moment he had been dreading was now upon him. He had to take the life of a man he had promised to set free.

Lethbridge-Stewart readied himself. He was about to creep closer, when he felt a hand on his arm. Pausing, he turned back to the journalist.

'What is it, Chorley?'

'Brigadier, I've got an idea.'

The noise was becoming unbearable, so Wallace withdrew into himself letting his mind wander and sanity fray. How he longed for a brandy. The cavernous church caused the howls of the besieging corpses to echo and reverberate, intensifying his uneasiness.

The scientist sat alone on a pew, his hands over his ears to block out the sound. He wanted to scream for silence. At times he even thought it would be worth dying just to have blessed relief from the unnerving moans, but it was just a passing fancy. Suicide was not an option. He owed it to the world to live. His precious research had been destroyed in the fire, but all the important facts were stored in his brain, bursting to be published for the greater good. If he could find the money to do so, he was sure that his medical discoveries would save countless lives.

Outside, the corpses were building in strength. There had to be hundreds by now. At this thought, his scientific mind reasserted itself. There was no way there could be that many. There weren't that many people in the village.

Removing his hands from his ears, Wallace fumbled in his waistcoat and pulled out his silver pocket watch for the umpteenth time. Flicking open the polished cover, he checked the dials. Only a few minutes had passed since he had last looked, but it seemed much longer. Earlier, he had tried to keep active to take his mind off his predicament. He had busied himself with Oscar's wounds, but had been able to offer only limited help. His only option was to wet a handkerchief in the font and cool the wounded man's brow. At least this enabled him to deduce that holy water was no more effective than normal water.

And to think Lethbridge-Stewart had put a negro in charge. As if such a man could tell Wallace what to do. He was Samson's better, regardless of this nonsense about him being an officer in the British Army. God knows what that black man had done to poor Oscar. Some witchdoctor's remedy no doubt. Wallace had even tried to assist Lethbridge-Stewart with the rescue of Mortimer Hartley from the hungry cadavers. Hadn't he proved his worth?

Resentment built up inside. He glared across the church to where Samson stood guard, and thanked his lucky stars that he no longer had the man's continual beatings of *Goosy Goosy Gander* to contend with. It had been almost as raking to his nerves as the persistent moaning from outside.

Wallace hated to admit it, but Samson looked alert and watchful for any sign that their defences were breached. It was a stark contrast to Reverend Cunningham, who sat silently in a pew looking forlorn. Earlier Wallace had been tempted to throw the reverend to the bloodthirsty cannibals outside just so he would shut up, but now Wallace simply felt sorry for him. Wallace had never seen the man so quiet. Gone were the words of fire and damnation. Those words were now obsolete. To all intents and purposes, hell was directly outside his place of work and clamouring to break in.

While he ruminated, his eyes scanned the church hall. Something wasn't right...

Cunningham was supposed to be looking after Zara, while Samson stood guard. Where was the damned girl? Quickly his eyes skimmed the room, but she was nowhere to be seen. Astonished at his own concern, he cast his mind back to when he had last seen her. It was before Lethbridge-Stewart had left.

A though struck him. Samson had chastised Cunningham for not locking the door properly, but the revered had insisted he did lock the door. What if Zara had unlocked it, snuck out when nobody was looking?

Wallace wasn't sure why he should be surprised. Only a black child would be so stupid as to go out in that!

He was about to alert the others to the problem, when a cry of warning diverted his attention. At first he didn't see what Reverend Cunningham was pointing at. Then he saw the tiny black shadows squeezing under the solid door. By their manner of movement, Wallace concluded that they were not ordinary church mice. Reaching to the pew for the kitchen knife, the scientist readied himself for the attack.

The building's defences had been breached.

Anne and Jeff arrived at the site and were greeted by Bill and Dashner. Pleasantries and commiserations were shared, before Anne explained that they were going to try again.

'That's the spirit, Miss Travers,' Dashner said. 'Keep calm...'

'...And carry on,' Bill added.

A smile passed between the two officers, and Anne assumed it was a private joke.

'Okay, this is how it goes,' she said. 'We're only doing this under one proviso. I'm going through this time.'

'Anne!'

'I agree with Bishop, I don't think—'

Anne held up a hand and cut Dashner off. 'I won't risk anybody else. Your men may be willing to lay down their lives, Lieutenant, but I won't have any more deaths on my conscience.'

Dashner took that with good grace and nodded curtly. 'Very well then.'

'I'm going too,' Bill said, his jaw set firm. Anne knew that expression. He looked at Dashner. 'We can't allow Miss Travers to take all the risk, sir.'

Dashner narrowed his eyes, and looked between the two of them. 'Of course not,' he said, a knowing tone to his voice. 'In that case I have stipulation of my own. You and Miss Travers may enter the Triangle, but not without a small squad. I won't have our Head of Scientific Research and our commanding officer's adjutant going into potential hostile territory unprotected.'

'Now see here, Lieutenant, taking Bill is one thing, but—'

Now it was Dashner's turn to interrupt. 'It's either that or nobody goes.'

Anne placed her hands on her hips firmly. 'And so,

Lethbridge-Stewart remains trapped in the Triangle. Perhaps I should call General Hamilton, see how that sits with him?'

Bill stepped between them. 'Anne,' he said, and looked at Dashner. 'Sir. A compromise. Anne and I, and two others. Between the three of us, I'm sure Miss Travers will be protected enough.'

Dashner appeared to chew this over. 'Very well,' he said, 'that's the final word on it.'

With that he walked off, leaving Anne with a feeling that the she had been manoeuvred into the outcome Dashner had wanted anyway.

Bill must have noticed the look on her face. 'Never try to win an argument with Tom Dashner. He's a legend for getting his own way.'

Anne narrowed her eyes, but said nothing.

'This does rather mess up my plan,' Jeff said, as the three walked across the field.

'What plan?' Bill asked.

'He was going to create an accident, a way for me to enter the barrier.'

Bill chewed his lip. 'Well, ignoring the fact that I'm not happy that you were willing to go in without me, I do have a way to take us all through. But you're not going to like it.'

Anne didn't doubt that. She hadn't liked most of what had happened since first arriving in the field outside Keynsham.

'Chorley, so nice to see you.'

The croaky dry words emitted from the flickering shadows near the main entrance of the once-proud manor.

From his hiding place, Lethbridge-Stewart watched Chorley approach the possessed Toussaint.

Lethbridge-Stewart steadied the flintlock pistol on an upturned barrel.

'Still have a bit of a speech impediment there, I see,' Chorley said flippantly, as he casually strolled closer.

Not for the first time, Lethbridge-Stewart had second thoughts about Chorley's plan. Using Chorley as bait didn't sit well with Lethbridge-Stewart, but it was far too late to back out now. However foolhardy the plan appeared, he had to admit he was impressed. It took guts.

Chorley halted at the top of the steps, prompting Toussaint to move a pitiful few feet away from the manor's front door. He was still bathed in shadows, but now his eyes pierced like daggers from the darkness.

'To what do I owe this pleasure?' the entity said through the stolen lips, sounding almost friendly. 'You're not here to complain about my cows, I hope.'

'To be honest, I didn't really like them. All those dead things walking around. It's so unhygienic.'

'All life is unhygienic,' rasped the Loa, giving a throaty gurgle that could only have been a laugh. 'How clean would you look to other creatures in the galaxy? They would wrinkle their noses in disgust.'

'Yes... well I suppose I could do with a bath, but with all the running away from the zombies... you know how it is.'

The outline shifted in the gloom, and Toussaint lumbered a little closer. As the hijacked body left the shadows, Lethbridge-Stewart at last had a clear view of the previously proud man.

Toussaint's hands were a mass of blisters from the heat of the fire, and his brown skin was covered in a layer of fine white ash. His whole body was tensed, like a stretched elastic band on the verge of snapping. Toussaint took two more steps forward, and Chorley stepped back, blocking Lethbridge-Stewart's line of sight.

'As far as I'm concerned, Mr Chorley, you're just food. It is every creature's right to eat, is it not? Why do you meddle with what is mine by right?'

'It's what I do, I'm afraid. I just can't stop meddling in things. Anything to get a good story.' Chorley was babbling. Lethbridge-Stewart willed him to be quiet and step back slightly. 'So, if you would be so good as to leave poor Toussaint's body and never return, I can go and meddle somewhere else.'

The journalist retreated another few feet and at last he was out of the line of fire.

Carefully Lethbridge-Stewart aimed the flintlock. He'd be lucky to get a second shot, and so this one had to count.

'If that is what you wish, then so be it!'

Immediately Toussaint's muscles relaxed. And just like that the Loa was gone, leaving a confused Toussaint gazing at the burning manor with bewildered eyes. He collapsed to the ground.

'Has it really gone?' Chorley asked, his voice full of worry.

'It might be a trick,' Lethbridge-Stewart replied gravely, stepping out of his hiding place, the pistol still levelled at Toussaint's prone figure.

It didn't feel right. It felt too easy. He found it hard to believe that the Loa would have left the old slave of its own free will, but he found it impossible to gun down Toussaint while he lay unconscious on the cobblestones.

As the flintlock wavered in his hand, the scrape of loose gravel alerted them to the presence of someone else close by. Lowering the gun, Lethbridge-Stewart peered into the night. Someone was heading in their direction. A silhouette solidified out of the darkness, and the features sharpened as the person came closer. He recognised her. It was the manor's cook, cradling her arm before her. From the angle, Lethbridge-Stewart surmised that it was broken. She had probably been attacked by one of the Loa's corpses.

'Miss Nash, are you alright?'

There was no reply, and then he saw the dark red blotches that soaked through her clothes.

The dead cook opened her mouth and omitted a long moan. Lethbridge-Stewart stared at the corpse and sadly realised that his instincts were correct. It had been a trick all along. If the Loa had indeed left Toussaint, all the corpses would have become unmoving hulks of flesh.

Behind him came another unearthly groan. He spun around and saw the mutilated body of Tom Sawkins stumble from the opposite direction. Alongside the dead body snatcher's ankles lurched the corpses of the cat and dog.

As Chorley backed away from the approaching monstrosities, Lethbridge-Stewart raised the pistol once more and aimed it at Toussaint. If he was quick, he still had a chance to complete the mission. All that he required was one clean shot.

He was too slow.

Before he was able to pull the trigger, his line of fire was suddenly blocked by the huge sightless dog. It gave a bubbling growl and glowered at him with empty eye sockets. Drool and blood dripped across its canine teeth, and Tom Sawkins and Miss Nash stumbled to Toussaint's side.

The two corpses helped the old slave to stand.

This was it.

Lethbridge-Stewart aimed the pistol.

Then the screaming began.

He watched as the slave regained consciousness and cried out in abject terror. There was no sign of the Loa in the old man. The undead dug their nails in under Toussaint's rib cage and pulled. Too late, Lethbridge-Stewart realised their intention.

The screaming abruptly stopped as probing fingers delved inside the terrified man's torso. Tom's hands returned with the prize – Toussaint's heart.

The lifeless body dropped to the floor, and both the animal and human cadavers turned to devour their meal.

Lethbridge-Stewart's dropped his aim limply.

Their one chance was gone. And now, with Toussaint dead, they had no idea where the Loa was. That it had another host was certain.

But who?

Before Lethbridge-Stewart could consider the options, from darker and murkier shadows rang the clear voice of a young girl.

'Goosy Goosy Gander,' Zara said. 'Whither do I wander?'

— CHAPTER FOURTEEN—

Goosy Goosy Gander

S amson struck down heavily with his heel, flattening the skull of the nearest rodent. After grinding the fragile bones underfoot, he raised his leg to survey his work. He half expected the unnatural creature to scurry unharmed from beneath his shoe. Instead it lay, twitching and pulsating, on the stone floor. It was still full of undead life, but now no longer able to function in the same deadly manner. Gradually the vole became motionless. Many more rodents squeezed under the oak door to replace it; perhaps too many to be held at bay for long.

Two of the creatures launched themselves at Samson's wrist. He twisted, catching a glancing blow to the first. It fell to the floor, and quickly he stamped down hard. One more rank harvest mouse was no longer a threat. In retaliation, its comrade's razor-sharp teeth bit in deep and hard. Crying out in pain, Samson grasped its body and ripped it off, bringing a small chunk out of his arm in the process. He flung it to the ground, and his leather shoe crushed it underfoot.

'Stamp on them,' he yelled to the others.

Nobody responded, but Samson knew that both men had heard his words. Wallace was too busy holding back a wave of mice to answer. The scientist slashed at the rodents with the kitchen knife. Samson found the stern look of concentration on Wallace's face unsettling. By contrast, Reverend Cunningham was on tiptoe, perched on top of a pew as far away from the marauding rodents as possible.

Fortunately, the rodent corpses could only squeeze under the door a few at a time, so maybe they had a chance. Many of the creatures must have already passed into the building, but it was anyone's guess how many more waited their turn. They were fighting a losing battle, and Samson knew it. There had to be a way of stopping their entrance altogether.

In a flash of inspiration, Samson slipped off his army jacket and crammed it into the gap underneath the door. The rodents trying to get in nipped at his fingers, but he ignored them. It was nothing in comparison to what would happen if the whole hoard entered. Soon the gap was completely blocked, and the trickle of rodents dried up. He knew that a simple piece of cloth wouldn't be able to hold back the tide for long, but it was better than nothing. He could already hear the chomping of many mouths feverously working their way through the jacket.

A house mouse tried to run past, and he stomped down hard. Two others tried to follow and met the same fate. Samson frowned. All the undead rodents were running in the same direction, so where were they going? He followed one with his eyes and realised that they were headed for the pew where Oscar lay resting. There, Wallace was frantically fighting over the butler's dozing form.

Samson watched as two water voles scurried up the sleeping man's leg. For a moment he wondered why, then the truth hit him.

Wallace grabbed one vole in a powerful grasp, but the other slipped past and into Oscar's open mouth. Immediately Samson rushed to help, but before he reached Wallace, Oscar sat bolt upright, spluttering awake. Gasping for air, Oscar breathed in only bloody fur and claws. Samson watched on helplessly as yet another rodent ran up the poor man's body, and its tail slipped past his teeth. There was one final choke, and it was over. The last vestiges of life ebbed away from Oscar's body, and he collapsed back onto the pew.

Wallace glanced over at Samson despairingly, but they both knew that they couldn't let Oscar rest in peace. Now he was simply another empty vessel for the Loa to make use of.

'Quick! Find something to bind his arms and legs with!' Samson said urgently, prompting Wallace into action.

The pair rushed to a tapestry hanging from a nearby wall. It was dark green, with woven cords tipped with delicate tassels encircling it. With Wallace's aid, he tore it down. Ripping off the woven cord, he rushed back to Oscar's corpse.

Samson blinked. He was sure he saw Oscar's hand twitch. But it had to be his imagination… right?

Not wishing to take the risk, Samson got to work. It was vital that Oscar's arms and legs were bound before the Loa took control.

Samson skidded to a halt by Oscar's side and reached for the corpse's wrist.

Then all hell broke loose.

There was a colossal shattering noise as the stained-glass window above the main church door exploded inwards. The saint that it had proudly portrayed was now little more than a shower of multi-coloured glass, raining down into the besieged church. Among the particles of blue, red and green tumbled a flurry of wings. The remnants of an owl and several pigeons half glided and half fell towards the surprised group. The Loa was no better at making its puppets fly than walk.

The undead birds forced Samson to raise his hands to protect his face. Their avian bodies had large patches of missing feathers, but their claws and beaks were readymade weapons for the Loa to exploit. The owl sank its curved beak into Samson's scalp, causing a trickle of blood to run down his forehead. It was joined by a pigeon, which aimed its scaly claws at his eyes. Gritting his teeth from the pain, Samson waved his arms desperately at the attacking bird. Lady Luck smiled upon him, as one hand connected and propelled the owl into the church wall. Delicate wing bones broke, and the bird slid to the floor in a heap of feathers. As the pigeon pecked mercilessly at him, he grabbed the small body with both hands and flung it to the floor. Mercilessly he stamped down, crushing its tiny skull underfoot.

A small distance away, Wallace was frantically defending himself from the final pigeon. Samson rushed to help. By the man's feet lay the reverend's craving knife. Snatching it, Samson plunged the weapon into the flapping bird. The dead creature hurtled to the ground, with its scattered feathers fluttering next to the tasselled cord from the tapestry.

The cord that was supposed to be used to tie Oscar down.

Samson's eyes swept to the pew, but the recently deceased butler was gone. Too late Samson realised the birds were a distraction.

There was an ominous creak, and the oak church door swung open. The Loa's new puppet withdrew its hands from the door handle and slowly turned towards them. Oscar's head lolled to one side, and a moan of triumph echoed around the church, intermingling with Wallace's cry of fright. The corpses that had been clamouring outside gathered in the doorway, advanced for their feast of living flesh.

Zara, or at least what had once been Zara, took a few steps forward. 'Oh, don't you want to sing with me then? What about a game instead? Guess who I'm going to eat first? Three guesses.'

Lethbridge-Stewart refused to answer the taunt. The Loa might have control of the slave girl, but that didn't mean he'd have to pander to the entity's whims.

'I'll give you a clue. It's not Mr Whittle. He's already a pile of walking bones. He let in my friends, you know.'

The church. Samson!

'You leave them alone!' Lethbridge-Stewart snapped.

'Don't want to play? Well I suppose you're all grown up, aren't you, Mr Army Man. At least Mr Whittle's useful now. Samson kept stomping on my mice, which was rather unkind. I think he was enjoying it, but my new butler puppet has put paid to that.'

'Why leave Toussaint?' Lethbridge-Stewart asked, refusing to be bated.

'Leave?' The girly laugh annoyed Lethbridge-Stewart. 'It was only a puppet, not my host body.' Zara twirled on the spot. 'This little girl had always been my host.'

'So, you have been with us all along. Ever since we escaped from the fire.' It was a statement of fact. Lethbridge-Stewart glanced at Chorley. 'The Loa has known what we were doing at every step. What we were planning.'

'I hid in this tiny frame, growing stronger and stronger,' the entity confirmed with a childlike giggle. 'But it was so rude of you to discuss overthrowing me out of earshot, while Samson kept me busy, repeating those prattling rhymes to me.'

'It was you that knocked him out on the way to the church, wasn't it?'

'Oh, well done. Figured it out all by yourself?' the Loa taunted. 'Samson let his guard down, and I made a break for freedom. If it wasn't for the unexpected arrival of that fool of a mill owner, he would have died then and there. I was *so* hungry. Goosy, Goosy, Gander...'

Zara's harmonious voice cut through the silence of the night, and Lethbridge-Stewart realised that for a brief moment the child seemed preoccupied, as if her concentration was elsewhere. Blessedly the singing abruptly stopped, and instead she let forth a sweet laugh.

'Revered Cunningham has fallen off his pew. Shouldn't play with my food really, but you know how children are. Grandfather wouldn't have been impressed.'

Chorley leaned in close, and whispered in Lethbridge-Stewart's ear. 'Have you noticed when she mentions the others, she sort of loses concentration here a little bit.'

Lethbridge-Stewart nodded. It certainly appeared that the Loa found it difficult to be in two places at the same time. If he could provide a distraction, it might give Samson a chance.

'Whispering to each other,' the Loa spat viciously, the laugh instantly disappearing at their mumbled conversation. Suddenly her voice returned to that of an innocent little girl, both playful and indignant at the same time. 'No fair.'

Quickly, Lethbridge-Stewart racked his brain for something to say. He had to keep the thing talking. 'When we first met you, Toussaint had performed some sort of ritual. He said it was simply a song, but I know he was holding something back. Is this ritual something to do with you?'

'Ah, the Dreamer's Lament. It's a prayer to the spirit Loa, for guidance and aid. Window dressing mostly.'

'Mostly?'

'Toussaint used one extra component; Wallace's chemical of dreaming. On the astral plane it was like a beacon of despair and hopelessness, but I didn't choose him to inhabit. He was far too inflexible. Zara on the other hand...'

'Are you saying she was at the ritual too?'

'Of course, Mr Army Man. She asked me to free her from Stedman and Wallace, and I was happy to oblige. But I had to create this place first.'

'Create it?' Chorley frowned. 'Well, that might explain the geography. But, look at this place, it's not the present.'

'Then if we're not back in time, where are we?' Lethbridge-Stewart asked the Loa.

'Wouldn't you like to know,' the Loa teased.

'Well, yes I would rather,' Lethbridge-Stewart said tersely. 'That is why I asked.'

'If you're not back in time, what's left?'

'The present, obviously.' Chorley nodded. 'Yes, yes.

That's why there are no old stories of strange people arriving in Keynsham's past. Why ghosts are seen in the Triangle.'

'What are you on about?' Lethbridge-Stewart snapped, irritated.

'Think about it, Alistair. We're *inside* the Triangle.'

The Loa sneered. 'You should watch this one, Brigadier. Not as dull as he seems.' The Loa clapped Zara's hands together in delight. 'I knew you would get there in the end. This place isn't really Keynsham. It is a mirror of it, where time runs so much slower. It was the past when I first created it, of course, but we're in your present now.'

Lethbridge-Stewart wasn't sure he followed, but nonetheless he asked, 'And where are from? You said the astral plane. Are you another part of Sunyata?'

Zara's face frowned. 'What is Sunyata?'

'It's an entity. In the void between realities. In… manifests itself as something called the Great Intelligence.'

'Ah,' the Loa said, and nodded Zara's head. 'I have met the Great Intelligence. No, I am not a part of it. So many… *entities*… exist in the void. More than your human mind could comprehend.'

One question answered at least.

'My construct started off small, just the manor house, but gradually over time it grew. So very slowly that nobody here noticed. They all thought they were still in their own village.'

The Loa seemed quite pleased with itself.

'But why? What's all this for?' Lethbridge-Stewart asked.

'To feed, of course. When Toussaint opened the door for me, and I consumed Zara, I realised I would need more than her puny lifespan to fully take control, so I created this

245

place. Here Zara would age only a few weeks, but I had over one hundred and fifty years to take over. All I had to do was create a hiccough in reality at *just* the right point. For Zara's benefit, of course.'

'How on earth is this all for Zara's benefit?' Lethbridge-Stewart said, amazed by the entity's warped logic.

'Her body is no longer a slave to Stedman, as she asked.'

'Stedman and his family stole her life, but she was free in her mind,' Lethbridge-Stewart said forcefully. 'Free to think what she liked, and dream what she liked. What good is a free body, if the mind is enslaved?'

'If you took my place you wouldn't be so fast to judge,' the entity seethed, anger rushing across Zara's face like a tidal wave. 'In the void, there is no body – just the hunger. I completed my end of the bargain, and now I need her. How else am I to eat?'

'You *need* her. You keep saying this. But, how exactly?'

'You're so full of questions. Will this take much longer? It's fun to hear Reverend Cunningham scream, but I really want to bite someone.' The entity let forth a girlish giggle and began to sing once again. 'Goosy, Goosy, Gander...'

Behind his back, Lethbridge-Stewart cocked the flintlock pistol. The others at the church were relying on him. There was only one way he knew of to end this. Zara had to die.

It took a few hours, but eventually they managed to spread a cable around the entire barrier, with the reinforced machine once again attached to the rail track. The idea was this time, if successful, to bring the entire village within the Triangle into phase with the rest of the world. Anne wasn't convinced that it would be entirely successful, but in theory at least it was sound. She expected a fraction of the village to reappear, at best.

'Wait until we're through, though,' she said to Jeff. 'I think the mistake we made last time was trying to…' She paused, and took a deep breath. 'Was using a person as a bridge, by altering their vibrational frequency. The human body couldn't take it.'

'Got it.'

'Hopefully enough of the village will appear that we can use it as a bridge back through the barrier. We can't risk dosing any of us with more of that concoction.'

Bill glanced up at that. 'When you say us…'

'…I mean you.' Anne smiled. That was the bit she hated the most about the plan. She had wanted to dose herself, but Bill had insisted that it should be him, after all he was driving and he needed to be able to enter. The rest of them would be secured in the back of the Land Rover, unable to run despite the urge to do so.

'Are we ready then, Lieutenant?' Corporal Fenn asked, tapping the needle.

'As I'll ever be.'

With a reassuring smile, Fenn inserted the needle into Bill's arm.

Anne watched the drugs take effect, a heavy feeling in her heart.

'Get behind me,' Samson ordered, as yet more corpses filed through the church door.

The reverend lay on the stone floor by the pew that he had unceremoniously fallen off moments before. As quickly as his heavy bulk would allow, the reverend scrambled to his feet and hurried towards Samson. Wallace waved the knife one last time in a vain attempt at bullying the dead villagers, and followed suit. Unperturbed, the corpses staggered towards them at their own leisurely pace.

The church would soon become a death trap. It was only a matter of time before the route to the side exit was cut off, and there was no way of knowing if more of the unholy creatures waited outside the side door. Still, Samson knew it was their best option.

He didn't relish going outside with civilians in tow, but what other choice had they? It was obvious that Zara was out there somewhere, and she had been left in Samson's care. He couldn't just abandon her to those creatures.

'They're getting awfully close,' Wallace said, his voice quivering as the undead lurched down the aisle after them. 'We need to get out of here.'

'Don't worry. We will be leaving very soon,' Samson said quietly. 'Head slowly towards the side exit. Draw as many of them in as we can.'

Slowly, they retreated past the rows of wooden pews until the side door was in sight. Samson drew his pistol from its holster. He had a couple more rounds, but what good would bullets be against the hoard of undead? Hopefully, enough had been enticed inside to make the escape easier.

'Now,' he ordered, and the trio bolted to the heavy oak door.

As they ran, he fished in his pocket for the key. Skidding to a halt, Samson rammed the key into the lock, and turned it. He held his breath as the lock clicked open. How many of the Loa's puppets remained on the other side?

He pulled the door open, and immediately a reanimated

corpse lunged out of the gloom. Behind it stumbled another. It didn't come as a surprise to Samson. There was bound to be a few. But for Reverend Cunningham it was too much. The reverend's nerve cracked, and he let forth a high-pitched wail.

'No, Rev!' Samson yelled out, but it was too late.

Before anybody could stop him, the panic-stricken man ran back into the church. Samson swiftly followed, just in time to see the reverend slam the door to the vestry shut.

The undead congregation were only a stone's throw away from the room's door, and immediately changed direction. In only a few minutes, the vestry was under siege, and there was nothing Samson could do to stop it.

'...Whither do I wander? Upstairs and downstairs...'

The rhyme's prose rang through Lethbridge-Stewart's head, hampering his concentration. Without Zara as a medium the Loa would be banished, but could he really trade her breath to save the world? He had vowed to help, but already her grandfather lay dead, and how many more would join him if she lived? He readied himself.

Chorley gave him a dejected look and the smallest of nods.

It was time, but could he do it?

She was just a little girl.

His eyes snapped up when the nursery rhyme abruptly stopped. There was a gurgling growl, and from behind Zara lumbered the undead dog. The Loa must have tired of their conversation and decided it was time for another snack. It came as no great surprise. It was a wonder that the entity had spoken to them for so long, and he couldn't help feeling

249

that there was something he was missing. The dead pet's blood-encrusted muzzle snarled cruelly, as it glowered at him through its empty eye sockets. It advanced closer until it was only a few paces away, taunting him. It pounced. Automatically, Lethbridge-Stewart swung the antique firearm from behind his back and fired. The shot was perfect, ripping into undead flesh, and there was a dull thump as the beast hit the cobblestones. The body twitched for a moment and then lay still.

'Oh, good shot, Brigadier! Right in the head!'

'Back away, Chorley,' Lethbridge-Stewart ordered, keeping his eyes fixed to the unmoving bulk.

He cursed himself for firing at the wrong target. He should have shot the medium, not the dog. It would take time to reload the flintlock, and now the entity was aware of the pistol he doubted he would get a second chance. As if on cue, the mutilated bodies of Miss Nash, Tom Sawkins and Toussaint emerged from the shadows. They surrounded the little girl like a macabre parade of overprotective relatives. The undead cat weaved around the slave girl's legs, leaving a trail of fresh blood on her bare ankles.

The entity giggled as other shapes came into view further down the road. A chorus of moans heralded the dead villagers' arrival. There were dozens of them, and Lethbridge-Stewart realised in horror that they now blocked the route back to the church.

'Brigadier, look behind us,' Chorley said, his voice trembling. 'I think we have a problem.'

Lethbridge-Stewart spun around. A short way behind them more lurching corpses blocked their retreat. There was a small opening, but it could very easily be a trap. There was a slim chance that they could get to the fields, but it was likely that the undead cows were waiting for them there. Crossing the countryside with the cows on their trail would be out of the question. The likelihood of their survival was minuscule.

He had to admit it; the Loa had planned its attack well. They were surrounded, with the circle of the dead closing in by the second. There had to be three quarters of the village population encircling them, with all realistic escape routes seemingly cut off. There had to be another way out. His mind worked overtime on the dilemma. Obviously that was why the Loa had been so chatty. As they had talked, it had been gathering its forces and blocking off all escape routes.

On one side of the road the manor burned, and on the other a row of terraced houses. Neither looked like a viable escape route, but if they remained any longer they would be done for.

He heard the Loa giggled uncontrollably as he pulled Chorley towards the houses.

They had almost reached the closest building, when its door creaked open and a corpse stumbled out. Its body was so mangled that it was completely unrecognisable as either male or female, almost as if it had been crushed and eaten simultaneously.

Chorley suddenly changed direction towards an adjoining building. It was swamped in darkness and looked like a dead end, so Lethbridge-Stewart hesitated. There was a sudden flare of flames; the smoldering manor found its final source of fuel, and for a fleeting moment he saw what the journalist was heading for.

Between the two buildings there was a thin alleyway,

and it was unguarded.

Together they scrambled down the tight space and into the deserted road beyond. There were moans of protest as the corpses followed single file behind them, but Lethbridge-Stewart and Chorley had a head start.

Reverend Cunningham held back the door with all his strength. The strain on his heart, from years of food abuse, notched up another level. The plague of mice and the birds' destruction of Saint Peter's image had rocked his sense of security in the hallowed ground. How could the Almighty allow such a blasphemy in his place of worship by the vermin of the land and sky?

The door inched open, and a flailing hand snaked its way into the small room, leaving a smear of dark burgundy blood trailing along the varnished wood. A set of ice-cold fingers brushed against Cunningham's wrist. Automatically he jerked away from the dead flesh, but the action caused him to lose his grip on the vestry door. Too late he realised his mistake. The Loa's puppets took full advantage, and forced the door fully open.

As the dead villagers pushed their way inside, the reverend recognised them all. It was a grotesque parody of his usual Sunday morning service, but Cunningham knew that the congregation were not here for his sermon. They had lost their souls to Beelzebub. There was no other reasonable explanation for what he saw.

For comfort, his hand clutched at the small silver cross that hung around his neck and he backed away from the approaching monsters. Morals and ethics that he hadn't contemplated since becoming a novice to his Godly work barged forward. At last he realised he had failed in his position as a messenger of God. His sight had been obscured by eighteen stone of fat and hazed by power. He should have been meek. He should have been praying. He should have been helping the weak and the hungry. No longer would he worship the meat and pudding, he vowed. He was born again. In his time of greatest need, the Almighty had shown him the way, but was there still time to make amends?

At the end of the vestry, he kneeled underneath the large cross and waited for his undead congregation. There was nowhere else to run, but the crucified image of Jesus of Nazareth gave him strength. He was ready to meet his maker. He clasped his hands together, and his lips moved silently in prayer.

Samson fired another round at the nearest corpse as it clamoured outside the vestry. The bullet tore through its back into dead flesh, but the creature hardly seemed to notice. When Reverend Cunningham's scream resonated around the church, Samson knew that he was too late.

Slowly, the congregation of the dead turned towards him, and behind them framed in the vestry doorway stood the reverend. His head reclined unnaturally, eyes stared ahead unseeing.

Swiftly, Samson made for the exit. Wallace was already waiting for him, but the way was blocked. Two corpses guarded the door. Both were dressed differently to the other people that Samson had seen inside the Triangle. One wore the uniform of a private from the Great War, and the other appeared to be a 1920s flapper.

Once again, Samson raised his gun and aimed it at the

closest cadaver. He silently gave the private honours, and pulled the trigger. Hot lead spat forth, speeding into the deceased private. Congealed blood and soft tissue spilled out the back of the corpse's head, and it collapsed to the floor as lifeless and still as the grave it belonged in.

'Aim for the head,' Samson cried out to Wallace. 'It puts them down for good.'

Wallace stared at the advancing flapper with a strange detached look. Suddenly, he lunged forwards and slashed at the undead woman's throat. Unperturbed, the Loa's puppet continued its stumbling walk towards them. Wallace struck again, and this time the knife dug neatly into the flapper's skull. The body slumped to the ground, and the two men fled into the night.

The plan had worked well. There were a few corpses stumbling across the church grounds towards them. It wouldn't be long before those inside filed out. Together, Samson and Wallace skirted around the back of the church to the road.

'Zara could still be alive out here,' Samson said. 'And I'm sure Alistair and Chorley could do with some help.'

Wallace looked at him as if he was mad. 'You can help if you want to, but I'm getting out of here.'

Samson stood dumbfounded, as Wallace ran off towards the boundary of the village. For a moment Samson contemplated following him, but the man was so blinkered that he knew that he wouldn't be listened to. With a sigh, Samson set off towards the manor.

— CHAPTER FIFTEEN—

Freedom

It was an odd feeling, passing through the barrier. All manner of thoughts bombarded Anne's mind, as she sat with the two men in the back of the Land Rover. Every excuse she could think of to turn back. *She had to help Alun with the funeral arrangements... She needed to speak personally to Chris Armitage's wife, apologise for killing him...*

She felt dizzy, and it was clear from Privates Donaldson and Yuen that they felt the same. Donaldson, the youngest of the two, tried to give Anne a comforting smile. She smiled in return, and looked out the back of the Land Rover, at the field where Dashner and Jeff were watching the Land Rover depart.

'We'll be through any...' Her voice trailed off as darkness abruptly fell outside, and Dashner, Jeff and the entire investigation site disappeared. The Land Rover juddered to a stop. 'We're through.'

'What happened to the day?' Donaldson asked.

'We've entered the Triangle. Different year, different day... technically.' Anne swallowed, and tried to ignore the sick feeling in her stomach. 'Are you feeling nauseous too?'

The privates nodded.

'I'm sure it'll pass, ma'am,' Yuen said.

'Let's hope so.'

The three of them waited for a few moments for Bill to join them. By the time he climbed into the back of Land Rover, the feeling of nausea had gone.

Bill stood there a moment, slightly crouched, looking around as if he couldn't even see them.

'Bill?'

He ignored her and reached out a hand. Testing the air.

The privates looked from him to Anne.

'Lieutenant, sir, are you okay?' Yuen asked.

Bill nodded his head slowly. 'Yes, Private, it's just...' He looked at Anne. 'This is incredible. The air particles inside the back here are so different to outside.'

'You can see them?'

'Yeah. I can see why people use hallucinogens now.'

Anne frowned. 'Okay, enough of that, soldier,' she said. 'Untie us so we can get on with the mission.' *And then we can get these drugs out of your system,* she added to herself, not keen on the idea of her boyfriend becoming addicted to narcotics.

'Yes, ma'am,' Bill said with a smirk.

He released the privates first, and ordered them outside. Once Bill and Anne were alone, he gently undid the ropes that bound her to the bench.

'What is it?' she asked, oddly disturbed by the way he stared at her face.

'I... I don't think I ever realised how beautiful you were until now.'

Anne stood up. 'So, I wasn't beautiful before the hallucinogens? Charmed, I'm sure.'

'What? No, I didn't mean...'

Her back to him, Anne smiled as she climbed out of the

Land Rover.

Finally, she was going to solve the riddle of the Keynsham Triangle. She looked up at the night sky. *I hope you're watching this, Father.*

Anne looked around, and found that the road she stood on was familiar. It was the lane that led directly into Keynsham, but it just didn't feel right. She walked over to a sign at the side of the road. For a brief moment she wondered what it was meant to say, then she saw. The letters, and thus the word, were backwards.

'Keynsham this way,' she said, noting that the sign was pointing in the wrong direction. 'Through the looking glass.'

'What's that?' Bill asked, coming up behind her. Then he saw the sign. 'Just like that Harris bloke said.' He looked down the lane, towards Keynsham. 'This is Durley Hill.'

'Thought so.' Anne nodded at the Land Rover. 'Shall I drive?'

Bill frowned for a moment, then nodded slowly. 'I think that might be best.'

'Yes. You just concentrate on what you're seeing. Reverse geography might be a bit confusing.'

Bill smiled. 'Not for me. Not like this. For some reason it all makes perfect sense.'

Anne said nothing and returned to the Land Rover. The sooner they found Lethbridge-Stewart and left the Triangle, the better it would be for Bill.

Chorley was alone. He didn't like it. The thought of the Loa and its zombie hoard just outside... It reminded him too much of being trapped in the London Underground. Lethbridge-Stewart had insisted it was all clear out there, but he still went to check upstairs, leaving Chorley alone downstairs.

He and Lethbridge-Stewart hadn't gone far. As soon as they were out of sight of the Loa, they had stolen into the closest house and had watched silently as the army of the deceased wandered past the window. If they lost sight of Zara, everything would be over.

Trying to keep his cool, Chorley idly fiddled with the arm of his glasses. He took them off and began to clean the lenses on the bottom of his shirt. As he was doing so, his ears picked up a faint rustling sound near the skirting board. He swung his head towards the noise, but the room was just a blur. Desperately, he attempted to thrust his glasses back on his face, but he only half successful. The skirting board was brought into focus, and he almost wished it hadn't been. Looking at him with dead eyes, was a tiny house mouse.

Forgetting about his crooked glasses, Chorley stamped down hard on the tiny creature. His concern growing, he scanned the floor to see if the thing was alone. He felt a draught on his neck and heard footsteps.

'Brigadier, I think we might have a...'

But it wasn't Lethbridge-Stewart.

The front door hung open, letting in a cool breeze, and behind him swayed the dead body of Tom Sawkins.

Too scared to even scream, Chorley shrank back from the corpse. He knew that he needed to run, but his feet didn't appear to want to respond. Tom seemed delighted to meet him, although that may of course have been due to the lack of skin on his lower jaw. The soot blackened teeth were forced into a wide grin.

Undead fingertips reached out and touched Chorley's

hair, causing him to flinch in alarm. In desperation, he lashed out with everything he had. His fists connected with dead bone and flesh, but the corpse took no notice of his frantic struggles.

Tom's fingers closed painfully tight on his fringe, and yanked. Pain sheared through Chorley's nerves as his head was slowly pulled towards the unyielding monster's slavering jaws.

Long dreadful seconds passed as Chorley stared death in the face. He was treated to the sight of a mixture of saliva and blood seeping down the corpse's chin. He whimpered when the string of crimson dripped onto his own cheek and began the slow trickle downwards.

The vacant dead eyes swivelled to stare at Chorley, and Tom's mouth gaped over his jugular vein ready to feast. Desperately, Chorley forced the deceased body snatcher's head upwards, buying him a little more time. He contemplated his own imminent death, and at last emptied his lungs.

There was a flash of fire together with the acrid smell of gunpowder, and his attacker's head jolted back as it exploded. Tom's blood splattered over his face. With a clump of Chorley's hair still in a clawed fist, Tom's corpse collapsed heavily to the floor.

Lethbridge-Stewart lowered the flintlock, and Chorley rubbed the tender bald patch on his head. 'That's one I owe you.'

'Only one? I must be slipping,' Lethbridge-Stewart said with what seemed to Chorley to be a genuine smile. 'Help me block off the doorway, before more of those things arrive.'

Together they manhandled a heavy bookcase in front of

the door. They were just in time. The large piece of furniture rocked alarmingly as the door was pushed from the outside.

'That's torn it,' Lethbridge-Stewart said, as he retreated towards the stairs. 'It knows we're here now, so we haven't got much time. Follow me.'

Before Chorley could reply, the bookcase wobbled again. With a panicked expression on his face, he immediately followed Lethbridge-Stewart's example and hurried up the stairs.

Wallace hurried up the road. He wasn't running away, he told himself. Of course, his research was too important to put himself in danger. That went without saying, but it was also crucial that he obtained help. A negro like Samson would never understand the importance of his mission. The magistrate needed to be informed about the creatures that had plagued the village. With luck, Wallace would be able to return at first light with a brigade of soldiers on his heels. He knew how to put these unholy monsters down for good now, so his expertise would be vital. He would be hailed as a hero.

Through the trees he could see the outline of the brass works to his right. That meant that Keynsham Bridge would be up ahead soon, and with it the end of the village. It would be a few miles until the nearest settlement, but hopefully he could hail a carriage there.

The bridge loomed up ahead, but in the gloom he didn't notice the loose cobblestone. He nearly lost his balance and only just stopped himself from tumbling into the road. He'd have to be more careful.

Composing himself, Wallace continued his brisk walk.

He had only walked a few more paces, when he found himself turning on his heels and walking back towards the village. Lethbridge-Stewart might need his help.

Abruptly he stopped. What on earth was he thinking?

Wallace pondered the situation, and realised that he had encountered this problem before. A few weeks ago Stedman had told him it was impossible to leave the house. In time that had been proved false, but his dear deceased friend had said that the issue had moved to the boundary of the village itself. Had Stedman been right after all?

Wallace walked slowly towards the bridge, and his alarm grew when he stopped suddenly in exactly the same spot. This time the scientist tried to extend his arms, but found that he couldn't. It was as if there was an invisible wall before him. He barely had a moment to contemplate the setback, before he felt a presence behind him. Wallace turned, but relaxed when he saw it was only Oscar. Precious seconds were wasted before he remembered that his butler was dead.

Readying the knife, he approached the corpse of his deceased employee. He was in striking distance, when once again his foot found the loose cobblestone. He stumbled, and the knife clattered to the road. Frantically, he searched for his weapon, but the dark hindered him. Realising that Oscar was nearly upon him, Wallace tried to flee. He had only travelled a few paces when he unexpectedly stopped. The only escape route was the road ahead – the road out of the village. Wallace's mouth ran dry. He was trapped.

Fear gripped him tight, and he stood there quaking as his former employee advanced. Oscar turned to leer at him through undead eyes, and cold hands grasped him. Wallace lashed out. He struck flesh but the corpse ignored his valiant struggle.

The dead butler's teeth were now so close that Wallace could see slithers of fur still clinging to the enamel, and he shuddered with horror when he realised that it was the remains of the Loa's rodent army. As Oscar bit down, blackness swept over him.

'What is that?' Anne pointed.

Bishop watched and felt his stomach curdle. On the side of the road a creature of some kind, one of those zombies he'd heard about, was ripping into a woman. If her miniskirt was anything to go by, she had to be one of the many who had vanished into the Triangle over the years.

The coppery taste of the blood hung in the air, and found its way up his nose. Bishop coughed violently.

'What is it?' Anne asked.

Bishop closed his eyes. 'A negative side effect of the hallucinogens. Increased sense of smell. Keep driving,' he added, wishing the scent in the air would change. 'The manor is where this all started.'

'Yes, and it's where Mr Harris saw Samson heading to.'

'Good,' Bishop said, eyes still closed. 'Then I imagine that's where we'll find him and Lethbridge-Stewart.'

Blood and brain fragments splashed onto the cobblestones. For several seconds the corpse remained upright, before collapsing face down into the middle of the street next to the rest of its fallen comrades. Lowering his gun, Samson gingerly stepped over the bodies and continued his journey. As he trudged down the street, he kept an eye open for Zara and Lethbridge-Stewart. So far, he had only encountered the dead; although for a brief moment he was sure he saw normal living person – a man in relatively contemporary clothes. But when Samson went to check, the man had gone. Samson wrote it off as his over-active imagination.

Through the billowing smoke of the manor, Samson could see the dying light of the fire. He was almost there. Ahead, he could make out figures in the gloom and then, suddenly, a child's voice rang out into the night. It was a nursery rhyme.

Samson felt a weight lifting from his shoulders. The little girl was still alive.

He fought down the urge to rush forwards. He didn't yet know who or what the other figures were. The last thing Samson wanted was to put Zara in any unnecessary danger.

So he kept close to the shadows, careful to keep himself as hidden as possible, and snuck up to the manor.

When he was finally close enough, he saw that a dozen or so dead villagers surrounded the child. They appeared to be guarding her. Perhaps the Loa was using her as a hostage? Well, he'd put an end to that. Silently Samson crept closer.

'Goosy, Goosy, Gander. Whither do I wander? Upstairs and downstairs, and in my lady's chamber...'

Lethbridge-Stewart filtered out the juvenile voice as best he could, and peered into the darkness of the night through the open window. From his vantage point on the second floor, he could see the little girl in the street below encircled by her posse of the undead. Zara looked up at him, and her sweet smile was briefly lit up by the glowing embers of the fire.

Suddenly the bedroom door juddered, and he realised that the corpses must have finally made their way up the stairs. As the undead fists beat against the pine wood, the door began to buckle. The iron bolt didn't look too substantial, so he knew that they didn't have long.

Apprehensively, Lethbridge-Stewart watched as Chorley gently shook gunpowder into the flintlock's barrel. There was a splintering of wood, and the bolt gave way. Abandoning his position at the window, Lethbridge-Stewart rushed towards the door. He was too late. The door swung open, revealing Sergeant Dovey, uniform streaked with dried blood. His lifeless mouth was twisted into a grotesque parody of a smile. The deceased soldier walked unsteadily through the doorway, just as Chorley rammed the shot firmly into the flintlock.

Before Lethbridge-Stewart could help, Chorley raised the flintlock. Squeezing his eyes shut, the journalist pulled the trigger. There was a flash from the muzzle. More by luck than judgement, the lead ball hit the walking corpse directly in the middle of its forehead. Dovey's body crashed backwards out of the door, and Lethbridge-Stewart slammed it shut, preventing more of the Loa's puppets entering. Immediately, he felt the weight of the undead on the other side as they clambered to get in.

Lethbridge-Stewart was impressed when Chorley instantly set about reloading the ancient pistol. At last the man was making himself useful, and not giving in to fear or panic. It took a few agonising minutes before the flintlock was reloaded. When Chorley finally joined his side at the door, Lethbridge-Stewart's arms were already beginning to ache with the pressure of holding it shut.

Chorley handed the gun over, and Lethbridge-Stewart found himself impressed once more by the man's fortitude.

'I think I may have misjudged you,' he said.

Chorley grinned. 'You judged me right. But that was a long time ago now... At least it feels like it. People change, Brigadier.' And as if to prove it, he continued; 'I'll take over here. You need to take care of the Loa.'

Aware that every second counted, Lethbridge-Stewart hurried back to the window. He peered into the road below and the door lurched alarmingly, pushing Chorley back a few inches.

Swiftly Lethbridge-Stewart located Zara, but to his dismay he no longer had a direct line of fire. The reanimated bodies of Stedman and Toussaint blocked his view of the little girl. The door rocked once more, and Chorley slid back another few inches. A dead hand forced its way into the bedroom.

Letting go of the door, Chorley backed away from the corpse of a blood encrusted train conductor. There was a ticket machine hanging around the corpse's neck, and it swung alarmingly.

Now or never, Lethbridge-Stewart thought. He had to end it now, in the only way he knew.

The road became alight by what could only be artificial light, but he didn't have time to wonder where it came from. Surprised, the possessed girl took a pitiful few steps forwards and into his line of fire.

Lethbridge-Stewart's finger tightened on the trigger.

'It's working, Erickson!' Dashner called.

Jeff looked up from the machine. The lieutenant was

right. The huge patch of land, never changing, forever looking the same as it did in 1815, had changed. Or at least a very small part of it.

'Is that Durley Hill?' one of the soldiers asked.

Jeff nodded. 'It is. And it should be over there,' he added, pointing towards where the investigation site began.

'Good enough for me,' Dashner said. 'I'll send more men in.'

'What?' Jeff walked over to the edge of the perimeter. And immediately a thought entered his head. He stepped away, distracted. 'As I thought, even if you wanted to, you can't. Not without those drugs we pumped into Lieutenant Bishop.'

'Damn. Then what do you suggest I do?'

'Wait,' Jeff said. 'And hope Anne finds the brigadier before this machine blows.'

The Loa smiled at the house. It could see Lethbridge-Stewart, looking through the window, aiming that ancient gun.

Its hunger had yet to be sated. But soon it would be. Even now it could feel its creation being brought back into the real world. There was a tear in the barrier, and more humans had entered. And beyond that tear... the whole world.

The Loa was curious about Lethbridge-Stewart's knowledge of the Great Intelligence. Was it out there? If so, the Loa had an old score to settle. But first it would devour the last of the humans inside the barrier, and then with its undead army, the Loa would spread out. Humanity would fall first, and then the Great Intelligence would know...

A shot rang out.

For a brief moment the Loa wasn't sure what had happened. But then it felt the pull. Zara, its host body, had been shot in the head.

Damn you, Brigadier! it yelled, but the words did not escape Zara's lips.

No. It could not end like this. It would be sent back to the howling void.

Holding on for dear life, the Loa reached out for the tear in the barrier. If the Great Intelligence could escape the astral plane, then so too could the L—

Samson peered through the smoke at the undead creatures surrounding Zara. He was in luck. They were all facing a small terrace house across the street. If he could take down the two closest to him, he might be able to reach the little girl and make good their escape. He knew that the things were slow, so there was a high chance of success. He raised his pistol and aimed its sights on the nearest corpse.

Samson was about to fire when the unmistakable rumble of a vehicle caused him to look down the road. It had to be Lethbridge-Stewart and Dovey. Perhaps he didn't need to do this alone.

Headlights lit up the street, and the sound of a single shot made him start.

All across the road the corpses collapsed. In their midst, Zara tottered on her feet.

There was a sob of pain, and to his horror Samson realised that the little girl had been shot. The child stumbled, and he rushed to help. He got there just in time, and caught her in his strong arms. He lowered her to the ground.

'Is that you, grandfather? I can't tell,' Zara whispered in a weak voice, looking up at him through blurry eyes. 'I dreamed I was a prisoner in my head. Am I free now?'

Samson looked up at Lethbridge-Stewart and Chorley approaching from the house, while from another direction came Bishop and Anne. Two Corps soldiers stood near the Land Rover, their rifles ready.

'The Loa was in her all the time,' Lethbridge-Stewart said, and kneeled down beside Zara. He looked at her, and smiled sadly. 'Yes, Zara. You're free.'

With a faltering smile, the child took her final breath. She finally had her freedom.

For a moment all was quiet, and then the air filled with a strange whooshing sound. Like a broken vacuum cleaner.

'What the devil?' Lethbridge-Stewart rose to his feet.

Anne looked around. 'I think the Triangle is collapsing. Look!'

The men watched as, like a glass ceiling, the dark sky began to crack and sunlight filtered through.

'We need to get out of here.' Lethbridge-Stewart ordered Samson to carry Zara's body into the Land Rover. 'I think we can safely assume everybody else in the Triangle is dead.'

Samson nodded. 'Yes. No one left to save.'

'Just ourselves,' Chorley pointed out.

'Yes. Let's go. Zara deserves a proper burial, and those who died here need to be remembered with honours.' Lethbridge-Stewart turned to Anne. 'I assume you have way out of here, Miss Travers?'

She smiled. 'I do. Bill here.'

Lethbridge-Stewart looked at his adjutant. 'Lieutenant, are you home?'

Samson could see it too. Bill appeared to be elsewhere.

'He's here. Just a little distracted.' Anne pulled Bill gently towards the Land Rover. 'I'll explain on the way out of here.'

Carrying Zara, Samson followed them to the Land Rover. He wasn't sure any explanation would make sense of the last couple of days.

— EPILOGUE —

The Mystery of the Keynsham Triangle

... perhaps we may never truly know what happened, and perhaps the legend will always overshadow the reality. But one thing is certain, whatever hocus-pocus was at the heart of the Keynsham Triangle, it has finally ended. Once again the land can be crossed. But, memory and tradition is a hard thing to change, so it may be that the land will forever be cursed. Never to know the footfalls of ramblers.

Regardless, let us remember all those who fell afoul of the Keynsham Triangle.

Barnaby Stedman. Isaac Wallace. Charlotte Bibby. Zara...

(Excerpt from The Daily Chronicle by Harold Chorley.)

Wednesday 25 March 1970 was the day Edward Travers was officially laid to rest. Of course, very few of the mourners attending the funeral knew that inside the coffin was really a little black girl called Zara. Of those attending, only Anne Travers, Bill Bishop, Samson Ware and Alistair Lethbridge-Stewart knew the truth. And while Anne said her final goodbye to her father, supported by her brother, Lethbridge-Stewart and Samson turned their thoughts to the little girl whose entire life had been taken from her. First by slave traders, then by Stedman's father, and finally by the Loa.

It had been only two days since they had escaped the Triangle, before it collapsed in on itself. For Lethbridge-Stewart and Chorley it had only been a matter of days, but for the the rest of the world two weeks had passed. Lethbridge-Stewart had tried to explain to Miss Travers what the Loa had told him, and in turn she explained what she had learned from her father's notes and a chap called Jeremy Harris. Lethbridge-Stewart wasn't sure he'd ever truly understand; it sounded very complicated, and there was far more science involved than his mind could take. In that way, at least, the mystery still remained. But Lethbridge-Stewart didn't mind. The day he understood everything was the day he would quit.

Chorley had been good on his word. He promised to write a small piece on the Triangle and get all those names of its victims out there. Even if some of them didn't really deserve to be remembered. Descendants of the dead still remained, never knowing exactly what happened to their relatives. They still didn't, but at least, for one day, the people of England would remember them all.

It was the least Lethbridge-Stewart and Chorley could do.

Actually, that wasn't quite true. There was one more

thing Lethbridge-Stewart could do – for Chorley at least.

The ceremony around the coffin complete, members of the Goff and Travers families began to make their way to their waiting cars, which would take them all to the wake. None of them would know the truth.

In his business, truth had become a valuable commodity.

Lethbridge-Stewart approached Bishop and Miss Travers. They were in conversation with Alun, who nodded at Lethbridge-Stewart as he joined their side.

'Thanks for coming. My dad would have appreciated it.'

'Least I could do. He was a good man.'

Alun smiled and excused himself, promising to see Anne and Bishop at the wake. Once he was out of earshot, Lethbridge-Stewart spoke.

'Again, thank you for allowing Zara this place.'

'It was either that or some unknown.' Anne gave a small smile. 'At least the poor girl gets some peace now, and she'll even get visitors over the years.'

'Quite.' At the far side of the graveyard, someone caught Lethbridge-Stewart's eye, and he bade his farewells.

'Did you see it?' Chorley asked once Lethbridge-Stewart had stopped beside him.

'I did. Surprisingly tactful.'

Chorley laughed. 'Like I said, Alistair. People change.'

'Yes.' Lethbridge-Stewart reached into his coat pocket and removed a slip of paper. 'They do, which is why I'm giving you this.'

'What is it?' Chorley took the paper and read the name on it. 'Sebastian Collins?'

'Understand, Chorley, that I am forbidden to tell you

what occurred at Dominex. Hamilton promised he would do his best to look after you in those days following your... breakdown, but it seems that wasn't enough.'

'Natural instincts, old boy,' Chorley said, no longer smiling. 'I smell a story, I have to follow it. Especially if it's the story of why I can't really remember what happened to me last summer.'

'Indeed. And this is your new lead. A name and number. It's the best I can do. *All* I can do. Find Sebastian Collins and you'll find Dominic Vaar.'

They passed some small talk before Chorley left. Lethbridge-Stewart watched him walk away. There was more he could have told Chorley, about what he had heard about Collins and Vaar, but regardless of how much Lethbridge-Stewart believed it, it was still mostly hearsay. No, Chorley would have to find things out for himself.

Lethbridge-Stewart turned away, leaving Harold Chorley to walk his own path in uncovering the truth about the alien Dominators.

Beware of the Mirror Man by Benjamin Burford-Jones

Bob flicked the remote control. The television's volume was loud enough to drown out the cry of a brightly coloured ball as it tumbled from a crack in the ceiling. The humans were too busy watching the screen to observe it land with a dull thud behind a crate of curtains. For a few moments, Hibbie lay motionless on the floor. The fall through the house had terrified him even more than the close encounter with the cat. He felt emotionally drained. The whole world spun around him. Best to lie still, he reasoned, until he felt better. Bit by bit Hibbie's head began to regain some feelings of normality.

'Oh, I'll come up all tartan coloured in the morning,' he moaned to nobody in particular.

When the ringing in his ears started to subside he became aware of voices – and they were not mimic voices. He pulled himself to his feet, and peered around. With shock he realised that he was no longer in the safe surroundings of the attic, but in a place completely unfamiliar. He was in a gigantic room, with a terribly high roof. On the walls hung peeling strips of wallpaper portraying badly drawn fish. If Hibbie's sense of humour had not been knocked by his ordeal, he would have smiled when he realised the fish wallpaper was pasted upside down. It gave the sense that all the fish were ill. Instead he grasped at a piece of knowledge passed onto him by Ethelbert.

'Upside down,' he said to himself. 'I must be on the other side of the world.'

Cautiously he peeked around the box that hid him from the view of the mysterious voices. To his amazement, he was confronted with four audiences. Seconds later he saw the television set that they were watching.

'Well I never! What a beautiful 'ome!' he exclaimed in awe. 'The mimics living there must be rolling in it. Been to 'Ollywood no doubt.'

Trying not to feel too jealous of the obviously talented owners of the magnificent set, who were so good that they had four audiences, Hibbie headed straight for the TV. When he got there, to his surprise the television was nowhere near as wide as his home in the attic. The reason for this came to him quickly. He had heard that people in Hollywood were always watching their weight, so they obviously only needed thin houses.

Hibbie paused for a moment. Last time he had seen Ell she was in the claws of a cat. Was she alright? Maybe the mimics that lived here could help him? Finding a small opening, he held his breath and squeezed in. Once inside the mimic crawled upwards, climbing higher and higher. He frowned. The bustle of everyday life, so familiar to him, could not be heard. There were no mimic voices, none of the racket associated with the moving of scenery, no sounds of rehearsals, not even any applause. Even worse, the layout was very different. There was no maze of passageways and rooms. Instead there were masses of wires, and many strange things that the young mimic's mind could not understand. Soon he was hopelessly lost. Then softly in the distance he heard a buzzing sound. The thought struck him – somebody kept bees here, just like Murb! And so it followed that the mimics from Hollywood must be nearby. Hibbie ran towards the sound. There was a crackle of energy and he disappeared.

The television blared out the news headlines into the living room. Barnaby was bored. Sophie was sprawled on the sofa, reading her magazine as she tried to ignore her parents' bickering.

'Who's that? What's she doing on the news?' Bob asked, pointing to a woman being interviewed by the newsreader.

'She's the one we saw in that other thing. You know. The documentary about thingy.'

'Thingy?' said a confused Bob.

'You know. Married to that MP.'

'No. I don't know.'

'You do. It was in the paper,' Ruth snapped. As Bob opened his mouth to question her further, she waved her hand at him irritably, 'Shhh… We've missed what she said now.'

'It's all over anyway,' sighed Bob. As his wife flashed a scowl in his direction, he sneakily flicked to the sports channel. 'Ah, this is more like it. Football!'

Bob was soon transfixed by the football results. When the highlights of the afternoon's matches began, he could hardly keep still. It was his team playing – an important match that he had missed due to the bustle of the move. Their best striker was in the perfect position for a cross, not far from the penalty box. The ball flew long, curving towards him. A goal was surely about to be scored. Suddenly an odd purple ball of fur appeared upon the grass, wandering as if in a daze in-between the players.

'Eh... what's that idiot in fancy dress doing on the pitch? Get off you fool,' shouted a dismayed Bob.

'They can't hear you, you know,' said his wife, absently. 'It's only a TV.'

Sophie smiled to herself. She knew better. The fur was a different colour to Ell, but it was obviously another mimic.

Her father watched in horror as the man wearing a silly costume roamed aimlessly across the penalty area. The football flew towards him, and he kicked it hard in the opposite direction with his oversized feet. The ball flew the entire length of the pitch and bounced neatly past the goalkeeper and into the goal. The watching crowd were aghast. The commentators were speechless. Bob was appalled. Just as his team looked as if they were about to pull a master stroke and score, the fool in the stupid purple costume had kicked the ball into their goal. They were now 1-0 down. Surely the ref wouldn't allow it.

'Idiot! He's ruining the game,' yelled Bob.

He was standing and shouting at the television, his face crimson. Ruth was losing patience. She picked up the remote control and changed channels. The cheers of football supporters became the opening titles of an Australian soap opera.

'Oi, I was watching that.'

'But, dear, I always watch this programme. Anyway all that excitement's bad for your heart.'

'Don't talk daft. What the... it's him again!'

Sophie's parents watched in amazement as the same strange man in furry fancy dress ambled into the pub. One good-looking hunk, sipping from a bottle of ice-cold beer, stopped his conversation with a beautiful blonde and turned to the unexpected visitor.

'Hey, mate,' he said, 'What you doing in that get up?'

'I appear to be lost. 'Ave you seen any mimics in 'ere?'

'Mimics? Ah, you mean parrots. Clever birds parrots. Can copy anything. Out in the bush, mate,' said the hunk. He turned back to the girl, and continued the conversation about the affair that her sister was having with his boss.

'Oh, Bob! Maybe it's an omen,' said Ruth. 'I knew that cat meant bad luck!'

'Don't be daft. It's got to be a publicity stunt. It must be.'

Sophie giggled as her dad flicked from channel to channel. Whatever programme he switched to, it never took long before the bizarre-looking fur-ball turned up. She listened to her parents argue about the meaning of this odd occurrence – her mother's superstitious reasons and her father's logical ones. She knew that both her parents were wrong. How the mimic had managed to get onto the television screen was the burning question. It should be impossible, but the little being's very existence had also seemed an impossibility.

Sophie slipped towards the door. She was sure this mimic was in trouble, and she wanted to offer her help to Ell. As she left the room, she glanced back at the screen. A spacecraft sped with a jet of fire past planets, stars and a purple-furred organism floating in space.

'Oh... stay on this channel, dear,' said her mother, 'It's Doctor thingy.'

'Who,' said her father.

'I just said! Doctor thingy! You know Doctor thingy.'

Hibbie did not like this one bit. He held his breath as he floated helplessly in the wake of the passing spaceship. Then suddenly he was somewhere else. The scene had changed, and he was inside a large control room. A many-sided panel covered with a dizzying array of buttons – both low tech and high tech – took up the centre of the room. Was it the bridge of another spaceship? He supposed it was better than the last place. He couldn't have held his breath for much longer.

On the other side of the control panel was a strangely dressed, gangly man. His clothes were eccentric and odd, but as he busied himself around the controls it was obvious that he thought he looked fantastic. He swept a lock of hair out of his eyes, and looked up. His eyes met Hibbie's. They burnt with an air of alien intelligence.

'Who are you?' asked the gangly man in surprise.

'Er... 'Ibbie,' said the mimic.

'Well hello, Hibbie,' said the gangly man politely. He flicked a switch on the control panel before whirling around towards him.

'Only a being of almost limitless power can breech the defences, so who are you really?' he said. 'Got it... you're the Great Soprendo! Let me know if I'm getting warm?'

'Just 'Ibbie,' mumbled the young mimic. 'I'm sort of lost. I didn't mean to come 'ere.'

'In that case I may be able to give you a lift home,' said the gangly man pleasantly. 'Where are you from? And what time?'

279

'The attic, about teatime.'

'Do you have the galactic coordinates? A postcode would help. Intergalactic taxi driver, that's me. By the way, you're looking a little fuzzy round the edges.'

Looking down, Hibbie was surprised to see that he was out of focus.

The man whipped out a silver tube from his pockets, and pointed it at the mimic. The tip glowed a brilliant green, and a high-pitched whine filled Hibbie's ears. He flinched. Was this some kind of weapon?

'No, no... this is impossible,' said the man looking at the silver device. 'According to these readings you don't exist. You're a mirage, a figment. If you really are here, you may be damaging the whole of space and time. Either that or I'm dreaming.'

The man pinched himself hard on his cheek, leaving a vivid red mark.

'Ow, I'm pretty sure I'm not dreaming.'

'It's you that don't exist,' Hibbie said as his heckles rose. 'You're just some illusion caused by that electrical television!'

'Now that was rude,' said the man, looking hurt. There was a gentle shudder as the machine ground to a halt.

'Ah, we're here,' said the man. 'I don't know who or what you are, but you'd better leave. Don't bother with the tip.'

The man strode over to a pair of doors, flung them open and pushed Hibbie out. The colourful world was gone, replaced with the dull grey of a black-and-white film. For a split second he felt at home. Black and white felt normal to him. Perhaps this place would be safer. The relief swiftly disappeared when bullets began to whistle past his head and explosions rocked the ground he was standing on. He waded through thick mud, carefully avoiding the vicious strips of barbed wire that encircled the area.

He couldn't see anyone around, although the sound of fighting was close by. It couldn't really be a battle, just as he couldn't really have been in space. He knew that it was simply an image created by the awful machine. Somehow his power of illusion had joined forces with this strange electrical beast's power to create a very convincing reality. And it was not a reality that he could control. Some of the places he had visited had excited him, and gave him fantastic new ideas for shows. Others were terrifyingly dangerous.

He looked again at his hand. It was still out of focus. Perhaps the illusion was breaking down and he would be able to find some way out of this horrible place.

Hibbie dived for cover when another bullet whizzed by. It missed him by inches and hit instead a blackened, peeling sign that read 'Warning – Land Mines'. Suddenly there was a tremendous explosion. As the German soldiers made their advance across the minefield, a few scraps of purple fur floated down from the sky and settled on the black-and-white mud, before being trampled by black-and-white feet.

Coming Soon from Candy Jar Books

THE FLAMING SOLDIER: A LETHBRIDGE-STEWART SPIN-OFF ADVENTURE

by Christopher Bryant

Brigadier Lethbridge-Stewart is investigating a series of cases of spontaneous combustion. How can an inferno start inside a brick wall? Who or what are the ghost-like creatures spotted in the area around Imber base? Does it have anything to do with Eileen Younghusband, hotel proprietor, whose ordinary day is about to be interrupted by secrets from her past?

Traumatic events from the Second World War impact upon the present day and a mysterious aircraft could hold the key to the identity of the flaming soldier.

Also available from Candy Jar Books

LETHBRIDGE-STEWART: NIGHT OF THE INTELLIGENCE
by Andy Frankham-Allen

Three men feel the pull of the Great Intelligence.

One; Professor Edward Travers, who was once possessed by it, plans to return to the Det-Sen Monastery to clear his mind of the Intelligence once and for all. But he never makes it. The Vault want him, but an old friend is waiting in the wings to help.

Two; Owain Vine, who carries the seed of the Intelligence within, is in Japan on a pilgrimage to cleanse himself of the taint he feels in his soul. Soon a happy reunion takes place, and Owain learns that past friendships are not what they seemed.

Three; Brigadier Alistair Lethbridge-Stewart, who finds himself haunted by the spectre of his brother, James, who refuses to stay dead.

The stage is set for the long, dark night of the Intelligence.

ISBN: 978-0-9957436-3-2